A Room at the Manor

Julie Shackman trained as a journalist and studied media and communication before turning her hand to women's fiction. She lives in Scotland with her husband and two teenage sons. When not reading and writing romance, she writes verses and captions for greeting cards.

A Room at the Manor

JULIE SHACKMAN

ALLEN&UNWIN
SYDNEY · MELBOURNE · AUCKLAND · LONDON

First published in 2018

Copyright © Julie Shackman 2018

Allen & Unwin
83 Alexander Street
Crows Nest NSW 2065
Australia
Phone: (61 2) 8425 0100
Email: info@allenandunwin.com
Web: www.allenandunwin.com

A catalogue record for this book is available from the National Library of Australia

ISBN 978 1 76063 286 1

Set in 11.6/16.5 pt Sabon LT Pro by Bookhouse, Sydney
Printed and bound in Australia by Griffin Press

10 9 8 7 6 5 4 3 2 1

The paper in this book is FSC® certified. FSC® promotes environmentally responsible, socially beneficial and economically viable management of the world's forests.

LOVE ALWAYS TO MY THREE SPECIAL BOYS:

Lawrence, Daniel AND *Ethan*

One

 'Have you been sprinkling your fairy dust again, Lara?'

I beamed across at Mrs Arnold. 'Thank you. I'm so glad you're enjoying it.'

My retired English teacher took a sip of her Earl Grey tea. 'Enjoying it, she says! Your red velvet cake is positively dancing across my tastebuds.'

I slid out from behind the dark wooden counter and approached Mrs Arnold. 'I was worried that it might be a bit on the dry side . . .'

Her chocolate-coloured eyes twinkled out at me from her carefully powdered face. 'You need to believe in yourself more, young lady.'

She delivered another forkful of cake to her mouth and let out a little sigh of contentment. Then she shifted in her bentwood chair, almost knocking over the laminated True Brew menu. 'I hope that Kitty Walker appreciates all your hard work and effort.'

A blush crept up my neck and decided to stay there.

'Since you started working here,' Mrs Arnold continued as she waggled her cake fork, 'your baking has been a godsend.'

She gave a small shudder from under her aubergine cardigan. 'I mean, Kitty's efforts are all well and good, but there's only so much Victoria sponge and apple tart a person can take.' She leaned over conspiratorially. 'Your Portuguese tarts last week were truly sublime.'

From a circular table nearby, two younger women sporting spray tans and slashes of red lip gloss interjected. 'So you're behind the cheesecake brownies?' grinned one through bleached teeth. 'They were excellent.'

I basked in their praise. 'Guilty as charged.'

Her polished companion nodded her blonde bob. 'It's about time this place moved into this century.'

Mrs Arnold opened her mouth again to speak but then clamped her lips shut. I turned to see my boss, Kitty, looming towards me in her plastic True Brew apron. 'When you've quite finished gossiping with all the customers, Lara, table three needs clearing.'

'I wasn't gossiping,' I explained calmly. 'These ladies were just complimenting me on my baking.'

Kitty's frosted pink mouth pinched. 'Yes. Well, I don't employ you to bake. That's my job.' She thrust out a wobbling chest. 'Your role is to serve customers and to clear tables, which, right now, you are failing to do.'

I made an effort to smile. 'But if you recall, Kitty, when you took me on, you told me that I could bake and experiment with some of my own—'

'I don't remember saying any such thing,' Kitty interrupted loudly, her jowls quivering as she hoisted her eyes away from me for a moment. 'Now, that table. It's positively a mess.'

I snatched up a tray and marched over to the cluttered table to tidy it. Mrs Arnold and the two glamorous ladies awarded Kitty disapproving glares, but she simply spun on her sparkly trainers and sallied back to the counter.

I could sense my face was as red as my corkscrew hair.

It was nobody's fault I was working for Satan's Mother except my own—and that had been necessity, not choice. Being made redundant from my civil service PR job had seemed like a blessing, especially when I then took off to Malta and met Anton. But upon returning to my hometown of Fairview in Scotland, there hadn't exactly been a wealth of employment opportunities. I'd been lured in with Kitty's unkept promise of the opportunity to contribute to the cake display, and the prospect of working on my baking skills. I realised I could have looked for work in public relations again, but the prospect of being trapped in some high-rise office filled me with dread.

If I owned a place like this, I thundered inwardly, it certainly wouldn't resemble its current state. I stacked the dirty teacups and glared at the dark wood panelling and sombre matching tables and chairs. What once might have been considered cosy had long since become dated and drab. The tea room carpet was a loud red and green tartan affair that shouted at you as soon as you stepped foot in the place and the dim glow of the carriage lights did nothing for the dingy Scottish landscapes Kitty had hung on the walls.

The tea room didn't even serve loose-leaf tea. Kitty bought cheap teabags and coffee that erred on the side of powdery. I promised myself that if I ever had my own establishment, customers would be treated to coffee that was rich and aromatic. I would stock a whole array of teas; French Earl Grey, Oolong, White Tea, Jasmine.

Baking had always held a fascination for me, but ever since I'd taken that night school baking class the summer before university, I'd fallen even more in love with it. The textures and smells. The meditative process of kneading and beating. And the way even the simplest of recipes could trigger the recollection of a special memory, or remind you of a precious moment, was something to be savoured. I glanced down at the silver bracelet dangling delicately from my wrist, thinking of when my late great aunt Hettie had given it to me after I'd completed the baking course.

I whisked away the tray bearing the dirty crockery, avoiding the sympathetic expressions from Mrs Arnold and the manicured ladies, and heading straight for the dishwasher. My new boss could be hard to take, but there were a couple of positives to this job. At least my best friend, Morven, lived nearby, and thank goodness I still had my flat just around the corner. I'd rented it out to a divorced lady in her forties for the past eighteen months, with a view to selling it after I'd moved to Malta to start life properly with Anton. My tenant had proved to be an ideal one, moving out six months ago to join her new man in London. Once my flat had been vacated, Morven diligently collected my mail, liaised with the estate agent when I couldn't and paid frequent visits to make sure all was well for my imminent return from Malta.

As soon as Malta entered my head, images of vanilla sand, sea foam popping like champagne corks against the rocks and Anton's dark eyes swam in front of me. I slammed the dishwasher door shut in an effort to send them packing. All the hours and effort I'd put into making his wine bar in Valletta a success and what did I receive in return? A gushing brush-off as though he'd swallowed a self-help book and the revelation that he'd replaced me with a burgundy-haired Russian. I just hoped he and his pneumatic barmaid, Tanya, didn't fall down any abandoned mineshafts.

Kitty pulled me out of my dark thoughts by bustling over to the mound of blueberry muffins she'd made and needlessly rearranging them. I'd suggested jazzing up the muffin selection by introducing other options, such as candied ginger and apple, dark chocolate and Guinness and pistachio and chai. My ideas were swiftly shot down with 'I know what my customers like and it certainly isn't any of that foodie fad nonsense'.

What was faddish about ginger was anyone's guess.

I'd returned to Fairview three months ago now and decided, in my lower moments, that members of the criminal underworld probably got more lenient sentences than working for Kitty Walker.

'Lara! Customer!'

I bit my lip at Kitty's bark and turned to a young mum and her bright-eyed toddler.

'How about one of my emerald biscuits?' Kitty called over to the little boy. 'I bet you'd love the icing. I made these, you know.'

His ash-blond head swivelled between Kitty's rather bland offering and the mini cupcakes I'd rustled up that morning, dotted with chocolate buttons and a dash of sparkles. Kitty followed the boy's blue gaze. 'Where did those come from?' she glowered.

'I made them,' I replied, defiant. 'I thought the little ones might like them.'

Kitty's lip curled up towards the tip of her wide nose. 'I don't think they're in keeping with the ethos of this establishment.'

I was on the verge of pointing out that this was a small Scottish tea room, not a worldwide conglomerate, when the boy chirruped, 'Can I have a cupcake, please, Mummy?'

I appeared from behind the counter and knelt down in front of him, my True Brew apron crinkling against my jeans. 'Seeing as you've asked so nicely, I'll find you the biggest one.'

His tired-looking mum nodded at me through a wide smile, but Kitty's expression was thunderous. I picked up the fattest of the mini cupcakes with the tongs and swiftly delivered it into a brown paper bag. That's another thing I would change: no cheap brown bags, but ones specially embossed with the name of my tea room.

Once they had paid and vanished out the door in a flurry of weatherproof jackets and pushchair, Kitty rounded on me. 'Well, seeing as you're so keen to be the boss, you can lock up again tonight.'

I buried a frustrated sigh. And there was me, thinking that what with all the happy customers, the old dragon might actually accept my freshly baked contributions as she'd promised. No chance. I grumpily folded up some napkins and stared out of the window at the afternoon sky, where shafts of sunshine were attempting to banish some milky cloud. I could bake and I loved doing it. I was also experienced in public relations. And yet here I was, working in a tea room that time had forgotten, undervalued and tongue-lashed.

'Customer outside, Lara!'

I poked out my tongue at Kitty's retreating back and snatched up my notepad. A quick glance outside reminded me that one of the outdoor tables was jostling with half-empty teacups and remnants of fruit scones. I reached for a tray and made my way outside where I was met with a sudden bellow.

'Open your eyes, girl!'

Two

 I clutched the tray a little tighter. 'I'm sorry,' I replied hurriedly. 'I didn't see you there.'

The elderly man's piercing grey gaze was unnerving. He stared at me for a few more moments before recovering himself. 'Well, obviously, judging by the way you were swinging that thing around.'

Okay, so I had been daydreaming a bit, but I certainly hadn't been careless with the tea tray. It was hardly a dangerous weapon, was it? While I tried to gather myself after this verbal onslaught, the man eased himself gingerly into one of our wrought-iron chairs. The tea shop overlooked the town square, with an excellent view of the higgledy-piggledy shops and the myriad old lanes between them.

He balanced his black and gold beech walking cane against the edge of the table. I noticed the handle was arched and carved in the shape of a thistle. Once settled on the quilted cushion, he eyed with blatant suspicion the tubs of daffodils I'd recently placed nearby.

I glanced nervously over my shoulder towards the tea room. Its bevelled windows reflected a duck-egg blue sky and golden April sunshine. I was keeping everything, including my fingers, crossed that Kitty hadn't witnessed this altercation.

The old man's voice barked into the air. 'You're not listening to a word I'm saying, are you?'

I turned my attention back to him. His grey combed-back hair framed an aggressive expression that was emphasised by a dashing, thick moustache. I glimpsed a moss green waistcoat and trousers beneath his grey raincoat.

'I could have sustained a serious injury just now,' he carped, still examining me through narrowed eyes. 'I think the least you could do, young lady, is offer me a complimentary tea and a slice of that Victoria sponge.' He raised a papery finger and jabbed it towards our cake display.

'But I didn't touch you,' I protested, pulling the tray protectively into my chest.

'You banged right against my shoulder! I could have sustained a life-threatening injury because of you. I'm very frail, I'll have you know.'

'Yeah, well, your tongue sure as hell isn't,' I hissed under my breath.

The man peered up at me. 'What was that?'

'Is everything alright, Lara?' Resplendent in her white and gold apron, Kitty barrelled past me.

'This girl almost knocked me flying,' protested the man from his seat before I could articulate a response. 'It's a bloody good job I was fit in my younger days.'

Oh good grief. I took a steadying breath. 'I am sorry but I'm quite sure I barely nudged you.' I opened my mouth to explain further but Kitty's death stare persuaded me otherwise. Instead I scooped a red curl behind my ear.

'I'm so sorry, Mr Carmichael,' gushed Kitty. 'Lara is rather inexperienced.'

My head whipped round to look at her. This was Hugo Carmichael? The old laird?

The Carmichael family lived at Glenlovatt Manor, just outside Fairview. They were a bit of a local enigma, stashed away in that butterscotch stone pile of theirs, keeping a distance from the great unwashed. They used to open up the manor to raise funds for local charities occasionally, but it had been closed to the public years ago, not long after the sudden death of Lydia Carmichael, the wife of the current laird, Gordon. Presumably the estate was now only occupied by the men of the family, Hugo, Gordon and Gordon's son, Vaughan, who had been sent off to public school years ago and was apparently now a sculptor. It was a rather depressing thought, three single aristocrats rattling around that sprawling estate.

My mum, Christine, would often accidentally fawn over images of Glenlovatt in the local paper before remembering she was anti-establishment, but I always viewed them as an unfathomable entity, living on the fringes of our little town and surveying everything from behind heavy velvet drapes overlooking acres of glossy woodland.

Kitty chose to ignore my reaction and clasped her hands across the gold teapot motif emblazoned on her chest. 'Can I treat you to some complimentary tea to apologise, Mr Carmichael?'

The man's expression rearranged itself into one of faux surprise. What a crafty old sod!

'Well, I suppose that would be acceptable.'

Kitty speared me with a frosty look. 'Lara, take Mr Carmichael's order and bring it out to him straight away.'

Both Mr Carmichael and I turned our heads slightly to watch her bustle back inside.

I clanked the tray on the empty table nearby and arranged my features into an expression of politeness. 'What would you like?'

'An Earl Grey and a slice of Victoria sponge—please.'

I presented him with a cautious smile, gathered up the tray and hurried back inside.

Three

It was a typical Scottish spring morning. Rain ran down the windows of True Brew, like diamonds racing one another.

I shielded myself as best I could under my umbrella and rustled around inside my handbag for the keys to True Brew. I suspected Kitty had only given me a spare set so she could skive off early at closing time or have some extra time in bed in the mornings, but I was determined to take the chance to prove to her she'd hired more than just a waitress.

Fairview was quiet except for the patter of the rain as I let myself in and switched on a couple of lights.

Once I'd shrugged off my raincoat, propping it over one of the radiators to dry, I unpacked the ingredients and switched on my iPod to listen to some mellow songs as I began to bake.

As I whisked the egg whites, sugar and salt in a large bowl, I imagined the rich, red river of raspberry jam gliding off the end of my teaspoon and into the careful indentation I would make for each macaroon. I laughed to myself as my stomach grumbled, even though I'd only just had cereal for breakfast. I was hoping the day's customers would show Kitty just how good my little golden islands would turn out to be.

I finished serving two elderly ladies their pot of tea and warmed cheese scones and weaved my way between the other tables and back to the counter, facing the glass-panelled door.

I couldn't help fantasising about how the place would be transformed if only the walls were painted a crisp white and some pretty gingham cushions added to the chairs. I pulled myself back to reality. That was about as likely as Hugh Jackman charging in to demand I abandon my post for a spot of uninhibited sexy time across the blueberry muffins.

While Kitty bristled about behind me, interrogating some poor customer about Mrs Strachan's marital affairs, I snuck a peek at the plastic storage container I'd secreted on a lower shelf. Taking a deep breath, I pulled it out of its hiding place and swung round to my boss, simultaneously awarding her a big smile.

She looked momentarily petrified. Taking an involuntary step backwards, Kitty jerked her tight grey hair at my container. 'What's that?'

'I came in a bit early this morning and did some more baking.'

Kitty's curled upper lip was now in danger of reaching her hairline. While teacups rattled over the murmur of conversation, Kitty leaned nervously over my proffered box. I eased open the blue plastic lid, which gave a satisfying 'phut'.

'They're raspberry and coconut macaroons,' I babbled. 'I thought we could try them out. See if our customers like them.'

Kitty's expansive bosom thrust itself forwards underneath her apron. For a moment I thought I was in danger of her taking my eye out.

I'd made them in large star-like shapes, with a rich, raspberry jam topping and a little glitter to make them sparkle. They looked quite magical under the tea room lights and rather tasty. Judging by Kitty's appalled expression, she didn't agree with me.

'I hope you haven't been using our ingredients. And they are *my* customers,' she boomed. 'Anyway, Lara, you know Fiona and I take care of all the baking.'

Ah yes. The two ugly sisters.

'I bought the ingredients myself,' I explained. 'I just thought it might be a good idea to offer something that's a bit . . .' My eyes discreetly swiped over the regular sponges and scones. 'Something a bit different.'

Kitty's fuchsia mouth quivered with indignation. 'What? You think my cakes are boring?'

'No! Not at all.' I scrambled around to choose my words carefully. 'I just thought it might be nice to offer something new.' I cleared my throat. 'And as you did originally mention that I could do some baking, I thought you might like to see more of my efforts.'

Kitty's eyes shone with annoyance. 'Oh, not that again. As you well know, Fiona and myself are the bakers. We don't need anyone else to contribute.'

'That's a pity,' rose a deep rumble from across the countertop. 'They do look rather delicious.'

Hugo Carmichael was peering expectantly out from under a black trilby, which he then removed with a flourish.

How wonderful: it was my least favourite customer back again. Could this day get any worse? Yes, was probably the correct answer to that. Still, he had complimented me on my baking, which was good of him. 'Thank you,' I smiled, slightly surprised.

'Miserable morning,' he sighed. Beads of rain hung precari-ously from his tweed coat. 'Think I'll treat myself to a pot of Earl Grey. Oh, and one of your macaroons, young lady. Thank you.'

Burying a shocked smile, I raised my eyes fleetingly to Kitty's face. The Elvis lip was back with a vengeance. 'Certainly, Mr Carmichael,' she managed through gritted teeth.

I busied myself preparing Hugo's tea tray and carefully placed one of my macaroons on it. Kitty's granite expression followed me across the tea room floor.

'There you are, Mr Carmichael. Hope you enjoy it.'

I turned to clear up the debris abandoned on a nearby table.

'Mmm, delicious!' I heard through an enthusiastic mouthful. 'Very melt in the mouth.'

I swung around, his words ringing in my ears. 'Thank you!'

He poured his tea and raised his eyes to me. 'So you like baking then?'

I nodded enthusiastically, sending my curly ponytail into a frenzy. 'I've loved it since school. I find it very relaxing, and rewarding too.'

I made a move to leave, but he reached out and gently touched my arm for the briefest of moments. He was wide-eyed. It was a little unnerving. His watery gaze fell on the silver bracelet swinging on my wrist. 'That's lovely,' he murmured. 'Where did you get it?'

I smiled down at my bracelet, its charms brushing against my skin. 'It was a present from my great-aunt—'

'Lara!' interrupted Kitty. 'Can you come here, please?'

I could still sense his gaze on my back as I retreated to the counter.

'I hope you're not harassing our clientele,' snapped Kitty as she fired up the coffee machine. 'Or pushing your baking onto them. It's not good for business.'

I tried to conceal my annoyance without too much success. 'Mr Carmichael asked for a macaroon. I thought baking was our business. This *is* a tea room.'

Kitty's jowls trembled ominously. 'You know exactly what I mean.'

Suppressing a sigh, I turned away. My reflection wavered in the bevelled window. I looked defeated. Grey, unenthusiastic eyes in a pale, freckled complexion stared back. The only part of me with any animation today was my hair. It spilled down my back as always, threatening to escape from its black band.

I was a twenty-seven-year-old redundant public relations officer who had been dumped by her Maltese lover. My life right now paled depressingly next to that of my mum, a glamorous widow living it up in Latin America.

I snatched up one of my macaroons and took a ferocious bite.

Four

The orange glow of streetlights pooled on the pavement and threw their hot reflections onto the closed shop windows opposite.

Kitty had got into the daily habit of clearing off early, normally trotting out either her weekly yoga class, her book club or a case of 'sheer exhaustion' as the excuse and leaving me to clean and close up on my own. I always thought people who did yoga were supposed to be peace-loving, kindly individuals who were channelled into their own inner calm.

As I swung the sign on the door to read 'Closed', my silver bracelet jangled. I looked fondly down at its 'lucky' silver charms, two cupcakes and two spoons, dangling against my skin. I'd started wearing it again upon my return to Fairview, hoping it would bring me good fortune as I chased my baking dreams. It was gorgeous, but I reflected a little despondently that it hadn't brought me much luck so far.

I buried a frustrated sigh at the thought. The empty cake counter glinted in the descending dark and the hideous carpet was so loud I would be surprised if they couldn't hear it in the Highlands.

I knew what would cheer me up.

I'd been thinking up a new recipe earlier in the day and now would be the perfect time to try it. My fingers positively tingled with anticipation as I flicked the kitchen light on again. Then I got to work, turning on the mixer and popping on a clean True Brew apron.

I started by grating a large carrot and two apples, sifting in some wholemeal flour and adding a generous perfumed dash of cinnamon. The machine turned the mixture nice and sticky as I beat in the sugar, oil and eggs. I allowed myself a good teaspoonful to taste-test, and, after deciding it called for some ginger and allspice, I rustled the muffin cases out onto a tray. The mixture eased off the tablespoon and into each muffin case with a satisfying plop. I took pinches of rolled oats and sprinkled them over the top of each muffin, before popping them in the oven.

The oven clock glowed neon red, marking down the time. While I waited, I hoovered over the tea room carpet, dashing back into the kitchen to check the muffins were rising as they should. Finally, a high-pitched 'ding' announced the baking time was over. Hitching on a pair of gloves, I sprang open the door, eager to see the result. I inhaled—the spicy apple aroma reminded me a little of Christmas. I allowed the golden muffins to rest on the wire rack for five minutes before taking a bite. The gentle spices teased my tastebuds and the oat topping added another layer of flavour. I placed the rest of the muffins in a Tupperware box to store in the fridge and reheat tomorrow morning. They should prove to be a nutritional start to the day for the busy commuters who often darted in on their way to the train station for a takeaway coffee.

'I will name you "muffins on the move" and you shall sell like proverbial hotcakes,' I declared, cleaning the dirty mixing bowl in the sink.

As I wiped down the kitchen surfaces, I imagined the reaction the muffins would receive from Kitty. Nevertheless, once I got a baking idea in my head, I couldn't dislodge it. If I didn't try it out, it would nibble at me until I gave it a go.

Once the kitchen was spotless, I grabbed my leather jacket and bag and headed for the door. With a sharp twist of the key I locked the tea room, leaving the place a silent and clean shell until it's day started all over again tomorrow.

Cursing the stabbing pains in my feet, I was about to set off for home when a noise from across the empty square made my head snap around.

A dark figure was stumbling towards me, muttering incoherently.

I clasped the strap of my bag tighter. Did I have anything on me that I could use to defend myself? I remembered I only had a tube of hand cream and a de-tangling comb. I must have left my bronze shield and Excalibur at home today.

The burnished light from the street lamps struck the silhouetted figure briefly. 'Bloody thing!' erupted a voice through the chilly air. 'Where the hell are you?'

Hugo Carmichael took a few more tentative steps. The familiar black trilby sat jauntily on his head. He broke into a relieved smile when he saw me walking towards him in my ballet flats. 'Ah! What a sight for sore eyes you are, young lady.'

My brow furrowed. 'What are you doing out here on your own?'

'I may be old but I'm not senile.' He gestured to the cobbles. 'I've only gone and dropped my blasted cane. Can you see it? The old eyes aren't what they were.' Then he paused.

Despite his attempt at a light-hearted tone, Hugo sounded uncharacteristically anxious. I wondered how long he'd been searching around out here.

'You stay where you are and I'll find it for you.'

Hugo's silver moustache twitched. 'Well, I was considering taking a brisk sojourn up the Fells, but alright.'

I cast my eyes around. After a few moments my attention rested on a flash of gold winking up from the darkened cobbles. 'Here you are.'

Hugo accepted his cane gratefully. 'Thank you so much.'

Above our heads, the sky was twisting into ribbons of blueberry black and a spray of stars began to arch upwards.

I pushed a curl away from my face. 'So, you still haven't told me what you're doing out this evening.'

Hugo's heavy lids blinked. 'Oh, I do apologise. I didn't realise I wasn't supposed to leave Glenlovatt without prior permission from the authorities.'

'You do that a lot,' I observed.

'Do what, precisely?'

'Use sarcasm to avoid answering a question.'

'Are you sure you're a baker and not one of those therapists?'

'Ha!' I snorted in triumph. 'There you go. You're doing it again.'

Hugo's watery eyes danced with mischief. 'Touché.'

I glanced around at the empty town square, fairy lights strung from the trees in a series of white gold loops. 'Okay then, if you're not going to tell me why you're back here, I'll be off. I can hear a hot shower and a hair treatment calling.' I gestured to the empty main road snaking up and out of town. 'How will you get home?'

'Travis is waiting for me up past the newsagent's.'

'Travis?'

'The family chauffeur and confidant.'

'Oh, I see.'

As I turned to go, he clasped a weatherworn hand on my jacket sleeve. 'Lara, my late mother always told me that if you follow your heart, your dreams will come true in the end.' A sentimental smile hovered at the corners of his mouth. 'Taking a big step is often frightening, but not taking a chance when it presents itself is even more terrifying.'

I stared at him, thrown by his unexpected words.

'Look, I'm grateful to Kitty for giving me this job, even if she is a right old cow to work for,' I replied uncertainly.

'But?' he enquired, staring at me.

I huddled further into my leather jacket. Before I could stop myself, I was confiding in Hugo. There was something comforting about his open expression that encouraged me to talk. The words eased out of my mouth as he stood there, listening and nodding. 'I want to achieve something on my own.' A sigh of exasperation escaped from my throat. 'Baking isn't like a job for me, not how it is for Kitty.'

Hugo's heavy black coat clung to his shoulders as he studied the True Brew sign with its gold steaming teapot emblem. 'If that tea room were yours, what would you do with it?'

I cocked my head to one side, wondering where this was going. 'Well, for a start I'd remove all that wooden panelling and the tartan carpet.' I paused. 'I can see white tables and chairs and starched tablecloths, delicate china and silver cutlery, and floor-to-ceiling windows.' I unfolded my arms, enthused now. 'I would have cake displays in the windows and local artwork on the walls. And we'd feature two modern cakes as bakes of the day but also retro favourites like Battenberg and chocolate gateau.'

Hugo stared back at me, eyes twinkling. 'Sounds as though you have a lot of big ideas, my dear. And to answer your earlier question, I sometimes like to come for a walk down here in the evening. Remember what Fairview looked like all those years ago when I was a lad . . .' His voice trailed off.

'Are you sure you are alright, Mr Carmichael?'

Hugo snapped out of his lost thoughts. 'Oh yes. Quite alright. Ah, there's Travis coming round the corner now.'

I hitched my shoulder bag higher. 'As long as you're sure. Look after yourself.'

As he made his way over to the newsagent's and the waiting car, I turned and walked back across the square and headed for home. The dark shop windows I passed gave only a teasing hint of their contents: strands of necklaces and watches sat on cushions in the jeweller's, and an assortment of elaborate candles and fringed cushions rested under the spotlights of the homewares boutique. Flowering baskets swung from the lampposts and further down the square a train was disgorging weary commuters onto the platform of our local station.

My beige ballet flats slapped along on the cobbles, leading me to my flat just ten minutes' walk from True Brew. I wearily clumped up the communal staircase and through the door. At least this was my own little oasis. Okay, there was no Mediterranean sun spilling through the curtains every morning but it was mine.

My sitting-room window looked out onto the tree-lined road, which snaked its way towards St Martin's Church. Its elegant gold-topped spire shot into the skyline and the ornate stained-glass windows reflected a distant greeting to me every day. A high stone wall ran around the church grounds like a grey skirt and the church's huge oak door had a look of toothy welcome about it.

Beyond the church I could see the rise and fall of the Fairview Hills, which were sprinkled with clouds of heather. A little market town on the outskirts of Glasgow, the pedestrianised town centre of Fairview housed an eclectic mix of shops, with echoes of its eighteenth-century history running down its cobbled side streets. The town was also fringed with several pretty woodland walks, and Kitty would often complain about the abundance of ramblers and hill walkers, even though she would happily take their money. She'd glare at their rucksacks and tut at their waterproof ensembles before plastering a sickly-sweet smile on her face and snatching their cash.

I dumped my bag on the sofa and clicked on a corner lamp, illuminating my powder blue sofa, stripy nautical cushions and cream carpet. I'd hung some pastel illustrations on the walls that reminded me of the Maltese coast: white buildings fringed with brightly coloured shutters and tropical flowers sat beside scenes of crashing waves and creaky fishing boats.

Perhaps a part of me was still there.

I'd already decided to take my work frustrations out in the kitchen. Battering and whisking up cakes might go some way to lifting my mood. I considered what I fancied baking this evening. Was it to be an Easter egg bombe, complete with sprinkled coconut, or would a banoffee pie be more fitting for a chilly spring night?

I had just dragged my navy curtains closed when the front buzzer crackled. 'Yoo-hoo!' came a exuberant voice through the intercom. 'Let me in!' Despite the prospect of my therapeutic baking session being cruelly interrupted, a huge grin spread over my face as I hit the button to unlock the downstairs door.

Heeled boots clattered up the stairs before a blur of Monsoon swing coat and blonde hair burst through the front door. My best friend didn't do subtle. Morven hurled herself at me like a heat-seeking missile.

'Sweetie, I'm so sorry I wasn't here for you when you got back.'

I raised my eyes to the ceiling. 'Don't be daft! Did you have a great time?'

Morven shrugged off her coat. The glow of her newly caramel skin against a short-sleeved white top and cream jeans told me the answer was most definitely yes.

'It was fab,' she grinned. 'Jake overdid it a couple of times with the ouzo. No surprises there.'

Morven and I first met as gangly twelve-year-olds. Despite her family's success in organic grain farming she'd insisted to her parents that she attend the local Fairview Academy and not the fancy public school they'd wanted. Her argument had been that she wanted a 'diverse' education, making friends with people of all backgrounds.

I knew better. The real attraction at Fairview Academy was the fact that it was co-ed, unlike the girls public school.

The Knight clan, although not as steeped in history as the Carmichaels, owned a considerable amount of land in the Scottish Borders. Morven's dad was a lovely messy-hair-and-glasses type while her mum was always bustling around, inviting people over to their rambling property on the outskirts of Stirling. They came from a long line of farmers, although the thought of Morven, with her river of highlights and her manicured nails, tilling the soil never failed to make me smile. She was far more at home on social media than on the land.

From the moment I met her we became firm friends. With her rolled-up school shirtsleeves and pale blonde hair, she was the yin to my yang. I was flattered and pleased when she confided in me about her privileged background.

'But please don't tell anyone,' she begged one school lunchtime. 'Half the kids will hate me and think I rate myself, and the other half will suddenly want to be my best mates.'

The desperation in her green eyes had tugged at my heart. 'I promise I won't say anything to anyone.'

Her face visibly relaxed under her stripes of blusher. 'Thanks. I just want to be liked for me, you know?'

I nodded and cupped her hand in mine, my glittery pink nail polish shining under the dinner hall strip lighting. We'd held our skinny wrists side by side to admire our friendship bracelets. I'd crafted Morven's from cotton threads in her favourite colours, purple and blue, and she'd done the same for me in red and orange.

'Friends forever,' we'd grinned cheesily.

My mum was enthusiastically embracing a late-arriving anti-establishment stage when Morven and I met. She'd come home from a long day lecturing at college, enthused about how her women's studies students were discussing her ideas. 'We had a terrific debate at lunchtime today,' she'd sparkled, unfurling her long cream scarf, 'about whether men are simply a vessel to support the greater demands of women in today's society.' I remember sitting there, nodding in what I hoped were the correct places while not having a clue what she was talking about. What would she think of Morven, daughter of the successful Knight family, with their organic food empire?

I need not have worried. Morven charmed my mother the first time she met her. I'd asked Mum if I could invite Morven round after school for dinner, and she duly arrived cradling a small wicker basket from an expensive skincare store. Sandwiched among the green ribbon and straw packaging were a bottle of peppermint foot lotion, a tub of satsuma plum hand cream and some honey body scrub.

Mum blushed with approval. 'So indulgent but, more importantly, ethically sourced. Thank you, Morven.'

Our semidetached house, at the time decked out in Mum's latest fad, African-inspired rustic, crouched at the end of a small cul-de-sac. The hall bookshelves sagged under the weight of autobiographies and literary essays, the newer ones mainly of a feminist bent. And despite Dad's sudden death years before, his presence still flitted from room to room like a ghostly whisper. His blue walking fleece hung expectantly from the coat rack. A pair of bashed-up old trainers he used to wear in the garden slouched among Mum's sandals. Even in our bathroom Dad's shaving kit was still perched beside the radio in a red ceramic mug.

My mother was fiercely independent, fired up to defend the female race. And yet she touchingly maintained 94 Hopetown Terrace in homage to her husband's memory and to the father I could barely remember. It was as if our house was in a state of perpetual alert, waiting for Paul McDonald to stride back through the door. On my bedroom windowsill there was a photograph of me and my dad. I couldn't recall when it was taken but I was small, with an expectant face and spools of red curls. Dad was smiling as he cradled me in his arms, his dark hair gleaming against his pale Irish complexion.

There was a constant scent of vanilla candles or spicy cranberry incense in our house. Morven appreciated the carefully draped mustard fabrics, textured print cushions and earthy cedar tables and chairs. Such a typically conservative home on the outside, with its paved drive and privet hedges, but an abundance of Serengeti-inspired culture on the inside.

Three months before, Mum had gone through a monochrome phase. Before that she was all about shabby chic. Often I'd come home and think I'd inadvertently wandered into the wrong house. Privately, I was sure the endless makeovers were a reaction to Dad's death—she seemed desperate to evolve. Officially Mum would say, 'A modern woman should regularly embrace her artistic desires,' conveniently forgetting how content she had been before losing Dad. There had been no frantic purchases of zebra throw cushions or distressed armchairs back then.

When Morven arrived that first afternoon for dinner, I offered her a plate jostling with my latest baking effort—chocolate-chip muffins. She eagerly took one, easing it out of its paper case and biting in. 'Wow! These are fab!'

My toes curled in appreciation as she rammed the rest of the muffin into her mouth and chewed ferociously. 'Thanks. The first time I made them they ended up a little bit dry.'

Mum had appeared in the kitchen, her mouth forming a firm line. 'Lara, I know you enjoy baking but please remember that it can limit a woman's potential by perpetuating a stereotype.'

'It's a chocolate-chip muffin, Mum, not a ban on freedom of speech.'

Morven held the last bite of muffin in her cheek like a greedy hamster. As soon as Mum's red kaftan swished out of the room again we erupted into giggles.

I'd told Mum about Morven's background but she never asked questions about her family success, or about her parents. Though I could see from across the top of our plates of shepherd's pie that she desperately wanted to.

Instead, Morven asked about Mum's college work and I brought up her growing interest in fair trade products. Between us, like a politically correct tag team, we managed Mum well.

After Morven left, having thanked my mum profusely for dinner ('The jam roly-poly and custard were delicious, Mrs McDonald'), Mum filled the kettle and said, 'She's a very likeable girl. I'm pleased you're such good friends with her.'

A glow of pleasure lit me up inside. 'Thanks, Mum. Me too.'

'After all,' added my mother, 'if we can lead more of these privileged youngsters to a political understanding we can topple the system from the inside.'

Oh good grief.

After leaving school, Morven got involved in the marketing side of her father's business, also taking on charity work whenever she could. I always feared we'd eventually lose contact, that she'd end up married to some guy who regularly popped up in *Scottish*

Society magazine, and produce four kids who always wore Alice bands (not the boys, obviously).

So far, it hadn't happened. Morven was dating Jake Ramsay, a rakish but likeable second-division footballer for Hawthorn United, who'd brazenly strode up to her at a sports charity do and exclaimed, 'Sorry for staring, but you look so much like my next girlfriend.'

Morven's parents weren't overly keen on Jake because of his rumoured track record with women. However, they knew from past experience, as did I, that Morven was likely to do the exact opposite of what you suggested, like drag Jake to Las Vegas for an impromptu wedding. Better to let her get Jake out of her system naturally.

My stomach decided to let out a rip-roaring gurgle. 'Do you fancy a stir-fry?' I asked.

Morven rubbed her hands gleefully. 'I'll say.'

She followed me into the kitchen and as I rattled the wok into action the interrogation began in earnest.

'So how do you feel about that arsehole now?'

I measured out the rice and pulled an agonised face. 'Angry. Hurt. I know that was all crap about our relationship coming to a natural end.' Switching on the kettle, I added, 'I think the natural end had a pair of 36C boobs and was called Tanya.' An image of her bronzed bosom looming across Anton's bar made my stomach tighten.

I shovelled the spatula over the chicken pieces with exaggerated aggression while Morven sloshed white wine into two glasses. 'Let it all out, Lars. I hate to see you feeling low.'

My shoulders slumped. The frustration of the last few days came tumbling out before I had a chance to think. 'I was made redundant from my job, the man I gave up everything for turned out to be a prize knob, and now I'm working for Darth Vader's mother.'

Morven opened her red mouth to speak but I cut across her. 'And my own mother is living in Spain with a guy barely older than me. She's having more bloody fun than I ever had.' Jealousy tapped me on the shoulder. 'Sorry for sounding so mean,' I mumbled. 'It's just I loved Malta and thought I could make a life there . . .' My voice tailed off into a whisper.

'Things will get better,' assured Morven, leaning across to squeeze my hand. 'You're an amazing, resourceful woman.'

'Who's currently working for a dictator,' I mumbled, slapping the chicken again. 'You should have seen the look that old bag gave my raspberry and coconut macaroons today.'

I turned to look at her. My best friend's face had broken into a wide smile.

I tried not to laugh. 'I'm glad you're finding my personal life so funny.'

Morven snatched up her glass, almost delivering a puddle of wine onto my kitchen floor. 'You're determined. You're enterprising. And you can bake a mean cake or three. You will get there and have your own place one day, I just know it.'

A little later, we sat down opposite one another at the kitchen table with our plates of steaming chicken stir-fry. I played with the stem of my wineglass. 'I want to feel like I'm achieving something. You know, doing something for me.'

Morven sat back, her green eyes brimming with concern. 'What if I talk to my dad? See if there are any opportunities?'

I shook my curls so fiercely I thought my head might drop off my shoulders. 'Thanks, but no. Being bankrolled by your dad defeats the purpose.'

Morven momentarily looked wounded. 'You don't want to be beholden to the likes of the great Richard Knight. I get it.'

My sigh bounced around the kitchen. 'I'm really grateful and it's very kind of you. But I need to do something on my own.' My face slid into a wry smile. 'It must be terrible for you, Morvs, having such a successful father.'

Morven pierced a piece of chicken on her fork. 'I really do understand your reasons. I would like to do something else for a change. Don't get me wrong, I enjoy working with my dad but it would be great to get involved in something that didn't have the Knight moniker stamped all over it.'

There was a companionable silence for a moment. 'Tell you what,' I suggested, savouring the tangy pineapple sauce, 'you can be my silent partner when I've got my tea room empire.' Morven laughed throatily, only to stop in mock indignation when I quipped, 'Only I've never known you to be silent in our entire friendship.'

Five

'Morning, Kitty,' I said brightly.

Kitty scowled from underneath her checked trilby. 'Morning,' she muttered back, alarming a couple of ladies as she stomped past into the back kitchen. I reached for my iPod to turn up the volume on the bright baroque music that gently danced through the tea room.

Kitty's head jerked back around. 'What is that racket?'

'I thought it added a bit of atmosphere.'

Kitty's expression darkened even further. 'This is my business, not a haunted house. Switch it off.'

Reining in my anger, I silenced the iPod with a jab of my finger. A triumphant smirk hovered at the corners of Kitty's mouth. 'That's better, don't you think?'

It wasn't. There was a heavy silence, except for the slosh of tea and clattering cutlery.

'And what are these muffin things in my fridge?' called Kitty from the kitchen. 'They look more like rabbit food to me.'

I popped my head around the door. 'They're healthy breakfast muffins. Carrot and apple with rolled oats.'

Kitty couldn't have looked more horrified if I'd robbed the till and made a run for it. She took a gulp of air, ready to verbally lambast me.

'Why on earth did you turn the music off?' questioned a clipped voice from behind us.

Hugo Carmichael was shuffling towards the counter. He raked a hand through his silvery hair. 'I was quite enjoying that.'

This was getting to be a regular occurrence. If I didn't know better I'd say the old grouch was becoming my guardian angel.

Hiding a smile, I addressed Hugo. 'Good morning, Mr Carmichael.'

Kitty barged past me like a grey battleship. 'Hello, Mr Carmichael,' she simpered, bent almost double. 'I just felt that music wasn't suitable.'

Hugo's grey brows looked like they were fencing. 'Why ever not?'

Under Hugo's and my own questioning gazes, Kitty reddened. 'Er, well, if you consider our clientele . . .'

Hugo scanned the customers currently seated at assorted tables. Cakes were being savoured amid the hum of chat. 'They might be elderly but they're not dead.'

I snorted with laughter.

'Yes, well,' sniffed Kitty, angrily fastening her apron. 'I'll consider our musical choices another time.'

Hugo gave me a conspiratorial wink across the top of today's centrepiece, a coffee and walnut cake.

Kitty thrust her hand out towards the heavily iced creation. 'How about a slice of this, Mr Carmichael? I made it myself.'

Hugo eyed it suspiciously. 'I've not long had breakfast but thank you all the same.' Then his attention alighted on me. 'I don't suppose you've rustled up any more of those scrumptious little macaroons, Lara?'

I could feel Kitty's eyes bore into my face as I turned to Hugo. 'No macaroons today but I've baked some cranberry and macadamia brownies.'

Hugo's expression reminded me of an excited child on Christmas Eve. 'Ooh, one of those, please, and an Earl Grey.'

Kitty scribbled up his order before thumping it onto the wall behind.

'We could sell the rest of my brownies,' I suggested to her retreating back.

She stopped short. I could practically see her hair bristling. 'Put out half a dozen and charge one pound fifty each,' she grudgingly bit out before disappearing into the storeroom.

Well, that was a small victory.

I prepared Hugo's tray and carried it over. Morning sun was feeling its way across the tea room, highlighting the snowy tablecloths. He took a careful bite of the brownie and closed his eyes. 'Just heavenly,' he sighed.

I turned to go but he pulled at my arm.

'Sit a moment,' he said, reaching for the teapot.

'I don't think Kitty would approve of that, Mr Carmichael.'

'Please,' he implored. 'And stop calling me Mr Carmichael. It's Hugo.'

I quickly sat down opposite him, checking that Kitty was still in the depths of the storeroom.

He regarded me across the table with those steely grey eyes. At first I wondered if I'd smudged my lipstick or had cereal caught in my teeth. Then he finally spoke again. 'Thank you for helping me find my cane last night.'

'Oh, you're welcome, Mr Carmichael. Sorry—Hugo.'

Hugo went to reach across the table for the sugar bowl but I got to it first and handed it to him. I caught him studying the bracelet as it slid up and down my wrist.

'Lara, can you answer the phone, please? I'm busy.'

Our heads jerked around to see Kitty inspecting her lipstick in the mirror of her gold compact. I offered Hugo a roll of my eyes and rose to answer the call, which was for Kitty anyway, regarding the latest milk order from her supplier.

'I've got to go out,' she bristled, patting her hair. 'I won't be long.'

'But it's almost lunchtime.'

Her chilly gaze appraised me. 'Yes, I'm aware of that, Lara.' She shrugged on a red jacket that made her look like a box. 'I've got to meet a friend. It's an emergency. See you shortly.'

And with that she was out the door in a blaze of sickly sweet perfume that reminded me of toilet freshener.

I proceeded to pace backwards and forwards from the counter to the floor, silently cursing not only Kitty but also the cheap plastic apron I had to wear. As I prepared a takeaway latte for a harassed-looking middle-aged man and slid two treacle scones into a bag for the elderly lady waiting behind him, a hunched figure trundled up to the counter.

'What can I get you?'

The scruffily dressed woman, swamped in a raincoat and with a shabby straw sunhat perched on her head, eyed the cakes hungrily as she plonked two carrier bags down by her old boots.

'Aren't these cakes pretty?' she gasped softly. 'They all look too lovely to eat.'

I nodded. 'I wish I thought more like that. It would help my waistline.'

The woman pointed a chipped fingernail at me. 'You've got nothing to worry about there, dear.' I was about to protest when she squealed, 'Oh! Those look good. How much are they?'

'These brownies?' I grinned, flattered by her enthusiasm. 'They're a pound fifty each.'

Her hands felt around her coat pockets. 'I've only got eighty pence,' she admitted after an embarrassed silence. 'Never mind. Maybe next time, eh?'

Before I could reply she had picked up her bags and turned to depart with a faltering smile.

'Good thing Kitty isn't here,' muttered Hugo over the rim of his teacup. 'She would have chased that unfortunate soul halfway down the street.'

I watched her hitch the collar of her coat up and tug down the brim of her floppy hat before opening the door.

'Hugo, would you keep an eye on the counter for me for a moment, please?'

Hugo's eyes widened. 'What are you going to do? Don't jeopardise your job, Lara. You know what Kitty is like.'

I pulled off my apron. 'Yes, I do know what she's like. And thank goodness not everyone in the world is like that.'

I slipped out the door, the clinking of cups and murmuring conversations disappearing abruptly as it shut behind me. 'Excuse me!' I called, pattering down the cobbles after the woman.

She turned and again thumped down her belongings, some of which I could now see were an assortment of clothes and dog-eared books and a faded duvet with yellowing pillow. 'Yes, dear?'

'The brownies,' I smiled. 'Would you really like one?'

The corners of her ice blue eyes crinkled as she smiled back. I noticed a lock of dirty blonde hair escaping from under her hat. 'I'll say I would. They look delicious.' Then a guarded tone crept into her voice. 'But I'm not a charity case, my dear. And I don't have enough money for one of your fancy cakes.'

I wafted my hand airily. 'We have far too many cakes for today,' I lied, 'and you'd be doing me a favour if you took one.'

Her lips tightened. 'But what about your boss? That Kitty woman?' She visibly stiffened as she mentioned her name. 'I came to your café once before and she threatened me with the police.'

'What for?'

''Cos I said her Marlborough buns looked rock hard—and I didn't have enough money to buy a slice of rocky road.'

I folded my arms in mock indignation. 'I'm sure that sort of talk normally carries a custodial sentence.'

We laughed, other shoppers weaving around us on the cobbles.

'Come on,' I urged. 'She's not there at the moment. Kitty, I mean.'

The woman's lips parted at the thought of cake. 'Those brownies do look tempting.'

'Well, then. What are you standing there for?'

I insisted on carrying her bags back up to True Brew and we left the strolling shoppers under a greying sky.

Hugo's bristly grey brows rose up to his hairline and hovered there when he saw my companion and me.

'You take a seat over there and I'll bring you a pot of tea and one of those brownies,' I said.

She sank gratefully into a chair by the window, where she stared at Kitty's assorted horse ornaments. 'But I can't pay for it.'

I shook my head. 'I'm sure we can stretch to a cup of tea too.'

With a tea bag stewing in the white ceramic pot, I dived into my purse underneath the counter and slid four pounds into the till. That would cover the cost of her cake and cuppa. Kitty accounted for every little item and I was not prepared to give her the satisfaction of blaming me for stealing.

Hugo ambled up beside me, balancing one gnarled hand on his cane. 'Kitty could be back at any moment.' Then he indicated the till. 'That was very kind of you.'

I tried to feign innocence. 'What was?'

He tilted his mouth. 'Don't be bashful, Lara. I just saw you putting money in the till.'

I raised one finger to my lips. 'Please don't make a big thing of it, Hugo. She is a proud lady.'

He studied me for a few moments before breaking into a warm smile. 'I suspect you can hardly afford to go throwing your money around.'

I gave a brief nod. 'My redundancy package wasn't exactly six figures as I was one of the last in, but it's enough to keep me afloat for now.'

Hugo adjusted his cane to give him additional support. 'I'm not trying to pry into your financial affairs, but knowing Kitty Walker as I do, I would imagine she isn't overly generous to her employees.'

I let out a dry laugh. 'Your assumption is correct.'

Hugo blinked a couple of times. 'Red hair, kind, generous and enthusiastic. That's an irresistible combination, young lady.'

'Thank you,' I blushed, transferring a meringue onto a plate. 'Try telling that to my ex.'

Hugo's fingers drummed against his cane before he suddenly asked me, 'When do you normally get your lunchbreak?'

'Are you asking me out?' I laughed nervously. Dating someone who must be about to receive their telegram from the Queen wasn't one of my priorities.

Hugo twinkled beside me. 'Believe me, if I were sixty years younger!' He rattled the tip of his cane. 'You haven't answered my question. What time is your lunchbreak?'

I stared at this intriguing old man. What was going on behind those intense eyes of his? He barely knew me.

'Usually around half-past twelve,' I replied with an edge of curiosity.

Hugo slapped his hand decisively onto the wooden counter. An elderly couple close by frowned over their zesty lemon cake.

'Right. I shall return at half-past twelve tomorrow,' he beamed. 'Be ready.'

'So, was today any better?' asked Morven that evening as I flopped down onto my blue sofa.

I clasped my mobile to my ear and waggled my freshly manicured shell-pink toenails. 'If you mean did Kitty hug me and tell me what a wonderful asset I am, then no, she didn't.'

Morven made a tutting sound. 'She's such a jealous old bat. You'd think she'd be grateful for how much business your baking is bringing in.'

I tightened the belt of my pink towelling dressing gown. 'Well, for now, I need that job, pure and simple. Hopefully something else will turn up or a TV station will spot my potential and give me my own baking show.' The very suggestion made us both giggle. As I sipped my cup of camomile tea I told Morven about my day, starting with my lunch date with Hugo. The thought of it was intriguing, to say the least.

Six

Outside the car window, daffodils swayed their dusty heads and trees spun glossy fingers into the air. Hills curved with blankets of green under a pale blue sky dotted with shreds of cloud.

My head was whirring. Hugo had collected me in his chauffeur-driven car, a purring Daimler in deep claret. The interior was a combination of dark wood and buttercream leather with impossibly comfortable seats.

The chestnut dashboard sparkled in the sunlight as Hugo's chauffeur, Travis, manoeuvred the vehicle to its destination. This car was the polar opposite of my dear little Cleo, with her silvery blue paintwork that had seen better days.

Hugo, seated beside me in the back of the car, wore a playful smile on his craggy face. 'Nearly there,' he said.

'Where are we going?' I asked with just a hint of trepidation.

'You'll see,' came the enigmatic response.

I drew a deep breath. I hoped I wasn't wasting my precious lunch hour on some weird whim to please Hugo. Normally at this time I'd be wandering around the shops or popping back to my flat to escape another tongue-lashing from Kitty. The morning had been the usual drudgery and frustration was still nipping at my heels.

The car ferried us around a sharp corner and I blinked at the sight greeting me. A black and cream sign announced 'Glenlovatt Manor' in sweeping letters. Behind that a huge and ornate gate peppered with wrought-iron thistles, protected the property with steely determination.

Why had Hugo brought me to his home?

I hadn't been anywhere near the Glenlovatt estate since primary school. I recalled the trundling coach disgorging its load of sticky, crumpled kids at the entrance along with our harassed teacher, Mrs Elvin.

The gate swung open and we swept through. The manor stood like a grand old lady, at the end of a long pink gravel drive. She was bathed in the beauty of spring, with buttery stone and bold windows glinting. The buttresses of ornate flowers and thistles reminded me of icing.

I glanced anxiously at my watch.

'Don't worry, Lara,' smiled Hugo as the car glided to a halt. 'I had a word with Kitty. She assures me she could manage on her own a little while longer.'

I sighed resignedly. Kitty was a snob so it wouldn't have entered her head to argue with Hugo Carmichael. She'd be saving up a tirade for when I got back.

As if sensing my apprehension, Hugo offered a cheeky wink. 'Don't give that woman any more thought for now. After lunch, Travis will return you to Fairview.'

Travis nodded politely as we got out of the car.

'Lunch?' I repeated, gazing at the steps that led up to the huge oval entrance.

'You still don't believe me? I wouldn't bring a young lady to my ancestral home without arranging lunch,' said Hugo with a smile. 'What sort of cad do you take me for? Now, let's press on, if we want to discuss this business proposition.'

'Business?'

'Do try to keep up,' he grinned again. 'I've brought you here to Glenlovatt because I want to discuss something very important with you.'

The two turrets of Glenlovatt sprang up either side of the entrance and I half-expected Rapunzel to drop her mane of blonde hair down from one of them. I suddenly felt quite underdressed in my jeans and ballet pumps.

My curiosity rose further when Hugo exclaimed, 'First lunch, then I'll give you the grand tour—and then we can have a little chat.'

Travis assisted Hugo up the steps and I followed behind. I didn't remember Glenlovatt being so impressive when I was a child, though I was then more preoccupied with Howie from the Backstreet Boys than the splendour of Scottish stately homes.

I watched Hugo's slightly bent figure disappear into the cool, dark entrance with Travis following faithfully behind him.

What on earth was going on?

Glenlovatt Manor, September 1955

'Have I told you that you're even more beautiful than you were yesterday?'

She laughed, the dusting of freckles on her cheeks bouncing. 'How long has it taken you to think of that line?'

He grinned, making the deep cleft in his chin pop. 'It isn't a line, my darling. It's true.'

Their fingers laced together in the autumn sunshine. Glenlovatt sat in the distance, its vanilla stone peeking out between the first russet leaves.

As her yellow cotton dress billowed out around her legs she drank him in, from the top of his slicked-back raven hair to the soles of his shiny brown brogues. Dressed in that combination of checked shirt and beige trousers, he reminded her of James Mason. His wide smile made her heart flip.

'The Silver Spoon is lucky to have a beauty like you, don't you think?'

Her mind conjured up an image of the tea shop, with its circular turquoise tables, high-backed wooden chairs and Art Deco diamond blue wallpaper. Maybe one day she'd have a tea room of her own. Then they could be together. Imagine that! She wouldn't be seen as just a waitress anymore.

As if reading her racing thoughts, he took her in his arms, erasing her concerns with a deep kiss. 'Nothing will change how I feel about you,' he murmured. 'You'll always be my Pre-Raphaelite girl.'

Seven

Good grief! I felt like I was expecting triplets. Although, given the generous serving of haggis and clapshot drizzled with whisky sauce, followed by a towering raspberry cranachan laced with whipped cream, I wasn't surprised.

I pulled my eyes away from the table and sleepily surveyed the dining room, which reminded me of something out of *Harry Potter*. The shining wooden floor reflected the impressive chandelier, which on closer inspection could have done with a dust. Decorating the walls were an assortment of austere portraits, military men with cut-glass cheekbones, women in flouncing, layered gowns, and haughty gundogs. Heavily embroidered rugs were scattered further along the room, leading to a heavy grey stone coal fireplace. A set of double doors permitted a peek into what must have been the drawing room, where I glimpsed mismatched furniture, a moss green chaise longue and two floral sofas.

Hugo sat silently to my right. Thank goodness he hadn't insisted on taking the seat at the other end of the table or I'd have needed the use of a PA system to communicate with him. The oak table sliced through the centre of the dining room and

I could imagine the likes of Robert the Bruce and his cohorts crowded around its lengthy expanse.

'Penny for them?' asked Hugo.

'It's a gorgeous room.'

Hugo's long fingers played with his linen napkin. 'Come. There's something I want to show you.' He gingerly rose out of his seat and in a moment Travis was at his side to assist him. 'I'll take you on a proper tour another time. Lunch took rather longer than I expected and I don't want to get you in trouble with your esteemed boss.'

We entered the hallway, which was lined by more portraits lit by carriage lights along the pale walls. A bust of a man with a stony expression glared at me as I tapped past his plinth. The floor was like a giant chessboard, solid squares of black and white tiles. I felt like Alice in Wonderland being led past a series of doors, each more mysterious than the previous one.

We passed a cabinet filled with family photographs. A selection of formal images showing men in dinner suits, then a couple of pictures of relaxed-looking people on a boating trip and a black-and-white shot of trendy partygoers in the sixties vied for my attention. My eyes were drawn to a colour photograph of a teenage boy in school uniform, his dark, floppy hair tumbling down over his brow and framing an intense, almost belligerent face.

Hugo's voice interrupted my nosiness. 'It's just through here.'

We reached a burnished door shaped like a church window. Segments of glass hinted tantalisingly at what was behind it. Hugo tugged a key from his pocket and made a few attempts to put it in the lock.

'Allow me,' I smiled, noting the tremble in his hands. 'Are you alright?'

The corners of Hugo's eyes creased like tissue paper. 'Nothing that a Drambuie won't cure.'

I crouched down with the key and felt a satisfying click as it slid into the lock. The door reluctantly eased open and a cloud of dust rose up to greet us both. The large room was almost empty and two huge windows with built-in seats allowed in pools of watery sunshine, which shone onto a bare beech floor. An image of Juliet reading some breathtaking romance while waiting for Romeo came immediately to mind and made me smile. A central pair of double doors looked out on to a small patio, with a view of sweeping green lawn, surrounded by a bank of trees. A set of short steps led into myriad paths and shrubberies.

I gazed upwards. The ceiling featured an apple green design of ornate hexagons, trimmed with a border of ivory flowers. It was stunning.

Hugo's eyes followed mine as I drank in the details. 'Gorgeous, isn't it?' he sighed. 'My late daughter-in-law loved this room.'

'I can see why,' I breathed, tracing my fingers along the nearest wall.

'Lydia used to love coming here to paint and draw . . .' His voice trickled to a sad whisper.

'I'm sorry.'

He quickly pinned a smile back on. 'Let's go out into the grounds for a moment.'

We walked back to the front entrance and out into the crescent-shaped drive. A path by the side of the house took us down into the patchwork of gardens and grounds. The sun had fought successfully against the clouds again and was now warming the chocolate brown earth of the flowerbeds. A perfume of mint rose up from the nearby herb garden. 'I used to love strolling around here in my youth.'

'It's a beautiful garden.'

Hugo shuffled forwards and opened his mouth to speak again, only to be interrupted by my trilling mobile.

'Excuse me,' I apologised, reaching into my back pocket. Kitty's name screamed on the screen.

'Where are you?' barked my disembodied jailer. 'Have you seen the time? I need a hand here. Members of the Fairview Players theatre group have just arrived and you know how demanding they can be.'

Before I could articulate a reply, Kitty continued, 'They've gone all thespian and I can't cope with it all!'

'I'm on my way,' I placated, giving Hugo an apologetic eye roll. I hung up.

'Travis will take you back,' said Hugo.

I gave him an appreciative smile. 'I'm sorry to dash off. Thank you for such a lovely lunch.'

Then a thought occurred to me. 'Hugo, did you want to ask me something?'

He paused. 'It can wait—for now.'

Eight

 Umbrellas popped open like multi-coloured mush-
rooms outside the window of True Brew.

It had been a few days since my strange rendezvous with
Hugo. As I'd departed Glenlovatt, Hugo promised to come back
to the tea shop to speak to me 'as a matter of urgency'. But so
far, he'd failed to appear. All I had to show for my lunch with
him was a severe ear-bending from Kitty for being half an hour
late back, and not feeling like I could eat another morsel for the
next twenty-four hours.

Funny how her attitude had been much more conciliatory
towards Hugo, when he'd rung her that afternoon to apologise.
From what I could hear of the snatches of conversation, Hugo had
insisted that my lateness was entirely his fault. Not surprisingly,
Kitty had spread herself prostrate across the tea room's carpeted
floor while emitting a series of sycophantic noises. It made my
skin crawl just to watch her.

In true Jekyll and Hyde form, she'd ended the call with a
girlish giggle before presenting me with one of her angry snarls.
'No more taking liberties' she'd threatened over the top of a fruit

scone mountain, 'otherwise you'll be out of a job.' She contorted her mouth. 'There are girls queuing round the block to work here.'

I looked out towards the tea room's dark bevelled door; all I could see were cobbles slick from another shower. With a heavy heart, I muttered an apology and occupied myself by rearranging some orange and chocolate fancies.

Unwanted pictures of Malta and Anton resurfaced in my mind. How much longer could I carry on working for Kitty before I impaled her with a cake slice? Okay, it was a job. It was local and just ten minutes' walk from home. But was being treated to daily tongue-lashings worth it? Jobs in PR were better paid but hotly contested, and did I really want to go back to that world anyway?

As Kitty's selection of Scottish pipe bands continued unabated from her dilapidated cassette player, my heart sank further towards the floor. I'd returned to Fairview in the hope of giving my life a jump-start. Right now, with more rain peppering the shop windows and the feel of Kitty's stare striking my back whenever I turned it, I felt my life had well and truly juddered to a halt.

Lost in a web of self-pity, I failed to notice Mrs Kendrick, a member of Kitty's coven, burst through the door in an emerald headscarf and tightly fastened raincoat until it was too late. Her heavily powdered face was alive with gossip. Oh no. The thought of being sandwiched between the pair of them was too much to bear. I dashed into the kitchen to remove the next batch of scones from the oven. They were like golden puffs of delight nestling on the hot tray.

I'd just started scooping them onto a cake stand when I heard a growing buzz of conversation from the tea room and the sudden scraping of chairs. I peered round the kitchen door to see a tide of customers abandoning their cakes and buzzing eagerly towards

Mrs Kendrick. She was in the centre of it all, a blue-rinsed beacon basking in the attention.

What juicy gossip was she announcing now? By the looks of it, it was something pretty spectacular. I abandoned my tower of scones and edged in beside Kitty.

I couldn't help but notice the inquisitive expressions of our customers transforming into ones of sadness and shock. Even Kitty, whose face normally only had two expressions—sour and very sour—registered disbelief.

'What is it?' I asked a man clutching his little boy's hand. 'What's going on?'

The young dad swiped a napkin across the child's icing-dotted mouth. 'Hugo Carmichael, the old laird, has passed away.'

His voice was light but the heavy words felt as though they were jumping up to slap me in the face. All I could manage was a strangulated, 'What?'

'The old laird has died. Such a shame. He was such a pleasant old chap.' He plopped a five-pound note onto the counter. 'Very sudden, by the sounds of it.'

I steadied myself against the counter, unable to focus clearly on anything, and watched in a daze as the man and his son wound their way through the chatting throng to the door.

Nine

The sun pushed through a bank of cloud, illuminating the windows of Hugo's ancestral home. I stood beside Kitty at the back of a large crowd of mourners in the grounds of Glenlovatt, where Hugo was being laid to rest in the family vault, a gated mausoleum protected by a huddle of leafy oak trees. The granite of Hugo's final resting place sparkled softly in the light. The family crest with its bright blue and gold carvings of thistles and roses brought warmth to the stone.

I was relieved when Kitty suggested closing True Brew after the morning rush so we could pay our respects. It seemed so sudden. In the very short time I knew him I'd become very fond of Hugo, and to have our blossoming friendship end so suddenly filled me with sadness. Despite his frailties, there was so much life and mischief in those wise old eyes. He may have been approaching ninety but he was such a force of nature, and I was really beginning to value his advice and kindness. I pushed back the lump collecting in my throat.

To the right of me, partly concealed by an assortment of black hat–wearing women and tall, sharply dressed men, was Hugo's son Gordon, the current laird. I'd never met him but had seen him zipping through Fairview in his Land Rover on a few occasions. He bore his grief well, smiling slightly at the words of comfort offered to him while pulling his black wool coat tighter and inclining his silver head.

More people drifted into my line of sight. There was the odd flap of a silk tie and the wink of designer handbags. Another man appeared beside the laird, all shoulder-length black hair and steely jaw. The collar of his navy coat was upturned, giving him a mysterious air. I raised myself onto my booted toes to have another look but at that moment a Scandinavian type modelling an enormous grey affair on her head stepped in front of me. My view of the tall, dark stranger was well and truly obscured by the trendy angles of her hat. I took a brisk step sideways for another view across the sea of bobbing heads but he'd gone.

Kitty nudged my arm. 'What are you doing, Lara?' she hissed out of the corner of her jammy red mouth. 'You're fidgeting about like a five-year-old.'

I took the opportunity to study my boss's funeral ensemble again. She too was wearing a hat, except hers was more like a hovering flying saucer. Any minute now I expected the black circular design to blast light over her steel curls and abduct her.

Well, I could live in hope, couldn't I?

She buried her gloved hands deeper into the pockets of her coat. 'Sharp breeze considering it's almost May. I wonder what we'll get for lunch.'

I rolled my eyes. 'I thought you wanted to get back to open the shop?'

Kitty answered my question with an indifferent shrug. 'There's no great hurry, is there? Hugo was a frequent customer. The least we can do is pay our respects.'

And partake of the Carmichael family's hospitality, I thought silently. Yes, the lure of a good funeral buffet and the throng of

Scottish movers and shakers were just too much of a temptation for Kitty. Losing out on lunchtime profits paled in comparison with the idea of networking with people from some of Scotland's most influential families. With one last lingering look at Hugo's burial place, I followed Kitty and the other mourners towards the house.

Despite the sunshine, Glenlovatt Manor seemed melancholy, somehow lacking the vibrancy of when Hugo brought me here just over a week ago. It felt like an eternity now, following him through the vast corridors under the watchful eye of his regal family portraits.

Staff directed us up the steps and into the dining room. My heart lurched when I thought about the decadent lunch Hugo arranged for us that day. Goodness knows what he had planned to speak to me about. I pushed my curls away from my face. Oh well. I would never know now.

The dining table had been transported to the furthest end of the room, allowing waiting staff to weave in and out of the clusters of mourners, proffering plates of finger food. The platters were filled with an assortment of gourmet treats: pasties sprinkled with toasted pistachios, mini roast beef and mustard rolls, cheddar and chutney on oatcakes, and hot smoked Scottish salmon with mascarpone cheese.

Kitty was off like a rocket on the fifth of November, using her octopus reach to gather an assortment of items. I didn't feel hungry but accepted a cup of tea and hovered in a corner with a large oval mirror opposite. I caught a glimpse of my reflection staring back at me from the gilt-edged frame. Red curls spilled over my shoulders, a bright splash against my plain dark coat. Thank goodness I'd decided to wear my bottle green scarf; I would have looked positively anaemic otherwise.

I buried my nose in the warm, familiar aroma of my teacup. Glancing up again, I caught sight of a short, spectacled man staring at my reflection in the mirror. He appeared constrained by his dark grey three-piece suit and slash of navy tie. He was clutching a briefcase. Surely a salesman wouldn't highjack a funeral, I thought incredulously.

He stared at me for a few more moments before skimming his hand over the top of his receding dark hair and moving towards me with fast steps. My teacup remained halfway to my mouth when he said in a soft Glaswegian burr, 'Excuse me, are you Ms Lara McDonald?'

'Yes?'

He extended his hand and I shook it after gingerly balancing my cup in my left hand.

'I'm Graeme Chalmers of Chalmers & Logie Solicitors. Can I have a quick word?'

'Er, yes. Alright.'

Confused, I handed my almost empty cup to a passing waiter and followed Mr Chalmers out of the buzzing dining room and into an alcove further down the great hall. The coolness emanating from the chequered tiles under my feet was a welcome relief from the stuffy room.

'I've been instructed by the late Mr Hugo Carmichael,' he began, running his fingers down his tie. 'Are you able to attend a meeting at my offices on Thursday morning at ten?'

I tried to process what he was saying. 'You're Hugo's solicitor? Why do you want to see me?'

He didn't reply. He merely stood there, waiting for a response.

'Um, yes, probably. Yes. Alright,' I answered, confused. 'But what is this all about?'

Mr Chalmers met my question with a sympathetic smile. 'I'm sorry but I can't divulge any information about Mr Carmichael's will until we meet.'

He pulled a business card from his inside jacket pocket and I saw a flash of blue satin lining. 'I look forward to seeing you on Thursday morning, Ms McDonald.'

Questions raced through my head so fast I thought my brain might implode. 'How did you know who I was?' I asked his retreating back.

Mr Chalmers' mouth twitched. 'Mr Carmichael told me to look for the Pre-Raphaelite girl.'

Ten

The train zipped into the outskirts of Glasgow, streaks of wide open spaces and Hansel and Gretel cottages now giving way to black ribbons of motorway.

As Queen Street Station surged into view, my stomach lurched in very much the same way as the train did. The last time I felt this nervous was when Anton had told me he needed to talk.

I'd made an effort for this meeting with Hugo's solicitor. A slim navy skirt skimmed my knees, topped off with a cream pussy-bow blouse and my leather jacket. I wiggled my toes in their sharp black court shoes. No pain, no gain, I suppose.

In order to wangle the morning off I'd had to employ every ounce of my mediocre acting ability to fool Kitty, ringing up as early as I could and feigning a headache. After a predictable stream of unsympathetic grunts, I promised to dose myself up with painkillers and plenty of water. 'I'll be in about lunchtime,' I assured her.

'Oh, alright,' came the snappy response, followed by a cacophony of clattering plates, 'but get here as soon as you can. I need reliable staff, you know!'

I'd slammed my mobile down before blowing an undignified raspberry. What an old bag!

Clutching my navy shoulder bag, I shuffled off the train with a stream of commuters, most preoccupied with their phones or studying the displays on the platform for their connecting service.

The Glasgow skyline was grey today against the sharp angles of tower blocks, glass offices and high-rise department stores. The offices of Chalmers & Logie Solicitors were only five minutes' walk from Sauchiehall Street, which my poor feet were grateful for. I looked like any other working woman as I hurried past shop windows alongside the churn of traffic, my hair tied back with some black ribbon. People darted across the pavement in front of me like out-of-control skittles.

As I reached the solicitors' offices, I took a deep breath to calm myself. Why on earth had the lawyer of an elderly Scottish aristo I hardly knew summoned me here? For the three days since Hugo's funeral my thoughts had catapulted from one theory to another until I decided my nerves couldn't take any more surmising. All the answers, I hoped, were behind this formidable façade of grey stone and black painted door.

My nervous reflection bounced back at me from the mirrored wall behind an immaculately groomed receptionist, who directed me to a plush waiting room furnished with a black leather sofa, white scatter cushions and monochrome paintings. I politely declined her offer of tea or coffee—the twist in my stomach suggested neither was a good idea I'd probably drop the lot and have to pay for the white carpet to be professionally cleaned— and instead tried to distract myself with the artwork on display. A pencil drawing of a young girl clutching a small sunflower caught my attention. I was studying its sweeping pencil strokes when the receptionist appeared in front of me. 'Ms McDonald, Mr Chalmers will see you now.'

I trailed behind her red heels to another black door. She rapped gently, offered an encouraging smile and then disappeared.

Pinning a shaky smile on my face, I pushed open the heavy door. Mr Chalmers rose to his feet from behind an oak desk that was overloaded with files and other clutter. A quick glance suggested that his office was expensively decorated, the deep beige walls boasting three large prints of Glasgow scenes in substantial silver frames. One showed the Clyde shipyards, with cranes lurking over the water; another, views of Sauchiehall Street at Christmas, snow and decorations illuminated by the glow of street lamps and car headlights. The third photograph was of George Square in spring, flowers bursting out of baskets and pigeons hovering near office workers lapping up the sun. A shelf of glossy-spined books ran the length of the wall behind his desk.

But my attention was soon taken by the three men sitting opposite Mr Chalmers.

Their faces were all familiar. One of them, the dapper, silver-haired man, was Gordon Carmichael, Hugo's son and the current laird. The second man was Travis, the family chauffeur cum butler. The other man seated beside him was the dark-haired, chisel-jawed figure from Hugo's funeral.

Surprise was drawn on all our faces at the sight of one another.

From behind a pair of gilt-edged spectacles Graeme Chalmers announced, 'This is Ms Lara McDonald. Ms McDonald, please meet Gordon Carmichael, Hugo's son. This is Vaughan Carmichael, Hugo's grandson, and this is Mitchell Travis, the family's chauffeur and trusted employee.'

As the three of them rose to their feet, an image of a sombre, dark-haired teenager popped into my mind. Vaughan must be the grumpy kid in the photograph, I thought.

Gordon and Vaughan shared curious glances as they shook my hand. Gordon smiled quizzically, at least, while Vaughan

Carmichael's jaw seemed to harden. 'I don't understand,' he muttered towards Mr Chalmers. 'I thought this was the family reading of the will.'

His steely blue gaze was upon me again. I took an involuntary step backwards.

'It is the reading of the will, yes,' replied Mr Chalmers.

'But she isn't family,' said Vaughan, his voice adopting a blunter tone and his dark brows gathering like storm clouds. He made me think of a bad-tempered Christian Bale. Embarrassment made my skin prickle. 'Look,' I said, tugging at my bag strap, 'I don't know why Hugo arranged for me to be here either. I'm as confused as you are.'

'Could everyone please take a seat?' suggested an anxious Mr Chalmers. 'Then we can get started.'

I sat down in the vacant seat next to Gordon and smoothed down my skirt nervously for something to do. The laird's mouth flickered a hint of a smile sideways but his grouchy son merely stared straight ahead.

As Mr Chalmers proceeded to read out Hugo's will in a clear voice, ghostly pictures of him floated before my eyes and I smiled fleetingly. Unsurprisingly, he had left Glenlovatt Manor equally to his son and grandson but seemingly not as much money as they had envisaged, judging by the surprised rise and fall of their eyebrows.

Then a paragraph was read out for the attention of Travis. The Carmichael employee looked genuinely touched as Mr Chalmers read out that Hugo always considered him a 'much loved and respected friend and employee'. Travis dropped his dark head slightly and sucked in a mouthful of air as Mr Chalmers carried on reading. '"I therefore bequeath my cellar of Dalmore whisky to Mitchell Travis with my gratitude and appreciation for his service over the years."'

'I can't accept that, sir,' he protested to Gordon. 'It's too much.'

Gordon dismissed his words. 'Yes, you can accept it, and you will. My father would be most offended if you didn't. He thought a great deal of you, Travis, as we all do.'

Travis nodded gravely. 'Thank you, sir.'

Mr Chalmers turned to me. 'Now, the late Mr Carmichael has left specific instructions for you, Ms McDonald.'

I ignored Vaughan, who shot forwards in his seat as if he'd had an electric current fired up his backside.

Mr Chalmers cleared his throat as he read. '"I, Hugo Carmichael, leave my late daughter-in-law's art studio at Glenlovatt Manor to Miss Lara McDonald."' He looked up.

I stared back at Mr Chalmers, whose expression was expectant. 'Art studio?'

He nodded briefly. 'Yes. Lydia Carmichael's art studio in Glenlovatt Manor,' he repeated.

I stared back at the surprised faces examining me. 'Why?' I asked. 'Sorry. I don't understand.'

'There's more, Ms McDonald,' clarified Mr Chalmers. He turned his attention back to the papers he held in his hand and began to read again. '"Lydia's art studio must be turned into a tea room for both the benefit of Glenlovatt Manor and as a business opportunity for Miss McDonald."'

Vaughan was appalled. 'Tea room?' He threw his hands into the air. 'Is this some sort of joke?'

Mr Chalmers eyed him carefully. 'No, sir, it most certainly isn't. Shall I continue?'

Vaughan folded his suited arms across his chest. 'Oh, please do. I can hardly wait to hear the rest.'

Gordon gave his son a withering look.

'"Glenlovatt Manor,' continued Mr Chalmers, 'was my family home for ninety years. However, as with many ancestral homes, modern demands and ever-increasing costs mean that it is in danger of falling into disrepair. I therefore direct that the art studio be converted into a tea room."'

Mr Chalmers ignored Vaughan's snort of derision. '"This tea room business will be part-owned and operated by Miss Lara McDonald."'

The breath caught in my throat. I swivelled my head in disbelief, first looking at Gordon and then at Vaughan. The only face that carried a modicum of enthusiasm about the announcement was Travis's.

Mr Chalmers paused for dramatic effect before resuming reading out the remainder of Hugo's instructions. '"Lydia, wanted Glenlovatt to move with the times, as do I. Therefore, this new venture will not only benefit Miss McDonald but also the future of Glenlovatt Manor and the Carmichael family."'

Vaughan opened his mouth angrily but Mr Chalmers silenced him with a simple lift of one finger as he continued. '"I wish for the gross profits from the tea room to be split between Miss McDonald and Glenlovatt Manor in a sixty to forty per cent arrangement."'

Mr Chalmers snapped up his head from the clutch of papers at the sound of me gasping. He smiled as he finished: '"I wish Miss McDonald every success in her new venture. I only knew this young lady for a short while, unfortunately, but I know she will make a huge success of it. I have every faith in her."'

He flicked his glasses off, placing them carefully on the desk.

Tears clustered in my eyes. I turned to read the faces of Gordon and Vaughan. Gordon was gaping at me. Vaughan was firing deadly lasers.

I couldn't make sense of it. It was crazy—wonderful, surprising but utterly bonkers. Was poor Hugo expecting to pass away so quickly? He must have written his will much earlier, and then changed it very soon after meeting me. What had possibly possessed him to do that?

I flicked my anxious eyes towards Gordon and Vaughan.

'But why me?' I croaked in response to their reactions. 'I don't understand any of this. I'm not family or anything.'

'You're telling me,' spat Vaughan, tugging at his gold silk tie. 'The old man must have lost it towards the end. I loved him a lot but this is crazy, even for him.' He gestured towards Hugo's will. 'My grandfather must have explained why he's done this. What else is in there?'

Mr Chalmers steepled his hands together. 'All I can tell you is that your late grandfather telephoned me shortly before he passed away and was most insistent that the nature of his will be changed.'

'But why?' asked Gordon. 'He certainly never gave any indication to us that he intended to alter his will.'

'I'm afraid your father has left specific instructions not to divulge any further information—for now.'

'For now?' echoed Gordon incredulously. 'No disrespect to this young lady but as Hugo's next of kin, I do think . . .'

Mr Chalmers pulled an apologetic face. 'I'm sorry, sir, but I'm fulfilling the strict instructions left by your late father.'

'Which are?' sighed Vaughan with an exasperated air.

'That the reasons for bequeathing the art room to Miss McDonald will be revealed on the twenty-seventh of October this year.'

'The twenty-seventh of October?' scoffed Vaughan. 'That's months away. Are you kidding me?' He appealed to his father. 'So this means we have to go along with this bloody charade while we wait for further instructions?' Vaughan shot to his feet. 'This is madness. Not only do we have a bloody tea room inflicted on us but that means we will have to open Glenlovatt up to the public again. We've been closed for twelve years now.'

Gordon leaned forward in his chair and ran a finger around the cream collar of his shirt. 'Why on earth has he stipulated the twenty-seventh of October? Do you happen to know the significance of this date at all?'

Mr Chalmers shrugged his shoulders. 'I don't know the significance either. What I do know is that your father has left a letter addressed to you all.'

There followed a pause so pregnant that I half-expected a midwife to be called. Mr Chalmers lifted an envelope and spoke again. 'This is the letter which is to be opened on that day.'

Eleven

As I stared up at the two men towering in front of me, a scary realisation clutched at my heart: I was now in business with two strangers I knew nothing about—except that the younger one was a total knob.

Traffic blasted past the three of us while we hovered uncertainly on the pavement outside the solicitors. Travis had cleverly excused himself from the icy atmosphere and was on his way to collect the car to take us back.

'So,' I exclaimed a little too brightly, 'that was unexpected.'

Vaughan's mouth slid into a grimace. 'You can say that again.' He turned to his father. 'Do you think Grandfather was all there at the end, Dad? I don't mean to sound callous but . . .' His indignant words trailed off.

'Of course he was,' sighed Gordon, dashing an impatient hand over his silver hair. 'My father was sharper than most people half his age.'

'Then why decide to turn Mum's old art studio into a tea shop?' pushed Vaughan, giving me a sideways glare. 'Unless, of course, he was cajoled into doing it?'

The inference hung like wintry mist in the Glasgow air, between the beeping horns and darting shoppers. I drew an angry breath. He thought I'd manipulated his grandfather into handing over that studio for my own purposes? What a bloody cheek!

'Are you accusing me of influencing Hugo?'

'I'm not accusing you of anything,' he snapped. 'I'm simply wondering what your exact involvement with my grandfather was.'

Gordon raised his palm. 'This isn't helping anyone.' He placed a hand on Vaughan's shoulder. 'Your grandfather was never cajoled into doing anything he didn't want to do. Not once in ninety years.' He rested his silvery grey eyes on his son. 'He loved Glenlovatt but he thought we weren't moving with the times. He said so often enough.'

Vaughan's dark brows knitted. 'What do you mean? Had Grandfather mentioned this ridiculous idea before?'

Gordon gave a light shrug. 'Once or twice, yes, but I thought he was just having random thoughts, especially when he didn't make a move to do anything about it.'

A couple of shoppers manoeuvred their way around us on the pavement, swinging an assortment of carrier bags in garish colours.

Vaughan jerked up the collar of his coat. 'So why wasn't I told about this? Am I no longer part of the family?'

'Stop being petulant,' said Gordon. 'I had as much of an idea as you that Hugo was going to do something like this.'

Vaughan's jaw set like concrete.

I could feel myself shrinking a little further. Here I was, caught between two warring aristocrats in the centre of Glasgow.

'If I might say something,' I managed, smiling shakily. 'I don't really understand all this either. In fact, I feel as though I've suddenly jumped on a merry-go-round that refuses to stop.' I twisted my fingers together. 'But what I do know is that I was very fond of Hugo. I also know how much Glenlovatt meant to him.' I raised my face in a slightly more confident gesture. 'If you support me, I promise to put every ounce of energy I have into making this tea room a success.' Then I added carefully, 'Not just for me but for Hugo's memory, and for the benefit of Glenlovatt.' Gordon adopted a small smile when I added, 'And I will respect the late Mrs Carmichael's studio.' Choosing to ignore Vaughan's silence on the matter, I concentrated all my attention on Gordon.

He nodded gratefully. 'Miss McDonald, large old homes like Glenlovatt are expensive to maintain, as I'm sure you will appreciate. Any other income we can generate would therefore be very helpful.'

Thank goodness I had at least one of these men on side. I nodded enthusiastically as I spoke. 'I'm determined to give it my all, sir. And, please, call me Lara.'

Gordon warmly extended his hand, which I gratefully accepted. 'Call me Gordon.'

But the new ease soon evaporated.

'Well, isn't this cosy?' sneered Vaughan. 'What next? Is Miss McDonald going to move in? Change the wallpaper? Operate a theme park in the dining room?' He pinned me with his hard blue eyes. 'Unfortunately, we don't have any other choice. Grandfather made sure this was all sewn up.' He pushed a lock of dark hair off his forehead. 'It doesn't mean I have to like it, though.' He turned and walked away from us.

'Where are you going?' called Gordon. 'Travis will be back at any minute with the car.'

Vaughan shrugged his broad shoulders. 'I fancy a walk. I'll see you back at the estate.'

Gordon watched as his son was swallowed up by the milling pedestrians while I tried to compose myself.

'Thank you for the offer of a lift home, Gordon, but if you don't mind, I'll catch the train back. I'd really like to clear my head.' I gave him a nervous smile. 'This has all come as a bit of a shock.'

Gordon nodded in agreement. 'Yes, it most certainly has. For all of us.'

My head churned with thoughts as the train rattled me back to Fairview. Why on earth had an elderly laird put all his faith in me?

I remembered confiding in Hugo about how much I desperately wanted my own tea room, and every time he shuffled through the door of True Brew he'd witnessed firsthand how difficult it was working for Kitty. But to let me use his late daughter-in-law's art studio and make the necessary financial provisions for me to make a living from it was a huge leap of faith that I was both grateful for and struggled to comprehend. Tears of happiness at this unexpected chance threatened to spill down my cheeks. Having to deal with Vaughan Carmichael, though, was going to be a huge challenge on its own, let alone making Glenlovatt Manor's new tea room a viable business.

As the train continued to Fairview Station, I considered Gordon Carmichael. Although the will had been a shock, at least Vaughan's father had the good grace to wish me well and offer his support.

'I have to admit,' he'd said, smiling ruefully after Vaughan's frosty departure, 'what I know about tea rooms you could write on the back of a postage stamp.'

The train slid easily up to the platform and unloaded a handful of passengers. It was lunchtime and gaggles of schoolkids were milling around the town square, devouring their sandwiches and rolls.

I glanced down at my office-style outfit. It would have to be a quick dash back to the flat to throw on some jeans before going to work. Then, I thought ominously, it would be a case of telling Kitty my news. Visions of a glowering Vaughan Carmichael and a snarling Kitty Walker converged into one terrifying monster in my imagination. I teetered faster in my heels.

Deal with one horrific apparition at a time, Lara, I told myself.

Then a thought struck me: I couldn't do this on my own. This required the *Thelma & Louise* approach—although hopefully we wouldn't end up over a cliff at the end. I pulled up the contacts on my phone.

'Morven,' I gabbled before she could say more than hello. My voice as I spoke sounded disembodied. It was as if the words bursting out into Fairview's afternoon air belonged to someone else. 'I've just inherited a tea room,' I gasped, dodging the people drifting past me, 'and I want you to work with me.'

Twelve

'You are what?' gasped Kitty. She clutched a shelf behind her in the storeroom for added support. 'After all the help and training I've given you and you stab me in the back like this?'

I racked my brain for examples of the training she'd given me, or situations where she'd freely given help, but couldn't recall a single one. 'I'm grateful to you for giving me this job when I came back to Fairview,' I explained politely. 'But I owe it to Hugo to give this my best shot.'

Kitty glared at me with her moon-like face. 'I don't understand this,' she muttered. 'Why on earth would Hugo Carmichael do all that for the likes of you?'

I dipped my head around the corner to see if any new customers had come in. Thankfully the lunchtime rush had subsided, leaving a man bashing away at his laptop in the corner and a couple with their grumbly toddler.

I knew I had to choose my words carefully. 'I haven't got my head around it all yet either. But from what was in Hugo's will, he was adamant Glenlovatt must move with the times.'

'By opening up a bloody rival tea room!' supplied Kitty, clasping a hand to her forehead in horror.

I tried to reassure her. 'It won't be like that. Glenlovatt isn't in Fairview itself. It's a few miles out.'

'I know that!'

I collected my thoughts and did my best to ignore Kitty's amateur dramatics. 'The new tea room will be specifically for Glenlovatt Manor visitors,' I carried on, growing more confident. 'Hugo was keen to open up the house again to bring in some revenue. The tea room would help with that.'

Kitty's hard eyes fired killer beams so I decided to try a different approach. 'I've read some things about these stately homes and how the upkeep of them is phenomenal. Leaking roofs, heating, structural wear and tear—'

'Oh, so you're an expert on stately homes now, are you?' she interrupted, folding her arms.

My shoulders slumped. This conversation was going downhill fast but I decided to try one more time. 'What I'm trying to say is—'

Kitty shook her head. 'I've heard enough. I'll pay you until Saturday.'

My mouth popped open. 'Sorry?'

She jutted her powdered jaw defiantly.

'You're letting me go? Right now?'

Kitty's frosty pink lips twitched.

'But I'm more than happy to work out my proper notice,' I insisted.

Kitty pushed herself away from the shelf, her apron crinkling angrily against her floral blouse. 'No need,' she assured me airily. 'I can manage. And anyway, there's a long list of—'

'Girls who are keen to work here,' I finished for her. I probably said that in my sleep, she'd said it to me so often.

She stuck out her hand and made a beckoning motion to me. 'Apron.'

Had I expected Kitty to be so ruthless? Part of me had. The other part had clung to the hope she'd show some element of understanding.

I slowly untied my gold and white apron, which she snatched back.

'Good luck,' she hissed, raining me with spittle. 'You'll need it.'

Glenlovatt Manor, August 1957

Rain coursed down the windows of Glenlovatt like tears. If the old manor was weeping for something precious she had lost, he knew what that was. He was suffering too.

The laird, Lachlan Carmichael, blinked up at his son from the comfort of his moss green velvet chair. 'Straighten your face, man.'

There was no response. Lachlan watched his son's shoulders tighten under the sharp cut of his dark blazer. 'Don't tell me you're still mooning over that shop girl.'

'She's not a shop girl. She's a baker.'

Lachlan twitched his bony fingers. 'Same difference, if you ask me.'

'That shows your ignorance then, Father.'

The young man swung around as he received a roar from his father. 'Don't you dare address me in that manner! Kindly remember who you are talking to.'

His dashing son smiled grimly, the silvery raindrops suspended from the window behind him like a jewelled curtain. 'It's not difficult to remember when you're constantly reminding me.'

Lachlan glowered at his son as he stalked around the drawing room. 'Why don't we throw a huge bash at Hogmanay? We could invite the Murray-Hamiltons. That pretty daughter of theirs seems rather keen on you.'

Visions of the girl simpering at him in some marshmallow-style dress set his teeth on edge. He couldn't contain his pain a moment longer. It was burning inside his chest, threatening to erupt. 'Do you know what happened this morning, Father?'

Lachlan's white face with its pointed expression infuriated him further.

'This morning I watched the woman I love marry someone else.'

Lachlan slammed a clenched fist on the quilted arm of his chair. 'Why the hell did you go? What's the matter with you?'

To compound Lachlan's fury, his handsome young son laughed. It was dry, bitter and inflected with hatred. 'What's the matter with me? Let me tell you. I'm still in love with her and I always will be.' He bent down and pressed his jaw towards his father's surprised face. 'But I'm so much of a coward, I let her go.'

Lachlan was dismissive. 'Don't be so melodramatic.'

His son's mouth twisted. 'You've never felt like this, Father. How could you possibly begin to imagine how I'm feeling?' He pulled back from the stench of cigar smoke emanating from his father's breath.

'I was not prepared to allow you to give up Glenlovatt for some common nobody,' spat his father. 'You should just have had the little tart and got her out of your system.'

Lachlan Carmichael let out a startled whine as his son seized his collar with both hands. 'If I ever hear you refer to her in that way again I won't be responsible for my actions.' He let go of Lachlan's grey shirt and the older man fell backwards into his chair. Aiming one more contemptuous stare at his father's shocked visage, he barged out of the door and into the garden. A cluster of yellow roses met him as he angrily rounded the corner, and triggered painful recollections of that morning.

The sight of her framed in the church doorway was one he'd never forget, her red curls spiralling gently beneath a short fountain of veil and her white dress pooling to the floor in layers of thick lace. She wore short white gloves and clutched a bouquet of yellow roses.

The church gate was heavy with white satin ribbon wound through the black wrought iron. Then the bells pealed their rusty joy and his stomach clenched. He dipped behind a cluster of wedding guests, unable to bear the pain of her seeing him. Nor did he want to set eyes on her new husband, but curiosity reared its head and he moved slightly to one side to get a clearer view.

The groom lingered protectively behind his wife, one hand placed on her bare upper arm. He had a ready smile and brown hair swept severely to one side. Longing lunged through him as wedding rice cascaded down onto her upturned face. He'd seen enough. He should never have come.

Rain was forecast for that afternoon but at that moment the summer sun dazzled down on the wedding party, illuminating floral hats, bare shoulders and Brylcreem-slicked hair. Barging into a female guest, he muttered an apology and raced to the other side of the road. He caught sight of his reflection in the milliner's window, haunted grey eyes staring back out of his sharply chiselled features. He had to live with the consequences of being weak, of not defying his father. But what he didn't have to bear silently anymore was Lachlan's intolerance of emotion.

He continued to examine his reflection in the glass, oblivious to the startled looks from the stern woman behind the shop counter.

One day his time would come, and he would ensure Glenlovatt would have what might have been.

Thirteen

 'Thank you for agreeing to see me.' I smiled at Gordon across his desk.

I was back at Glenlovatt just two weeks after the formal reading of Hugo's will, to meet with the family about moving things forward with the tea room. Well, when I say family, that grumpy sod Vaughan was nowhere to be seen. He was probably off somewhere biting some innocent virgin's neck.

As Gordon started to speak, his mobile rang and he indicated to me to sit down. 'Please excuse me, but I should take this.' He rolled his eyes good naturedly as he left the study.

I nodded and smiled again.

As I waited for him to return, I clutched at the notebook I'd spent the past fortnight jotting down ideas in—everything from possible colour schemes and layouts for the tea room to a suggestion for resuming tours of the house. Then there was the issue of recruiting staff for both the baking and cleaning. Thoughts about our opening hours leapt up at the front of my mind too. I had envisaged opening 9am to 4pm Monday to Saturday, with a slightly shorter day of 10am to 4pm on Sundays. I scrambled through my pages of notes, where I'd scribbled 'rotational days off for staff' so that everyone would have the benefit of a break.

'Sorry about that,' came Gordon's voice as he returned and clicked the door closed.

His study was reminiscent of him, a calm and discreet exterior of solid wood panelling with polished redwood furniture. Yet I sensed that underneath it all there was a desire to succeed.

A large sash window boasted views of the side grounds, where a border of Scottish bluebells in the deepest shade of lavender jostled for attention beside white clusters of star-shaped cuckoo flowers. I cleared my throat and cast a glance at the notes in front of me.

Gordon seemed to sense my nerves. 'Let's start with the food, shall we? I'm sure that's the most important part.'

I relaxed a little due to his friendly demeanour. 'That's a good idea.'

I referred to the menu section of my notes. 'I don't know what you think about this but I was going to suggest we include simple items on the menu to cover breakfast and lunch.' I fiddled with my pen. 'I wasn't going to suggest full cooked breakfasts or anything like that. I imagine Thistles to be a classy tea room.'

A glance at the silver tea set already seated on Gordon's desk reminded me of another point. 'There will be no tea bags, only good quality leaf tea, and I thought we could offer traditional fruit and plain scones, toast, salmon and cream cheese bagels and maybe some quiche.'

I referred to my notes again to ensure I wasn't missing anything important. 'That should keep all the bases covered so we can concentrate on the baking side of things.'

Gordon smiled encouragingly and scribbled down some notes with his fountain pen. 'This all sounds wonderful. You're making me rather peckish!'

Pulling my gaze away from him for a moment, my eyes rested on a portrait of who I guessed must be Gordon's late wife, Lydia. Her elfin face was enhanced by the pale blonde curls piled haphazardly on her head. An ice blue satin gown melted over her milky shoulders. She was stunning.

Gordon caught me staring at the painting. 'It's a rare one because she didn't like to pose for stuffy portraits,' he murmured. 'She wasn't at all pretentious.' I turned to him and saw a distant longing cloud his face.

'She was very beautiful,' I said softly.

Gordon's grey eyes twinkled. 'Yes, she was. She must have been about your age when we had that painting commissioned.'

My attention slid away from the white gold features of Lydia. Another oil painting hung beside it, this one of Vaughan. He was all raven black hair and hard cheekbones. A black jacket and white shirt clung to his broad frame. Unlike his mother, there was no mischievous smile flirting on his lips. Instead, his defiant jaw exuded his usual air of provocation.

As if reading my thoughts, Gordon raised a grey eyebrow. 'He isn't as terrifying as he likes to make out. He's just very protective of his family—well, what family we have left.' My suspicious response must have been obvious, causing Gordon to lean forward on his desk. 'Vaughan was very close to Lydia, and when she died he struggled for a long time. My son isn't keen on the idea of reopening Glenlovatt to the public either.'

'I would never have guessed,' I smiled. 'Why isn't he?'

Gordon raised his hands in a helpless gesture. 'He's a very private young man. I think he believes that by opening up Glenlovatt again to the public, we're somehow exposing ourselves and belittling the family name.'

'But if the tea room is tasteful and does well, only good can come of it, surely?' Aware that nerves were beginning to nibble away at me, I placed my hands in my lap. 'I just wanted to let you know that I'm keen to move things along with the tea room as quickly as possible.'

'Oh, so are we,' assured Gordon. 'But with your current job working for Kitty Walker, I don't want you taking on too much.'

'I don't think that will be a problem. I've been fired,' I blurted, heat spotting my cheeks.

Gordon blinked. 'Fired? But why?'

'Oh, it's nothing to do with anything underhand,' I gabbled, anxious to reassure Gordon that I hadn't done anything terrible, like sticking my hand in the till. My shoulders slumped in a defeatist manner. 'I think Kitty viewed me as the opposition when I told her about what Hugo had done and she just wanted me gone after that.'

'But that's terrible!'

I shook my head. 'I was relieved to go, actually. She was very difficult to work for.'

'Well, her loss is our gain.'

Gordon slid open one of his desk drawers and produced a creamy envelope. Dark, spidery writing danced across the front. 'It would appear,' he explained, 'that my father was very busy letter-writing right up to before he died.' He dipped his fingers into the already open envelope and tugged out a letter. 'Talk about thinking of everything,' he said in a voice carrying more than a hint of admiration. 'Before he passed away, Hugo arranged the legal and financial provision for Lydia's art studio to be converted.' His modulated Scottish burr mingled with the faint smell of ink and leather.

'Sorry, what does that mean?' I asked.

'It means, young lady, that we are, in effect, raring to go. No bank loans, no planning permission, no red tape.'

Gordon eyed my puzzled face from across the desk. 'Let's just say my late father knew the right people. These people owed him a favour or three and he didn't hesitate in calling them on it.' He shook his head. 'He's even arranged for the best builders in the west of Scotland to do any conversion work.'

I leaned back in my chair. The very thought of all that negotiation and paperwork had been a real cause for concern. Then I realised something, which triggered my face to break into a grin. 'He knew I would say yes.'

'He did indeed,' agreed Gordon. 'So it really is just a case of you making this tea room something special.'

'So no pressure then,' I gasped, still grinning like an idiot.

Gordon put the letter back in the drawer. 'I just wish Vaughan would get on side. It would make things a bit easier.'

I aimed a pointed look at Vaughan's broody painting while I nervously fiddled with my silver bracelet. Perhaps it was proving to be lucky for me after all, now that my baking dreams were slowly becoming a reality, although I knew I would need all the help I could get dealing with that git!

As I prepared to leave, I casually glanced across at a couple of newspapers lying to the side of Gordon's desk. Their pages were open, revealing two different photographs of Vaughan, one with a blonde hanging on his arm and the other with a moody-looking brunette draped around his neck.

Gordon's gaze followed mine and he became grim-faced.

'I'm afraid my son has this morning appeared in two separate gossip columns.' He shook his head. 'Goodness knows what happened to that American brunette he was seeing.'

An awkward silence settled across the study. I couldn't imagine the very proper Gordon would ordinarily share such details with a near stranger; he must have been worried.

Beyond the ruby red curtains, a May morning was blossoming and I suddenly longed to be out there in it. 'Well, I'd better be off,' I exclaimed, clumsily jumping to my feet. 'There's plenty to do.'

I'd only just started off across the great hall when I saw Vaughan striding up the corridor from the other direction and enter his father's study.

Gordon's muted tones reached me from his desk. 'I've just had Lara in to see me about the tea room.'

The breath lodged in my throat when I heard my name mentioned. I hovered beside a grumpy looking grandfather clock and pretended to myself that I was interested in antiques, not eavesdropping.

'Well, thank goodness I can be excused from discussing cake recipes,' came Vaughan's reply. 'I've got a prospective client coming round to discuss an installation piece.'

I heard Gordon sigh as he replied, 'Do you know what your problem is?'

'No, but I think I'm about to find out.'

'You haven't met the right woman yet.'

Vaughan started to protest but Gordon ignored him. 'When you do, you're not going to know what's hit you.'

In my mind I saw Gordon nod over at the black-and-white photograph of his late wife that sat on his desk. Lydia was posing on a windswept cliff top, her head thrown back and hair whipping around her animated face. 'Believe me, son, there is no feeling like it.'

'Yes. Well, until this mythical creature arrives, I'll try to be more circumspect, okay, Dad?'

I heard the rustle of newspapers and decided it was time to complete my exit. Something told me Fairview's resident grouch would refuse to play nicely.

Fourteen

'Have you seen it, Dad?' blazed Vaughan, barging into Gordon's study. 'It's looking like something out of a bloody doll's house!'

I opened my mouth to defend myself but Gordon got there first. I clutched at my scribbled notes, from which I'd been about to give Gordon an update on how things were progressing.

Gordon tugged off his square spectacles, plopping them onto a pile of papers. 'I don't know how you can come to that conclusion yet, son. The floor has simply been resanded and polished, and only the cake counter is in.'

Vaughan's dark brows gathered together. 'I'm telling you,' he growled, 'this tea room, and opening up Glenlovatt again, is a big mistake.'

I watched nervously as Gordon studied the beams of sunlight coming through his study window.

'I don't understand why you're so against this,' he puzzled. 'Your mother adored this house and we were open to the public up until she passed away.'

At the mention of his late mother, Vaughan pointedly turned

towards the window. 'Exactly,' he said after a long pause. 'Our grief was private and it should stay private.'

I shifted uncomfortably in my chair.

Gordon smothered a sigh and stood up. In an instant, he was beside his son. 'She's been gone twelve years now.'

'I'm only too aware of that,' replied Vaughan, sounding pained.

'And we'll never forget her,' soothed Gordon, placing a hand on his shoulder. 'But your mother wouldn't want Glenlovatt falling into disarray or, even worse, having to be sold.'

'Maybe I should go,' I muttered, gathering my notes.

Vaughan raised a dark brow at me from over his shoulder.

'No, Lara,' directed Gordon. 'You're doing everything you can to help and I'm grateful to my father for bringing you to us.'

Vaughan sprung round to face his father, as though Gordon's words had suddenly illuminated something for him. 'Things aren't that bad, are they?'

Gordon let out a dry laugh. 'Nobody would guess you've been so hard at work for these past few months.'

'That's right,' prickled Vaughan. 'I've been working bloody hard on my sculpture commissions, Dad.'

'I wasn't talking about your sculptures,' clarified Gordon with a pointed lift of his eyebrows.

Now it was my turn to stare emphatically out of Gordon's study window. The emerald lawn rippled in the slight breeze and heavy headed daffodils bobbed their golden crowns as if in deep conversation with each other.

I could imagine Vaughan's wolfish smile as he said, 'Europe is full of beautiful treasures, and I'm hardly going to leave them unappreciated, am I?'

'Yes, alright,' snapped Gordon. 'I'm sure Lara has even less interest in hearing about your exploits than I do.'

'If you'll excuse me,' I smiled tightly. 'I've got things to do.'

'Of course, Lara. Thank you.'

As I turned to close the study door I saw Gordon resume his seat, staring up at Vaughan as if admiring the fine angles of his son's face. Perhaps he was thinking Vaughan could turn heads, just like Lydia did.

'All I meant to say was please be careful,' I heard him warn. 'And try to take other people into consideration. Some of these girls you've hurt had genuine feelings for you.'

I paused outside the slightly ajar door at these words. Even as I hoped this eavesdropping wasn't going to become a habit, I was too intrigued to move.

Vaughan dismissed his father's cautionary words. 'Oh, come on, Dad! It's all just a bit of fun.'

'For you, perhaps. As I've told you before, the problem with you, son, is that you've never been in love.'

'And how would you know?' barked Vaughan.

Gordon's voice was heavy. 'Believe me, if you'd ever been in love the way I was with your mother, you'd know.'

I pictured Vaughan grinding his teeth. 'We're straying off the subject again here, Dad. And, as you say, we've discussed my love life before.'

Then Vaughan asked a question that made my chest flutter with concern. 'Are things that bad financially?'

I could detect resignation in Gordon's tone. 'Yes, things are pretty bad. Why do you think your grandfather went to all this trouble in his will?'

'But why didn't you tell me, Dad? I could have helped.'

'What, from your art studio or your latest conquest's boudoir, perhaps?' There was a chilly silence.

'Sorry,' apologised Gordon after a pause, 'I didn't mean that. I wanted you to concentrate on your commissions. They're a great opportunity for you. The last thing I wanted to do was burden you with our leaky roof and dodgy heating.'

Vaughan made a short grunting sound, but Gordon continued, 'Listen, son, some extra income would be more than welcome and the tea room could very well be the answer.'

There was another period of silence. 'We have to do this for the sake of Glenlovatt,' Gordon said eventually. 'It's what your grandfather wanted and, if she were here, I know your mother would have wanted it too.'

'Okay,' Vaughn agreed tightly. 'If there is no other way.'

'Believe me, son, there isn't. And you never know, the new tea room could be the making of this place.'

Vaughan said pessimistically, 'I'm reserving judgement on that for now.'

I was sorely tempted to burst back into the room and deliver a swift punch to that angular jaw of Vaughan's as I heard him mutter, 'Well, just make sure Lara McDonald doesn't turn Mum's studio into Santa's grotto.'

'Now, is there anything that I've missed?'

One of Morven's carefully plucked brows arched. 'Are you trying to be funny, Lars? You've got everything covered and, as you said yourself, dear old Hugo made sure all the basics were in place before he passed.'

We both looked around Lydia's old art room. There was a sea of shelving waiting to be put up, and tins of glossy white paint sat with their lids gaping open like greedy mouths, as the decorators got to work with thick paintbrushes. The crackle of a radio could just be heard above the whizzing and whirring of drills.

I pointed to the patio doors at the end of the room. 'I suggested to Gordon that we use those as another entry point to the tea room, as well as through the great hall—at least to begin with.'

'What do you mean?'

I dropped my voice a little lower as I answered Morven. 'Well, I was thinking that we should keep visitors coming to us via the great hall for now, as it might pique people's interest and make them want to see the rest of the house.'

A slow smile spread over Morven's face. 'You mean if they bring back guided tours?'

'Absolutely. And of course that would generate not only more income for the house, but more customers for us.'

'I like it,' said Morven. Then she gave me a sideways look. 'Why don't you go and take a break? You look like you could be doing with a dose of fresh air.'

'But I've got to confirm a time for the delivery of the dishwasher and I wanted to get another quote from that local laundry company.' I let out a gasp. 'Oh, and we said we'd talk about the social media side of things too, didn't we? I mean, we're going to need Facebook and Instagram accounts for the tea room.'

With one push between my shoulder blades, Morven had me out of the patio doors. 'All that social media stuff is in hand, Lars.'

'But what about job adverts for staff?'

'Right you! I've had enough! Go and take a breather for half an hour. I am capable of using a telephone, you know.'

'But I also need to speak to the local paper about advertising costs,' I bleated, mentally running through dates. 'If we want to open on the sixteenth of July—'

'Out!' roared Morven, planting her French-manicured hands on her hips.

With a faux wounded expression, I mouthed a grateful 'Thank you'.

The gardens of Glenlovatt were positively frothing with colour. Thrusting heads of golden and cream daffodils had given way to pushy lavender wallflowers, tufty pansies in watercress green and rose pink magnolias.

Meandering around the manor's grounds was a far more enjoyable way to spend a lunchtime than the forty-five minute respite from Kitty I had at True Brew. I glanced down at my watch. I could spare another ten minutes. Morven was doing her best impersonation of Wonder Woman. I didn't know what I would have done without her.

I inhaled, sending a deep wave of mint and fresh grass coursing into my lungs. I skipped down a set of steps, the faint tinkling of water from an angel-topped fountain ringing out like tiny bells.

The grass sprang beneath my jewelled ballet flats and I lifted my face upwards to feel the sun's rays as they battled their way through a bank of stubborn cloud. I kept strolling aimlessly, ducking and weaving between stray branches until, without warning, the Carmichael mausoleum rose before me, its ornate stonework sharp against the sky.

A sudden image of Hugo sprang into my mind, twizzling his grey moustache and declaring, 'It's a good day for it.'

I swallowed hard and blinked furiously, taking a few more steps before suddenly darting behind the nearest tree in alarm.

Vaughan was standing with his back to me at the mausoleum entrance, clutching in one hand what appeared to be a single white rose and a couple of thistles bound with a tartan ribbon. The combination of flowers matched those in the Carmichael family crest, carved into the stone above the mausoleum door. He bowed his head. 'These are for you, Mum,' he said softly, placing the posy against the grey arched door.

I pulled myself back behind the tree trunk, my heart thudding. Should I reveal I was there? Somehow, I didn't think my appearance would be appreciated. I guiltily stole another glance.

'You always used to say you were a rose between two thorns,' Vaughn said.

I smiled sadly to myself.

His deep voice was laced with sorrow. 'I'm really trying not to be as much of a dick, Mum. Oops. Sorry. I should have said "idiot", shouldn't I?' My eyes widened as a faint chuckle rumbled from him. 'I can just see your disapproving face right now.'

I angled my head just a little further out to see him.

'Love you, Mum,' he whispered hoarsely. 'We miss you.'

I wrapped my arms around myself, feeling strangely cold despite the dappled rays of the sun snaking down through the branches above my head.

As Vaughan continued to stand there, his long jean-clad legs firmly planted on the ground, I quietly padded away before picking up a swifter pace once I reached the first roll of lawn. Soon I was a blur of white cotton shirt and black capri pants as I headed back, Vaughan's heartfelt words to his late mother circling in my head.

Fifteen

'Well, what do you think?' Ben Wallace said.

The local carpenter who Hugo had organise for the tea room's woodwork, gestured proudly with a calloused hand.

I couldn't help but let out an appreciative gasp. The cake counter he'd custom-built for the tea room was a solid oak-panelled design, painted a glossy white. I'd suggested it would be a nice touch to acknowledge the Carmichael family crest, so Ben had recruited the artistic talents of his graphic-designer daughter.

She had adorned the top edge of the counter with a row of painted thistles, their prickly beauty and green-veined leaves popping against the snow-like background. They ran the whole length of the counter, drawing your eyes to the glass panel directly above. This was where all the cakes would be displayed. On imagining it filled with cherry-studded scones, carrot cake smeared with buttery icing, and glazed muffins, my stomach fizzed with excitement. I smiled to myself as I visualised our cake of the day taking pride of place in the centre—perhaps a glistening salted caramel cake, or a lemon and thyme olive oil cake, with lemon rind and white icing . . .

'I love it,' I breathed. 'Thank you so much, Ben. And please tell your daughter she's a marvel!'

Ben's broad face was a picture of delight. 'Glad to hear it.'

I approached the counter and tentatively ran my fingers along the painted thistles. They were so lifelike that I half-expected their prickles to sting my skin. 'I'm sure the Carmichaels will love it too—well, at least, one of them will.'

Ben folded his beefy arms. 'Aye, that son is a bit of a dour bugger, isn't he?'

I rolled my eyes in agreement.

The last couple of weeks had seen a flurry of renovation activity. A couple of Ben's juniors were busy with some snagging work, their tools clattering over the sound of a crackly radio. Voices echoed around the chaos. Bizarrely, the smell of paint and dust made me even more excited.

While I was imagining cream and white high-backed chairs surrounding circular tables, and ornamental thistles dotted around the shelves, a voice carried through from the far end of the room.

'Come and have a look at this,' called Craig, one of the decorators. He crouched in front of a dusty chest, which looked like an old-fashioned dressing-up box.

'What is it?' I asked, leaning forward.

Craig winked. 'Let's open it and take a look, shall we?'

'I don't think we should. It doesn't belong to us.' Ignoring me, Craig began to tamper with the lid. 'We can't open it,' I protested, even though my curiosity was rising. 'It must belong to the family.'

Ben nodded. 'I agree with Lara, lad. Where did you find it?'

Craig jerked his dark cropped head towards a previously concealed cupboard that was now swinging open from a side wall. 'The chest's already open, folks. Look.'

Sure enough, the lid of the chest was slightly ajar, layers of pink tissue paper peeking out. The air was now filled not only with the dulcet tones of the radio presenter but also anticipation.

Slipping his paint-daubed fingers under the heavy arch of the lid, Craig released a puff of musty scent. Our eager faces craned forwards to glimpse whatever might be inside.

Before I could stop him, Craig peeled back the top piece of tissue, revealing a layer of thick art paper covered in sketches.

I felt an obligation to step in and at least ensure they were treated gently. He stood aside as I knelt to uncover the top few artworks, coloured sketches of flowers, ranging from sunny daffodils to purple pansies nestled in among more elaborate drawings of regal white lilies and creamy orchids, their trumpets almost seeming to reach out of the paper.

I dug a little deeper into the chest and felt my fingers brush against what felt like wooden carvings, again swathed in sheets of pink tissue paper. Still feeling guilty but now totally unable to contain my curiosity, I unwrapped a gorgeous carving of a thistle. The wood had been finely honed before being painted in vibrant purples and moss green. The veins on the leaves were intricately expressed, the grooves gentle under my touch.

Craig rocked back on his boots and gave a short whistle through his teeth. 'Someone's got a real talent.'

'Had a real talent,' I corrected after turning the thistle over in my hands. Painted in shiny black on the reverse was a discreet 'L.C.', matching the initials underneath each of the sketches.

'They were done by the late lady laird,' I said with a sad smile.

Craig's dark brows shot up. 'I bet they'd be worth a few quid, especially with her being dead.'

My mouth tightened. 'Craig!'

'Well, you know what I mean,' he said uncomfortably. 'Artists' work always goes up in value when they're six feet under. Everyone knows they don't earn a penny when they're still alive.'

Ben's face hardened. 'Have some respect, lad.'

But Craig carried on, eyeing the artwork speculatively. 'I'm only speaking the truth. The lady laird has been gone years, so this lot is bound to be worth something.'

'I don't think that's any business of yours.'

Vaughan's growl boomed across the bare room.

I spun round to see his steely blue eyes land on the open chest, now spilling forth its contents.

'What are you doing?'

'Craig just found it inside that wall,' I explained, pinning on a nervous smile. 'I think it may have belonged to your mum.'

Vaughan crouched down beside the chest, tenderly picking up one of the thistle carvings. I watched as his fingers traced the carved lines, his gaze melting.

A lump formed in my throat. 'I was just thinking that it would be lovely if we could put up some of your mum's artwork in the tea room,' I ventured carefully, 'especially the thistle carvings.'

Pulled back to reality, Vaughan studied me from under those thunderous dark brows of his. 'Oh?'

I was aware of the expectant faces of Ben and Craig staring at me as Vaughan rose to his feet, carrying the weight of suspicion in every inch of his towering frame. He stood over me, all dark hair and attitude.

I coughed nervously. 'As the thistle features heavily in your family crest, I thought it would be nice to have that as a theme in the tea room.'

I just prayed he couldn't hear my heart repeatedly bashing against my ribs. Why the hell was I turning into a nervous wreck every time Vaughan Carmichael was in the vicinity? Yes, he was part of the aristocracy, of sorts, but he needed some urgent lessons in manners and communication skills.

He studied my face for a moment before muttering through a granite jaw, 'That's a good idea. I like it.'

I watched in surprise as he stalked off. Then he stopped abruptly at the door, where the hallway was bathed in spring sunshine. 'Make sure it's tasteful, though, won't you? We don't want you going all My Little Pony, do we?'

The workmen buried grins as I fiercely stuck my tongue out at the lord and master's disappearing back.

'Er, excuse me?'

Loitering where Vaughan had strode out was a young lad carrying a couple of new shelves for the kitchen.

'Oh goody,' I grinned, hurrying towards him. Enthusiastically taking them out of the alarmed lad's arms, I started to rip off the bubble wrap.

You've got to be joking.

Staring back up at me was not the ivory white of my dreams but the stuff of nightmares: avocado green that a 1970s situation comedy would have been proud of.

From over my shoulder, Ben let out a cackle. 'Don't think we'll be finishing off the kitchen anytime today, lads.'

Sixteen

That night, I sat at home nursing a mug of steaming hot tea and imagining certain parts of Vaughan Carmichael trapped in a vice.

After an afternoon of hectic phone calls to the avocado-green-shelving supplier, during which my ears were ritually abused by cheap jazz tracks, my mind was racing between Hugo and his surly grandson.

Dear old Hugo. I was so determined to do well by him, it almost caused me physical pain. Glenlovatt was such a beautiful old house and to play a part, even a small one, in keeping it a going concern was the very least I could do.

But more than that, Hugo Carmichael had given me hope and a belief in myself that I thought had been well and truly extinguished after Malta. I turned my attention to the assorted seashells perched on my windowsill that had travelled back with my shattered confidence and broken heart. They sat in creamy Mediterranean splendour like mini moons, a bright spot against my petrol-blue curtains. I tried to push away pictures of inky black sky dusted with stars, waves tickling the sandy shore. The nautical theme of my flat wasn't lost on me.

I gave myself a sharp mental prod and turned my attention to the scribbled notes balanced on my lap. I'd been trying to come up with some more ideas for not only the tea room but also for Glenlovatt Manor in general. Vaughan might be an intimidating, rude sod but I owed Hugo a great deal, and I couldn't allow a scowling sculptor with a chip on his shoulder the size of the River Clyde to spoil Hugo's hopes for its future. Bloody hell, at times I felt like I was some sort of vampire hunter, fighting the dark forces of Dracula. I could understand his reluctance about the tea room—it was a huge change—but if he wanted to keep the heart of his ancestral home beating, he'd have to adapt.

I smiled grimly. Vaughan adapting to anything would be painful for him, not unlike root canal treatment.

Why are you still thinking about the Prince of Darkness? Something to tell?

I gripped my ceramic mug tighter, and waggled my feet, perched on which were fluffy red slippers. Come on, Lara, back to business. Hang on. Prince of Darkness?

Ideas tumbled around my head, competing for attention. Snatching up my notebook, my pen began to dance across the lined pages. Vaughan would require blood pressure monitoring when he heard my suggestion but Gordon might be more amenable. Something like this would be a great way to reintroduce Glenlovatt into the Fairview community. With excitement hammering in my chest, I got to work on my idea.

I was just beginning to get into my stride when the entry buzzer made me jump.

'It's me,' said Morven.

'Is everything okay?' I asked, but I could already hear the clatter of her wedges negotiating the communal stairs.

I opened the door wide and she whirled in, a blaze of Burberry trench coat. 'I need you!' she bleated. 'Right now!'

'No offence but I've always fantasised about a roguishly hand-some man standing there saying that, not my best mate,' I said.

Morven dashed some rain droplets from her sleeves. 'I can assure you that I need you more than some sex-starved hunk does.'

'Okay, okay, take a pew and I'll stick the kettle on.'

Morven shook her head. 'There's no time for that.' She clasped her manicured hands together. 'Do you remember what I'm doing this evening?'

'You're currently standing in my hallway.'

Morven's red lips pursed in frustration. 'It's that summer fashion show at the Lomond Hotel I organised. To raise funds for Fairview Library?'

'That's right,' I nodded politely, hiding the fact I'd been so preoccupied with the tea room that I'd forgotten. 'So why aren't you there?'

Morven threw her hands up in the air, making her armful of gold bracelets ring like church bells. 'One of our models has let us down at the last minute. Apparently she's pulled a hamstring at Zumba.'

'And?' I pushed.

Morven's steady gaze under her perfectly plucked brows should have alerted me. 'Can you do it?'

'Do what? Oh no . . .' I started to back away.

'You're perfect,' she assured me. 'All of our models are ordinary girls.'

I folded my arms. 'Keep digging. You're about three feet down already.'

'No, no, I didn't mean it like that,' she placated. 'All the models are gorgeous, normal ladies, not a bunch of fake-tanned twiglets.'

'Morven, I really don't think . . .'

She assumed a pleading expression. 'This is to raise money for our local library. It's to benefit our community. Imagine all the children holding brand-new, glossy books in their little hands.'

I hooked my thumbs into the pockets of my jeans. 'Next you'll be telling me it's for abandoned dogs and orphans.'

'If I did, would you say yes?'

'You're something else.'

Morven took a step closer. She widened her green eyes.

'Oh, don't do that,' I begged.

'Do what?'

'That wide-eyed pleading thing that you do when you want something.'

Morven was theatrically appalled. 'I've got no idea what you're talking about, Lars.'

'This,' I explained, contorting my eyes and mouth.

'I don't do that,' she insisted. 'And if I did, it would mean I was constipated.'

There was a momentary stand-off.

'You've only got to model a total of two dresses at the end of the show,' promised Morven, 'and they are both stunning.'

'Are they short?' I sighed, aware I was being systematically worn down.

'One is shortish,' she said defensively, 'but you've got fabulous legs.'

'Can't one of the other models do it?'

'That's the problem. The rest of them have to shoot off. Two have got young kids, one is heading down south for a work meeting before the show ends and the other has got elderly parents she needs to get back to.' She dropped down on one knee. 'I'll beg if you want me to.'

'Oh, get up,' I ordered. 'You're making my flat look untidy.'

'So you'll do it?'

I glanced down at my paint-flecked hands. 'Alright, but you owe me one big time.'

Morven squealed like a baby pig as I started to move towards my bathroom. 'Just give me a few minutes to tidy myself up.'

'No time for that,' she said, wheeling me towards my coat stand. 'We've got hair and make-up students standing by to attend to you.'

Before I knew it I was sitting beside Morven in her buttercup yellow Audi TT, streaking through the wet streets of Fairview. The dark pressed around us, only occasionally broken by a flash of hot orange street lights.

I tugged down the passenger visor and flipped open the mirror. That wasn't a good idea. I looked like Ronald McDonald after a particularly nasty electric shock. What remained of my eye make-up was smudged on my tired face.

The allure of my cup of camomile tea and a box set of *Modern Family* was all I wanted, not waddling down a catwalk in a tinfoil dress.

I snuck a glance at Morven. She was concentrating on the road ahead, but there was definite relief in her expression now. I supressed a sigh of frustration. Oh well. At least it was for a worthwhile cause and I could throw my sacrifice back at her at the next opportunity.

The Lomond Hotel was only fifteen minutes' drive away, otherwise I would have been in real danger of falling asleep in Morven's warm, plush and patchouli-scented car. We swung into the huge car park, which was illuminated by white circular lights that reminded me of Christmas baubles. The hotel itself sat up on a grassy embankment, its dark stone façade almost as black as the trees stretching behind it. I'd driven past it on numerous occasions but never had reason to pay a visit. Sash windows, heavy with crimson velvet curtains, cast slivers of light onto the grass outside. Two small pine trees stood to attention either side of the glass main doors, each glowing with a tangle of silver icicle lights.

The rain was dive-bombing us now. I tugged up the collar of my navy trench coat.

'Follow me,' called Morven, splashing through a puddle.

She led me through the brightly lit reception area, resplendent with squashy toffee-coloured leather sofas and walnut furniture. There was a large function hall at the rear of the hotel from which music was pumping.

All I could make out from the doorway was circular tables and chairs draped in rose pink tulle. The silhouettes of guests made my stomach zing. Crikey! How many people were at this thing?

The catwalk (or 'runway' as Morven repeatedly corrected me) was decked out in pink carpet. To the sound of rapturous applause and a chorus of appreciative wolf-whistles, a shapely black woman sashayed down it. A red maxi dress moulded to her curves, and her braided hair was piled up in an elaborate style.

'You're on in twenty minutes, Lara,' beamed Morven. 'This is Abbey. She'll take care of your hair and make-up.' From a side door, a young girl with a choppy blonde bob had appeared.

'You didn't tell me the entire population of Fairview was at this thing,' I hissed hopelessly out of the corner of my mouth.

Morven waved away my concerns. 'Knock 'em dead, kid!'

I know who I'd like to knock dead, given half a chance.

Abbey guided me through to a small room where another model was just departing for the runway. She had a cap of silver hair that framed her face and was sporting a Katharine Hepburn–style suit.

Abbey sat me down in a chair. 'Are you ready to be transformed?'

I gulped back a ball of apprehension. 'Do your worst,' I said, smiling thinly.

Having smoothed, smeared and dusted my skin from an array of pots, Abbey examined my hair.

'For your first dress, I'm going to put your hair up. When did you last wash it?'

'Last night.'

'Great. It holds better when it isn't freshly washed.'

Like a dextrous octopus, Abbey scooped my curls in all directions, pinning and securing with grips. Then she directed me behind a screen to change into my first outfit. It was a long, floaty, almost angelic-looking number in cream, with a V-neck and fluted sleeves. A pair of matching cream ankle boots completed the outfit.

When I stepped out, still fiddling with the sleeves, Morven almost collapsed. 'You look gorgeous,' she grinned. 'Like a character out of *The Great Gatsby*.'

I swallowed mouthfuls of air. 'I think I'm going to be sick.'

'Can you wait until you've modelled first?' said Morven, sticking her head round the curtain. 'Right, you're on!'

With a gentle push between my shoulder blades, I was out in front of the pink circular tables under dazzling spotlights. I could just make out shadowy faces and various silhouettes.

'Go for it,' grinned Morven.

As pop music boomed out of the speakers, I knew I had to do something. Standing there looking like an utter tit wasn't an option. Pasting on a serene smile, I walked steadily to the front of the runway. Inside, I was a manic duck, paddling for dear life in deep water. With a quick swish of my skirt, I turned to the left and then to the right (I'd seen it on some modelling-competition show on Sky) before marching my way back up the runway. Applause thundered in my ears.

'One down, one to go,' called Morven from the sidelines. 'You were great out there.'

With my heart thudding in my ears, I tumbled through the curtain. Abbey and another girl peeled the floaty cream dress from my clammy skin.

'Here you go,' said Morven. 'Outfit number two.'

I blinked at the black and silver handkerchief she was holding. 'Are you kidding me?'

'What's the matter with it?' puzzled Morven, holding it higher in the air. 'I think it's stunning.'

'Well, you wear it then.'

'What, with my boobs?'

She did have a point. Morven had her own chest plus everybody else's, whereas I had always been more modestly endowed in that department.

Nevertheless, I planted my hands on my hips. 'I wipe my kitchen surfaces with cloths bigger than that.'

'Rubbish.'

Abbey loosened my hair from its piled-up tower and removed the myriad grips. It fell down my back in a relieved array of wild curls. She fired a comb through the roots and aimed a generous skoosh of hairspray at the finished result. 'You're good to go, Lara.'

'No, I'm not,' I argued, glaring at the dress. 'I'm a baker, not a Christmas turkey.'

Morven's fine jaw clenched under her foundation. 'Remember why you're doing this.'

'Because you bullied me into it.'

'No, not that. The real reason.'

A wave of guilt washed over me. How come Morven could make me feel like Cruella de Vil when she wanted to?

If I walked quickly, I reasoned, it'd be over in a minute. 'Oh, alright,' I snapped. 'Give it here.'

I dived behind the temporary changing screen and eased into the dress. I had to admit, it was beautifully cut. It was off the shoulder and slid effortlessly to the top of my thighs.

Morven slung a pair of silver strappy heels over the top of the screen. Great. Not only would I be struggling to breathe in this thing, I'd have a nosebleed due to the teetering height of these ruddy shoes.

I pulled them on, gave one last ineffectual tug on the hem of my dress and stepped out, like a newly born baby deer on stilts.

If my mother could see me now, trussed and glossed like a Sunday roast, she'd require immediate medical attention, followed by a lie-down in a darkened room, I thought.

Morven clapped a hand over her mouth. Abbey simply sighed. 'What is it?' I asked.

'You look incredible,' beamed Morven. 'Honestly.'

'Stunning,' added Abbey, moving forwards to tease a stray curl from my face.

From beyond the folds of black curtain, I could hear a tinny voice announcing the last outfit of the evening.

I rolled my eyes and stepped out.

A huge round of applause and exclamations rose in the semi-darkness. With a slight smile, I did my best to swing my hips and strode as carefully as I could, trying not to appear to have wet myself.

I was acutely aware of my big hair and expanse of leg, but the crowd cheering and clapping made my confidence grow a little, so I adopted a small pout. Reaching the end of the runway, I again angled my body this way and that. As I moved, the silver panels of the dress shimmered like rainwater. I raised and dropped my bare shoulder, which Abbey had smeared with some glossy body cream.

I performed one more turn to the side, smiling more naturally this time—and froze.

Standing by one of the tables closest to the stage was a stunned Vaughan Carmichael staring back up at me.

Seventeen

I don't know who was more shocked.

I stood frozen for a few more moments before Vaughan eventually blinked and broke my trance, his face impassive. Then his attention slid from my face, pointedly lingering on my legs. I tugged down the hem of my dress and clattered quickly back up the runway to retreat behind the curtain.

'You were wonderful,' gushed Morven.

I tapped my silver-heeled foot. 'Thank you for the compliment, but at the moment, I've got more pressing matters on my mind.'

'Like what?'

I jabbed my finger towards the audience. 'Vaughan Carmichael just got an eyeful.'

'Oh, he's here? I do hope his family have made a generous contribution.'

My mouth sprung open. 'Are you for real, Morvs? Did you hear what I just said?'

Morven raised and dropped her white lacy shoulders. 'Please calm down. Your ears are going that strange raspberry colour.'

'My ears are the least of my sodding worries. The laird's son has just had a good glimpse of this!' I swept my hand up and down my bare legs to illustrate the point. 'Can you begin to understand how humiliating that is? I want to be viewed as a serious businesswoman. Flashing my anaemic Scottish skin at a business associate isn't really conducive to that!'

Morven ignored me. 'Your ears always turn that weird colour when you get annoyed or stressed.'

'No, they don't.'

'Yes, they do. Remember at school when you said you didn't fancy Adam Scoular? Every time he walked past, you looked like Spock with an earache.'

'No, I did not!' I protested hotly. 'Wait a minute. Why are we still talking about my bloody ears? I repeat, for those who are hard of thinking—Vaughan Carmichael just got a good old look at my thighs.'

'Calm down, will you?' laughed Morven. 'You are totally rocking that outfit.' She gave my arm a reassuring squeeze. 'He probably couldn't believe his eyes. Maybe he didn't realise it was you anyway.'

I wrapped my arms protectively around my waist. 'Oh, he knew it was me, alright. He was having such a good look I'm surprised he couldn't read every word of this ruddy outfit's washing instructions.' I shoved my way past her to hide behind the changing screen. 'Oh, stuff it. I couldn't give a toss what the Muppet of the Glen thinks.'

'Yeah, right.'

I bobbed my head back over the top of the screen as my dress slithered off me to the floor. 'What do you mean by that?'

Morven ignored me.

I kicked my heels to one side. 'I just don't want the likes of Vaughan Carmichael thinking I'm some kind of airhead. He already suspects I manipulated his late grandfather into altering his will. Goodness knows what he thought just now.'

Morven muttered, 'I bet he was thinking a lot of things.'

'You've got to be joking!' gasped Vaughan in horror. 'Dad, don't tell me you've agreed to this?'

Gordon was sitting against the backdrop of his study window, smooth and silver-haired. He shrugged his shoulders. 'I like Lara's idea,' he answered simply. 'It sounds fun and will be a great way for us to reconnect with Fairview.'

Vaughan looked as though he'd been punched. He pushed a hand angrily through his hair. 'Fun?'

'Yes,' I smiled tightly. 'Something that makes you smile—or heaven forbid, even laugh.'

Gordon's eyes glittered with amusement.

'Very funny,' ground out Vaughan. 'Believe it or not, I do know what fun is—and this isn't it.' He turned to me pointedly. 'Anyway, what did you get up to last night? Do anything interesting at all?'

Heat scored my cheeks. Smug sod. 'I was helping a friend out, actually. At a charity event.'

I knew he would be incapable of keeping my catwalk appearance to himself. I flicked a quick glance at Gordon but he was preoccupied momentarily with papers on his desk. Then he muttered an apology. 'I'll be back in a minute.' He darted out the door.

When I glared back at Vaughan, he was still studying me. What was with all these unfathomable stares this morning?

'What were you doing prowling around there last night, anyway?' I asked, irritated. 'I wouldn't have thought a charity fashion show was your kind of thing.'

Vaughan arched his eyebrows. 'Prowling? You make me sound like some predatory wolf.'

'You said it.'

He tilted his head to one side. 'Want to see my big, sharp teeth then?'

I ignored his playful smirk. 'No, thanks.'

He let out a short laugh. 'For your information, I only dropped by to hand in a cheque from Dad. We wanted to contribute to the library funds.'

'Oh. I see.' I disguised my awkwardness by examining my shoes.

'But I'm glad I popped by when I did,' he added after a long pause, 'otherwise I would have missed seeing your fantastic performance.'

He's trying to provoke a reaction, Lara. Just ignore the prat.

I was relieved when Gordon strode back into the room, clutching a couple of invoices. 'Sorry about that, folks. I remembered I need to get these paid urgently.' He resumed his seat with a smile. 'Now, where were we?'

'It will be a great way to kick off getting more revenue for Glenlovatt,' I explained nervously, clasping my fingers together. 'And most people love fancy dress.'

'Indeed. And you need to promote your work more,' said Gordon, turning to his frozen-faced son. 'This is an excellent way of doing that and it benefits this place at the same time.' Vaughan opened his mouth to protest but Gordon carried on enthusiastically. 'We can invite contacts in the art world, as well as the local community.'

'And you don't have to get involved if you don't want to,' I said to Vaughan. 'I can organise it.'

'With my help,' insisted Gordon. 'My experience of fancy-dress balls is somewhat limited but I'll do what I can.'

With the morning sun striking Vaughan's dark hair, he was one intimidating figure. He swung his head between the two of us and then threw his hands in the air.

'Okay! Okay. It's like being sandwiched between a bloody tsunami and an earthquake.'

Ignoring Vaughan's reluctance (and it isn't easy to ignore a brooding six-foot-three sculptor), we agreed to hold the Glenlovatt fancy-dress ball in six weeks' time, prior to the opening of the tea room. We'd been assured that all systems were well and truly go for the tea room to open officially on the sixteenth of July.

Despite the curled lip of Vaughan, Gordon was also enthusiastic about my suggested 'Ladies and Rogues' theme.

'There are plenty of rogues in Fairview,' muttered Vaughan.

Gordon tilted a silvery brow at his son. 'That's the pot calling the kettle black if ever I heard it.'

Vaughan looked suitably uncomfortable. He slid a look in my direction, before letting out an exasperated 'Dad!'

Gordon gave him a serene smile in return. A family joke, I presumed. Getting the Ladies and Rogues Ball organised was not going to be an easy task, but, with Morven's offer of help, I was determined to manage it. I turned back to my online search for an alcohol supplier.

Thankfully, Ben, Craig and the rest of the tea-room squad could be trusted to get on with things, even if their tea breaks seemed to go on a little. I took advantage of their morning tea sit-down to tell them about the ball, and Ben squared his beefy shoulders in response. 'Don't you worry about a thing, Lara,' he beamed confidently. 'Me and the rest of the A-team here know exactly what we're doing.'

Every morning I got a kick out of seeing how things were progressing. The studio was becoming more and more like a tea room with each passing day. The cake counter took centre stage opposite the windows and patio doors, and the restored floor was a beautiful blank slate awaiting the placement of tables and chairs, which would be arriving soon.

New kitchen shelves had been delivered, thankfully in the right colour this time. Two of the carpenters were busy installing white open-shelved cabinets at one side of the room. I'd suggested to Gordon they could house a selection of local produce, such as jams, honey and marmalade—there were a few local businesses I was sure would be interested in getting involved, and it would all be extra revenue for the tea room and the house. I'd also considered the idea of selling china tea pots customised with the Glenlovatt coat of arms, but whether we could organise all that as well as everything else before the opening was another question. I was bursting with enthusiasm!

First things first, I needed to find a quiet spot away from the hammering and read through the applications I'd received after advertising online for staff.

Just then, the third carpenter, Oron, arrived, his arm around an apprehensive young woman gripping a large Tupperware box.

'Morning, Lara,' he began. 'I'd like to introduce my sister, Jess. We saw your ad about needing staff for when this place opens and I reckon Jess is your girl.' He smiled encouragingly at her.

The nervous young woman moved her box to one hand and shook mine with the other. 'Jess Murdoch. I used to work for a large bakery in Glasgow. I sent you an email, but thought I'd drop by with something I'd made—just to show you ...' She trailed off, uncertain.

'Fantastic! We love initiative here,' I beamed. 'Let's talk more outside. I've got a bit of time before a phone call to one of our suppliers. Bring those goodies along,' I added.

I led her out of the tea room through the patio doors. We walked down one of the garden pathways together until we reached a tired but charming-looking wooden bench, overlooking the first bank of trees. The summer sun weaved in and out of shreds of cloud as we sat down.

Jess smiled, obviously still a little nervous, her chestnut hair blowing around her freckled face in the light breeze.

'So,' I started, 'You were saying that you used to work for a bakery in the city?'

'Yes, for four years. The details and my references are in that email. I was baking a bit of everything but my specialty is savouries—quiche, pies, bread.'

As she said this, she eased open the lid of the Tupperware container, and the homey smell of warm Emmental and pumpkin quiche waltzed up to me. Sitting next to the generous slice was a mini pie and a quarter loaf of ciabatta.

I smiled in admiration. 'May I?'

'Please do.'

I accepted a napkin from her and savoured each of the delicious samples in turn. The quiche melted in my mouth, the steak pie was wholesome and comforting, while the ciabatta tickled my tastebuds with its airy softness. 'Wow,' I gasped. 'These are seriously good.'

Jess's dusting of freckles danced across her cheeks as she smiled. 'Really?'

'Really,' I emphasised.

Emboldened, she added, 'Oron said he would put in a good word for me, but I wanted to do this on my own. Your ad mentioned that the tea room would be serving lunch as well, and I thought some of these would work well.'

'That's right,' I replied. 'We're after someone to be there early in the morning until just after lunch.' I hoped I was framing my words carefully. 'So, as you must have seen, it wouldn't be a full-time position. Early morning to mid-afternoon instead.'

'Oh, that would be perfect,' enthused Jess. 'That means I'd be able to fit my work day around Harry's school hours. That's my son.'

'But what about weekends?' I asked. 'Obviously, there would be a rota so that all the staff get sufficient time off.'

'Oh, Harry's dad can look after him on weekends but if there was a problem, my mum or Oron said they would help out,' she assured me. 'It's just late afternoons that would have been a problem, with my son now at school.' Then she reddened. 'Listen to me. I sound as if I've got the job already.'

'Well, there's nothing wrong with thinking that,' I replied, 'This is all very promising. Anybody who can make a quiche as mouth-watering as that gets my vote!'

Jess froze for a second.

'I'll just have a read through of your application and check your references, of course, but I have a good feeling about this.'

I couldn't help but smile as I saw Jess leave Glenlovatt in her little white Fiat, wearing one of the broadest grins I'd ever seen. I'd promised to let her know within the week.

Eighteen

 'Morven!' I panted down the line. 'For pity's sake, help me!'

My best friend's calm, measured tones slid into my ear like warm honey. 'Take a deep breath. You sound like a heavy breather.'

'I have been taking deep breaths,' I moaned. 'I've taken hundreds.'

Morven sighed. 'This is your area of expertise, organising everybody. In fact, organisation should be your middle name.'

I stared forlornly at my to-do list. 'I wish I had your faith. I don't think I can do this.'

'Do what?'

'Any of it. The tea room, the ball. Hugo had so much faith in me . . .'

I looked around my kitchen with a doleful look. 'You should see the state of my lemon and lavender fondant fancies!'

'What?'

I eyed my baking efforts in despair. Yoghurt and egg were smeared on the kitchen worktop, and dirty glass bowls sat idly around in the carnage. Despite my carefully experimenting with a new icing recipe, each lilac and yellow miniature sponge resembled something out of a science fiction movie. And the sugar roses hadn't worked out at all.

'They're supposed to look like dainty little presents,' I wailed down the phone, 'Not these melted, lopsided lumps I've produced.'

There was a pause before Morven announced, 'You're just having a bit of a wobble—that's all and perfectly understandable. But you've forgotten one very important point. You are not on your own in all of this. I'm right by your side.'

I replied with a whimper.

'Now you listen to me,' continued Morven. 'What with your baking talents and my schmoozing abilities, this gorgeous little tea room is bound to be a success.' I heard her moving around at the other end of the line.' Give me twenty minutes and I'll be there.'

'Are you sure?'

'Of course. You need a bloody good talking-to.'

I headed for the fridge 'Thanks, Morvs. I'll crack open a bottle of white.'

A clean-up and two generous glasses of crisp Sauvignon Blanc later, Morven and I slumped further into my sofa.

She pushed her long blonde hair back. 'It's not like you to have such a crisis of confidence. What's brought all this on?'

'I don't want that Vaughan Carmichael standing there saying, "I told you so," even though he probably will anyway, whether things go tits up or not.'

Morven's green eyes locked with mine. 'That's the third time in the last ten minutes you've mentioned his name.'

I waggled my slippered feet. 'Is it?'

Morven crossed her arms, sending her array of gold bracelets jangling in unison. 'Uh-huh.'

'Well, you'd go on about it too if you had to deal with him,' I replied darkly. 'He's an arrogant, rude sod.'

Morven's lips twitched. 'He gets mentioned in the gossip columns a lot, you know.'

I cradled my mug. 'Does he?' I asked airily. 'I wouldn't know. I never look at them.'

Morven, on the other hand, devoured the social pages with relish. What she didn't know about socialites wasn't worth knowing.

She shifted slightly beside me and cast a long look from under her lashes. 'Do you know what they call him sometimes?'

'Go on. I know you're dying to tell me. It isn't Grumpy Git, by any chance?'

Morven's eyes twinkled. 'In a way, you're not far off. They call him the Heathcliff of the art world.'

'Heathcliff?' I spluttered. 'Well, I suppose that's one name for him.'

'And he's got a reputation with the ladies.' She picked at an imaginary thread on her silk skirt. 'He's a bit of a bad boy, you know.'

The echo of Gordon's recent remark rang around my head. Then I recalled those newspaper photos of Vaughan lying on Gordon's desk. A spark of annoyance lit up in my chest. 'Why are you telling me all this, Morvs?'

'I don't want you getting hurt again. Not after all that shit you had to deal with in Malta.'

I gestured dismissively. 'Anton is well and truly in my past. I'm moving on, or at least I'm trying to.'

Morven looked around my flat, with its blue stripes, nautical knick-knacks and clusters of shell ornaments.

'What?' I asked suspiciously.

'It looks like a Mediterranean harbour in here.'

'Thanks very much!'

'I'm not being rude about it,' explained Morven. 'It's lovely. I'm just wondering whether your heart is still over there.'

I shook my red curls defiantly. 'Don't get me wrong. I still miss Malta, but as for Anton . . .' I finished with a shrug. 'I loved him but he didn't love me. End of.'

'Well, I never liked him,' she said through a grimace.

'You only met him once!'

'And it was enough,' she added.

I laughed dryly as we slumped our heads back against my sofa, looking out at the prickly beauty of the Fairview landscape through my sitting room window. The evening sky was awash with dashes of pink cloud.

'My priority is Thistles from now on,' I said, cutting through the silence.

Morven was confused. 'Thistles?'

'That's what I was going to suggest for the name of the tea room.' I sat up, enthused. 'I've been struggling to come up with something suitable but original at the same time. I asked Gordon but he was more than happy to leave it with me. It came to me this morning. Thistles feature heavily in the Carmichael family crest.'

'And Vaughan is certainly prickly,' supplied Morven with a wry smile.

Although I couldn't deny what she had said, I gave her a withering look.

'Well, let's make a toast then,' said Morven, her wine glass aloft. 'Here's to Thistles and all who eat cake in her!'

I clinked my glass against hers with a grin.

Nineteen

After a productive evening of brainstorming ideas with Morven for the Ladies and Rogues Ball, I marched into Glenlovatt Manor the next morning, armed with a notebook's worth of suggestions. I was also going to tell Gordon and Vaughan about my idea for the name of the tea room.

'Let's go into the drawing room,' beamed Gordon as we concluded our morning tour of the worksite. 'We'll be more comfortable in there.'

Vaughan proffered me a frosty smile and indicated for me to walk in front of him. Tapping self-consciously across the black-and-white tiled floor, I risked a glance over my shoulder. For a split second I could have sworn Vaughan's attention was focused on my rear, but his angular face was so impassive I dismissed the thought. I wished now that I hadn't opted for the skirt I was wearing. It was a little on the snug side.

I'd only glimpsed the drawing room very briefly once, with Hugo. The easy chat we had that day, his dry sense of humour, the delicious lunch and his infectious love of his ancestral home came spilling back to me.

Gordon opened the dark wooden doors. Light sliced through the two sash windows, pooling on the green chaise longue and the two floral sofas. The drawing room reminded me of Hugo in so many ways: classic, warm and full of character.

Gordon indicated one of the sofas and I gratefully sat down. Vaughan and his father took up positions on the two bottle green armchairs opposite. As if by magic, Travis, Hugo's trusted chauffeur, appeared in a sharp suit, with a silver tray glinting with matching silver teapot, cups and saucers and a plate of shortbread. He delivered it to the table with an encouraging smile at me before retreating.

'So,' I smiled, straightening my notebook unnecessarily, 'before I suggest some ideas for the ball, I wanted to run a name by you for the tea room.'

Gordon clattered the teapot and paused. 'Go on.'

Taking a big breath, I announced, 'Thistles.'

For a moment, the only sound in the drawing room was the rattle of teaspoons.

'Thistles?' repeated Vaughan slowly, in that deep cut-glass burr of his.

Oh no. Had I put my size six feet well and truly in it? Maybe this suggestion was just too close to home for them, what with a thistle being part of Lydia's signature on all her artwork.

My fingers nervously tumbled over each other in my lap. 'Sorry,' I gushed. 'Perhaps that's not—'

'No,' interrupted Vaughan. His voice had adopted a surprisingly softer edge. 'I think that's a good choice.' He looked at me again before turning his attention to his father.

Surprised, I snatched up my teacup. I realised how important it was for me to get the Carmichael seal of approval. This whole crazy, exciting venture meant the world to me, and the very thought of doing something insensitive caused a nest of butterflies to career through my stomach. Over the rim of my cup I could see Gordon's wistful expression.

'Lydia loved thistles,' he mused aloud. His mouth curved into a wry smile. 'When you think of all the gorgeous flowers in those gardens and how she always had a thing for thistles. That was her all over. Seeing beauty in everything whether it was immediately apparent or not.'

'With the fact that thistles also feature in your family crest,' I supplied gently. 'I just thought it was appropriate.'

Gordon nodded happily while Vaughan studied me for a moment with a quizzical gaze. 'Right. Good,' he barked after a heavy pause.

I looked away. Good grief! Reading Vaughan Carmichael was like trying to understand the offside rule in football. I noticed a photograph of Hugo in a silver frame on top of a highly polished side table. He looked so dapper in a cherry red cardigan, cream shirt and navy tie.

Gordon's eyes followed mine. 'He was an old bugger at times,' he sighed, 'but we miss him so much.'

'I'm sure you do. He was a very special man.'

Vaughan's long fingers played with a thread on his black jeans. 'He was also frustrating at times. I don't know what this "Do not open till the twenty-seventh of October" is all about.'

'Well, none of us know, do we?' answered Gordon simply. 'We're just going to have to abide by his wishes, and come October twenty-seventh we'll find out.'

Vaughan's brows knitted. They showed more than a speck of suspicion.

I again shuffled through the notes I'd made with Morven about the ball and looked up, pinning a cool smile on my face. 'Shall we get on to the ball?'

I happily announced a local baroque group had been booked and pulled out a list of RSVPs from the guest list so far. I showed them photos of the flower arrangements the local florist was planning to do for us, and we went through sample menus from two different caterers, discussing the pros and cons of a canapé-style menu or a buffet.

'While the canapé menu looks the most appealing,' I added, 'the buffet menu is more budget friendly.'

Gordon perused the document. 'Let's decide by the end of the week.'

Vaughan's expression was unreadable. 'You really have thought of everything, haven't you?'

Not sure whether he was being complimentary or sarcastic, I flicked my notebook pages over and turned to the ideas I'd been brainstorming for Glenlovatt. 'Gordon, do we have time for me to run some other suggestions for the estate past you?'

Gordon took a sip of his tea. 'Please do.'

Vaughan looked positively horrified.

'Well, it's too late for this year but I thought next year we could have a ticketed Easter egg hunt in the grounds and maybe ask someone to dress up as the Easter Bunny.'

Mischief reared in Gordon's eyes. He pointedly turned to Vaughan.

'Don't look at me,' he growled, shifting uncomfortably in his seat.

Stifling a laugh, I referred again to my notes. 'We could make Thistles Easter themed too, with lots of yellow decorations, and I could bake Easter egg bombes, hot cross buns, ginger-bread bunnies, marzipan chicks; that kind of thing.' Spotting Gordon's smile of approval, I was encouraged to carry on. 'Then for Halloween, Glenlovatt could host a ghost trail. Obviously, not too scary for the little ones.' I leaned forwards in my seat. 'We could string little orange lanterns round some of the trees and give the children goodie bags. There would be an entrance fee for this too and perhaps a prize for the best fancy dress.' Then another thought came to me. 'We could even invite a local children's author to come up with a suitable ghost story to read to them as they went on their walk.'

Vaughan peered across at me as though I'd just landed from some alien planet. 'I can't wait to hear what you've got in mind for Christmas.'

Gordon silenced him with a weary 'Please continue, Lara. I can assure you we are listening. Both of us.'

'For Christmas,' I began steadily, 'we could have a reindeer ride around the grounds for the families.' I indicated with the tip of my pen the sprawling gardens outside the window. 'Pretty lights strung around the trees would look gorgeous here, and perhaps we could serve mulled wine, mince pies and hot chestnuts.'

'That sounds a great idea too,' agreed Gordon.

Vaughan stretched his long legs in front of him, folded his arms and said nothing.

'These sorts of events should make Glenlovatt more of a focal point again for the local community, especially as the estate has been closed to the public for a number of years.'

'Twelve years,' piped up Vaughan flatly. 'Glenlovatt has been closed to the public for twelve years now.'

He and his father swapped knowing looks.

Gordon gestured around the richly decorated drawing room. 'Your grandfather and mother thought the world of Glenlovatt and it is down to us to ensure its future.'

I sensed colour erupting on my cheeks, worried I'd put my foot in it again. Recalling the faith Hugo placed in me, I swallowed hard and spoke again. 'And for Mother's Day and Father's Day, we could run an afternoon tea in Thistles for the mums, and perhaps something like an Irish coffee and Guinness cake event for the dads.'

Vaughan glanced over when I said, 'I know this is a lot of detail right now, but I feel I owe it to your grandfather to give this my best shot.' I closed my notebook, resting it on my lap.

Gordon nodded enthusiastically while Vaughan tried and failed to stifle a bored sigh.

I really was so grateful to Hugo for believing in me, but at times like this I did question whether all the hassle from his unpredictable grandson was worth it.

I collapsed beside Morven into a chair by the tea room's patio doors. There were only three days till the Ladies and Rogues Ball. Papers lay scattered over the table in front of us, alongside discarded cups of tea and plates of half-eaten cake.

There were lists about lists, scribbled confirmations from last-minute guests and a couple of last-minute apologies, a list of items donated by local businesses for the charity auction, and details of the buffet and when it would be delivered.

Morven tipped back in her seat. Her blonde ponytail snaked down the back of her chair as she let out a loud yawn. 'I don't think I can eat another mouthful of cake.' She rubbed her non-existent tummy. 'I've had far too much.'

I eyed her flat stomach, concealed under a red ribbed top. 'Yes, I can see that from all the way over here. People will think you're pregnant.'

She stretched. 'I think we've got everything in hand. And if we haven't, well, tough luck. We'll just wing it on the night.'

I took a slurp of cold tea. 'Urgh! I'll make another pot.' I stood on weary legs. 'You think it will go okay, don't you?'

'Of course it will. And if it doesn't, you could always offer to be Mr Grumpy Pants' new nude model.'

I took an ineffectual swipe at Morven's head. 'That isn't even remotely funny.'

There was a sharp knock on the tea room door and Travis walked in with a cardboard box in his arms. 'There has been a delivery for you. I think it's your menus.'

We both jumped to our feet as he placed the box on the floor. 'Thanks, Travis,' I beamed while Morven eagerly ripped into the contents. 'I'll bring you one of our special coffees for the excellent service.'

'I wouldn't say no.'

I smiled after his retreating frame, and spun round with a clap of my hands only to see that Morven's excited expression had melted into one of mild panic.

'What's wrong? They're not avocado green, are they?' I laughed lamely.

'No, they're not green,' she faltered, turning one around to me.

I took it out of her hand. 'Then what's the problem?'

'Look at the top. Right there. Where it should read "Thistles".'

Oh, for pity's sake!

'"Fizzles"?' I gasped. 'How the hell did they work that one out?'

Morven patted me on the arm. 'Don't worry,' she assured me, 'I'll sort it.'

I dragged a tired hand down my face.

'I'll get on to the printers right now, okay?'

She strode off across the great hall and I turned back to the paperwork, silently praying there would be no more mishaps.

Twenty

My heart pounded against my ribcage.

Upstairs at Glenlovatt, I leaned out the guest bedroom window to see the manor house's façade looking spectacular underneath the scarlet July sunset. The stone and glass was highlighted by strategically placed torchlights that snaked the length of the gravelly drive. They licked the warm air, their flames of burnt orange like twisting exotic dancers. Stationed below on the manor steps were two impressive figures dressed in matching navy livery, ready to proffer flutes of pale gold champagne from solid silver trays.

I took a nervous gulp of the sweetly scented evening air before ducking back inside to put the finishing touches on my up-do.

The day had been a whirlwind of securing last-minute arrangements, but once Morven and I realised that we could do no more, we'd dashed upstairs to get ready. Gordon had insisted we make use of two of the manor's guest bedrooms, complete with ensuite showers. Although the plumbing made intermittent groaning noises like it was suffering from chronic indigestion, the hot needles of water were so soothing, I could have lingered in the shower for longer.

The room itself was dominated by a gorgeous carved oak four-poster bed, its pillows and bedding matching the long, fluted drapes' deep gold fabric. What with my sumptuous gown spread out across the bed, I felt as though I'd travelled back in time.

Once we were ready, Morven and I met on the landing and made our way down to the entrance to greet the guests. Standing just inside the doors, I caught sight of my reflection in one of Glenlovatt's magnificent windows. Morven had suggested we go to a fancy-dress boutique in Edinburgh owned by one of her mum's friends, and I was so glad we had, despite the cost of my outfit triggering a nervous twitch in my left eye. The sky blue satin overlayered with white lace made me think of crashing ocean waves, its frothing white bands travelling down to the floor. The material lapped to my elbows, where it was caught on each arm by a small ribbon. I'd piled my curls haphazardly on my head and secured them with a blue orchid decoration. On my feet was a pair of ice white Cinderella-style slippers. Clutching the blue scalloped purse that Morven had loaned me from her vast collection, I raised my chin in an attempt to look more confident.

I flashed a nervous smile at Morven. She had chosen a pale gold silk dress with solid panels of lemon. Her sleeves were also to the elbow but very discreetly gathered in, and she'd tied her hair to one side with gold ribbon. Buttercup yellow ballet shoes adorned her feet. She really did look like a princess.

Lights dazzled outwards from the great hall, beckoning in the eager first arrivals. Everybody from local journalists to members of the Fairview Business Consortium filed in on a sea of laughter and chatter. They had all made an effort, decked out in robes, gowns, tailcoats and sophisticated hats. Swathes of opulent satin and silk rustled around me, the shades of the costumes reminding me of the manor's heavenly flower garden, with passionate reds, golden yellows and mint greens. The men were wearing everything from tricorn hats and braided jackets to flowing overcoats and frilly shirts. It was an impressive spectacle, watching the liveried waiters guiding them into the dining room.

Morven's flirt radar seemed to have gone into overdrive for a tall man in brown riding boots, who was lingering beside her.

'I might catch you for a dance later,' he smiled, displaying a rather cute dimple in his left cheek.

Morven plucked a fan from her lemon silk purse. 'I wish you would,' she said coquettishly, batting her lashes across the top of it.

When he'd gone, I shook my head in disbelief. 'Where did you get the fan from? And what about Jake?'

'This old thing?' she asked, giving the floral fan a waft. 'It used to belong to my grandmother. And as for Jake, well, just because you're on a diet doesn't mean you can't admire a cream cake, does it?'

The great hall, and its chequered floor, was now a sea of guests, their jewelled colours dancing before my eyes. From the great hall, the dining room ran down on the right and along the length of the house in a column of spectacular colour and noise. We headed over, following the sound of the band, sending soaring notes of mandolin, kettle drum, harp and piano up into the cherub-fringed ceiling. A number of couples were already dancing, swinging each other gently round. The musicians, in their matching green velvet jackets and knee breeches, transitioned into an upbeat baroque piece to encourage more dancers.

With a wave, Morven sashayed off to join the man in riding boots. I stood and watched them from just inside the dining room doorway, gratefully accepting a glass of champagne from a passing waiter. I needed something to do with my hands. Then I exchanged a few words with some of the passing waiting staff, encouraged by their politeness and efficiency—everything seemed to be going to plan.

As I surveyed the guests, I noticed one of the musicians, the tall blond guy strumming the mandolin, was looking over in my direction. I buried my gaze in my champagne flute before sneaking another look. Yep. He was definitely checking me out. A slow, lazy smile slid across his face.

Suddenly, Gordon appeared beside me, resplendent in a midnight blue tailcoat and dark fitted trousers.

'Good evening,' he smiled, running a finger around the collar of his frilled shirt. 'You look simply stunning.'

I grinned with appreciation. 'And you look very dashing.'

Gordon rolled his eyes. 'This bloody shirt is itching like mad, but needs must.' He clasped his hands behind his back in a regal pose. 'I think this shindig is going very well so far, don't you?'

'It certainly seems to be,' I agreed, savouring the chorus of laughter, music and chatter. 'I just hope everyone has a great time.'

At that moment, Morven swept back over, linking her arm in mine. 'Lars, look around, everyone's having ball.' She chuckled at her terrible pun.

Gordon nodded, 'And most of it is thanks to you two.'

'Oh, I don't know about that,' I blushed, clutching my champagne flute a little tighter than I needed to.

Morven batted her eyelashes. 'Thank you, Gordon. I'll certainly take it even if Lara won't.'

Honestly. She was shameless at times.

Gordon patted my arm. 'Hugo would be very proud of you.' He thanked a waiter who handed him a glass of champagne and faced me, his lightly tanned face tinged with regret. 'I just wish you had been able to meet Lydia. You are alike in many ways.' With a mischievous grin, he added, 'She was one hell of a slavedriver too.'

I gasped in mock disbelief and was about to reply when my attention, along with that of most of the other women nearby, was drawn to a tall figure striding into the room. He was wearing a long black cloak, riding boots, a white open-necked shirt and a tricorn hat. A black Zorro-style mask concealed his features, and his broad shoulders and long legs were rocking the outfit for all it was worth.

I gave my dress a quick smooth, wondering who this specimen was, when Gordon took a step forwards.

'Vaughan!' he shouted jovially beside me. 'Over here!'

My mouth flopped open, not an attractive look on anyone, as Vaughan turned towards us, parting the clouds of dresses and swinging tailcoats.

'Hi, Dad,' he said, but his eyes behind the mask were on my face. 'Hello, Lara.' He took in my outfit, from my hair to the tumbling folds of satin and lace at my feet. His jaw, normally hard and uncompromising, seemed softer, with a shadow of a smile. 'You look amazing.'

Hang on. Was that a compliment? Surely not.

I bit back my surprise. 'Thank you. I like your outfit,' I croaked.

Great. Now I sounded like I had a throat infection.

'Thanks,' he said, giving his cape a brisk flick. 'A friend of Dad's works for a TV production company. She can magically lay her hands on this sort of thing.'

I wish you'd lay your hands on me. I took a nervous gulp of champagne. *Get a grip on yourself, woman! Remember why you're here.*

'Well,' Gordon declared, 'I think I'll leave you young things to it and go and mingle.'

Morven coughed discreetly into her champagne flute. 'I think I'll join you.'

I turned to her with a pleading look but she just grinned and gave me a small wave as she took Gordon's arm and waltzed into the crowd.

I quickly looked sideways at Vaughan, his angular jaw stippled with the faintest hint of dark stubble. He slowly peeled his high-wayman mask away from his face and slid it into his pocket. It was one of the sexiest things I'd ever seen.

Stop it.

'Are you alright?'

'Yes, yes, fine, thank you.'

He gestured towards the guests. 'You've done a great job.'

I played with the lace on my dress. 'Thank you. I did have a lot of help from Morven.'

Vaughan shook his head slightly. 'You really should learn to take a compliment.'

Words tumbled out of my mouth that I couldn't retrieve. 'Can you blame me? Compliments don't seem to come very naturally to you.'

Vaughan grinned, displaying white, even teeth. 'I guess I deserved that.'

I had never seen him smile like that before. It lit up his whole face.

Turning slightly to my left to escape his penetrating stare, my eyes fell on a small wooden sculpture on top of a nearby cabinet. Modern in style, it was of a naked couple embracing, the woman's head thrown back in joy, wavy hair spilling down her back, and a man holding her. The lines were simple but beautifully expressive. I was surprised I'd never noticed it before.

'Are you interested in art?' Vaughan asked, following my gaze.

I was so entranced by the figures I almost forgot he was there and an automatic defensiveness sprang back into me. 'Why, is a baker not supposed to appreciate art?'

Vaughan raised his hands in mock surrender. 'Don't be so prickly. I never said that.'

An awkward silence settled between us.

'What do you like?' he asked suddenly. 'Art wise, I mean?'

I gave a small shrug. 'Anything that catches my eye, really.'

Vaughan gestured to the embracing couple I had just been admiring. 'I made that when I was sixteen.'

'You did? It's wonderful,' I breathed, taking another lingering glance at the lines and planes of the two lovers.

'Yes,' he said slowly. 'I've always been good with my hands.'

A dry cough lunged out of my throat. Was he doing this deliberately? I disguised my scarlet face by pretending to search in my bag for a tissue.

'What do you know about sculpture?' he asked.

'Not very much, I'm afraid.'

'Oh, don't apologise,' he insisted. 'I know nothing about baking.' He moved a little closer. The cut of his jaw was striking. 'Two of my favourite sculptures are the Riace bronzes. Have you ever seen them?'

I cleared my throat, irritated that his closeness was having such an effect on me. 'I don't think so. What are they like?' I asked, trying to sound casual.

'They're ancient bronze figures of two naked Greek warriors. Very little is known about them, as they were found in the sea off the southern Italian coast, near the town of Riace,' he continued, 'but the sinewy details of their bodies and the character their faces hold are mesmerising.' His icy blue eyes sparkled as he went on. 'They really do epitomise beauty and strength.' His gaze flickered over me with an intensity that made me avert mine for a few seconds. 'Whether it's eroticism or jealousy, the art of sculpture captures it all.'

'What about modern art?' I asked, changing the subject from the human form to safer ground.

'My tastes are pretty eclectic, to be honest,' he confessed. 'I'm quite an admirer of Jeff Koons. Have you heard of him?' Vaughan continued when I shook my head. 'He tends to use things like inflatable figures and children's toys in his work.' He pulled his phone from the pocket of his tight jodhpurs and tapped on the screen. 'Look at this one,' he said, handing his phone to me. 'His stainless-steel Popeye figure is something else.'

For a split second there was skin-to-skin contact; it was like a small electric shock. Vaughan didn't seem to flinch and I smiled down at the screen, which showed a highly polished Popeye flexing his glossy muscles. 'I love how he's captured the facial expression,' I said.

'What, this?'

When I looked up from the phone, Vaughan was pulling a ridiculous expression, tilting his chin upwards and pulling his mouth tightly closed.

'If the wind changes, you'll stay like that,' I laughed.

He feigned a hurt look. 'I would have thought it was an improvement.'

I issued a small smile. *You're not getting any more out of me,* I decided silently. The last thing I wanted was to join his queue of fawning females, even though I was starting to see why there was one. He could be pretty charming when he wasn't being a creep.

'So what about you?' I asked. 'What kind of art do you work on yourself?'

His eyes glinted as he spoke. 'Well, I do enjoy dabbling in the contemporary side of things but classical sculpture is really my thing. Marble and clay, mainly. For me, moulding faces and figures out of my imagination is what it's all about.'

A shrill sound burst through the bubble from behind us.

'There you are!' brayed a woman in a blaze of orange satin. Her bleached blonde hair draped over her caramel shoulders in a plait.

Vaughan's mouth slid into a tight line. 'Petra,' he mumbled, 'I didn't know this was your kind of thing.'

She clamped a jewelled hand onto Vaughan's arm. 'Anywhere where you are is my kind of thing.'

Oh, please.

Her arched eyebrows knitted as she turned to me with a toothy smile. 'Who's this?'

I plastered my own, less extravagant smile on. 'I'm Lara McDonald.'

'Oooh, the tea lady!' she trilled, sending a sideways glance up at Vaughan.

'Lara isn't the tea lady,' he corrected sharply. 'She's the owner of Thistles, our new tea room at Glenlovatt.'

A glazed expression was already forming on her tight features. 'Well, seeing as Vaughan isn't going to introduce me, I'll just have to do it myself.' She thrust out a jewelled hand tipped with lilac nails. 'I'm Petra Montgomery-Carlton,' she said, squeezing my hand slightly more firmly than seemed necessary. 'Vaughan's fiancée.'

Twenty-one

The rich scent of venison tartlets and mini beef Wellingtons whirling past on silver platters suddenly made me feel nauseated.

Vaughan was engaged. To this blonde woman with the endless name. Okay, so what?

'Congratulations,' I blurted.

He took a faltering step towards me. 'Lara . . .'

I jumped in. 'If you'll both excuse me, I've got so much to do.'

I turned and pushed through braided shoulders and spools of lace, elaborate powdered wigs and trailing cloaks. The opening of the tea room on Monday was looming and I needed to concentrate on Thistles. That was my focus.

'Lara?'

Outside in the great hall, Travis was studying me with a look of concern. 'Are you alright?'

'Yes. Yes, thank you. I'm fine.'

He wasn't convinced. 'If I may . . . It isn't something to do with the young laird is it?'

I sensed my skin flush red. 'No, it's—'

Behind me, came an eruption of uncontrollable giggles.

It was Morven, accompanied again by the guy in the riding boots. Beside him hovered the flirty blond musician. Morven's green eyes were shining with mischief and I noticed she was rather breathless from more dancing exertions.

'Come on, you,' she trilled, catching me by the wrist. 'Let's get you on the floor.'

'No, Morvs. I really should go and check on things with the caterers. I'm not sure when they bringing out the food . . .'

Morven shook her head. 'Oh no you don't. It's time for Lara to shake her thang.'

My protestations were in vain. Morven's fingers remained tightly around mine until we were positioned among the other guests on the dance floor. The band tapped their instruments, thumped their feet three times and then the whirling strains of a Scottish reel struck up. Other guests twirled beside us, linking arms and swinging each other round. The colours of their gowns and tailcoats melted against one another as they moved. The musician grinned at me, spinning me backwards and forwards, until Morven and I came face to face again.

'Has he upset you?' she whispered in my ear.

I twirled the hem of my dress. 'Has who upset me?'

Morven rolled her eyes. 'Don't give me that.'

We linked arms and as I turned around, I came face to face again with the attentive musician. 'I'm Mark,' he smiled.

'I'm Lara.'

'Yes, Morven told me.'

Mark took my hands in his and as he swung me gently, my lacy skirts swishing back and forth, I spotted Vaughan staring from among the crowd. Petra was clawing at his arm. The music swelled as it rose to a crescendo, causing the delirious dancing to end in a riot of laughter. We all loudly applauded and the band basked in the appreciation. I spent the rest of the evening politely evading Mark's attention and making every effort to forget Petra's triumphant words echoing in my head.

The rest of the weekend evaporated in a haze of disappointment, anticipation and a feeling of utter stupidity. Why was I knocked for six by the news Vaughan was engaged? He was a stubborn and grumpy sod, and we had been nothing but disagreeable to each other to date. Petra was obviously a rich society girl. They were made for each other. I owed it to Hugo and to Gordon to concentrate on Thistles and nothing else. Whatever my funny turn over Vaughan had been, it was over.

On Sunday afternoon, I headed into Thistles to check everything was perfect. I entered through the patio doors, where the hazy sunshine was creeping through, creating artistic triangular shapes on the wooden floor. We'd placed a couple of tables outside, which would hopefully entice customers to visit us via the garden entrance, as well as making their way through the great hall.

With fresh eyes, I took in the shiny wooden tables and high-backed chairs. The cake counter now had several wooden shelves running along the wall behind it. Assorted screw-top jars of tea and coffee sat there, along with a large chrome coffee machine. A small blackboard, currently blank, was hung beside the coffee machine, ready to boast about our assorted treats. My heart lurched at the sight of the electronic till and credit card machine. I wasn't a seven-year-old playing shop. I was a twenty-seven-year-old businesswoman, charged with making Thistles profitable and securing the future of Glenlovatt Manor.

No pressure.

Then I spotted the boxes of reprinted menus piled neatly in one corner. Just in time. With the kitchen scissors I prised a box open and anxiously read through one of the menus, checking for typos. I breathed a sigh of relief. It was perfect.

I removed the rest of them from the boxes and began propping two on each of the tables, against the mini sugar bowls Morven had organised. They featured a ribbon of Clan Carmichael tartan of moss and sage green, decorated with squares of blue.

Then I brought out my to-do list and tried to calm my nervous excitement by walking through everything methodically. I triple checked the fridges, pantry area and barista's station were all well stocked; fired up the credit card machine and the till to make sure there wouldn't be any technical glitches; and made sure all the jams and marmalades for sale were stickered with prices.

Finally, I picked up my jacket and bag from a nearby table, knowing there was nothing else to be done until the baking the next morning. My stomach lurched at the thought as I made a move to leave.

'Ow! Bloody hell.'

I snatched my finger away from the patio door, where I'd managed to catch it as I'd pulled it closed. A dull ache was followed by a flash of red as my fingertip throbbed. That would no doubt turn into an impressive bruise by the morning.

'Are you alright?'

Vaughan was hovering just behind me.

'Yes, I'm fine, thanks. I just caught my finger in the door.'

I made a move to walk past him but he put his arm out and said gruffly, 'Let me take a look.'

Please go away, I pleaded inwardly. *Take your white shirt and faded jeans and just go.*

'It's fine. Really,' I insisted. 'I've only caught it in a door. I don't require resuscitation.'

A mischievous smile flashed across his face. 'I can do that too, if you like.'

I straightened my back. 'No, thanks. Big day tomorrow, so I should get going.'

Vaughan took a large step, blocking my path. 'Not until I've checked your hand is okay. You've got a twenty-minute drive home.'

'Oh, for pity's sake!' I shoved my hand out. 'See? It's fine.'

He gently took me by the elbow. 'I think that'll be a nasty bruise. Come on, there's some arnica in the store cupboard.'

He led me back through the tea room, into the great hall and down a short flight of stone steps that took a sharp turn to the right. His Timberland boots echoed loudly beside my trainers. He pushed open an old, battered door to reveal a narrow cupboard with a very dusty window and some cheap shelving. Below the window were a sink and a rickety cabinet.

Vaughan cranked the cold tap on and, before I could react, plunged my offending red finger under it.

'Aaargh! That's freezing! You could have prepared me.'

'By doing what, exactly? Placing a few scented candles around the place? Wafting essential oils in the air?'

I scowled up at him looming over me. 'There's no need for sarcasm. You know what I mean.' I snatched my hand out from under the water and Vaughan turned the tap off. There was a grumpy gurgle from the pipes.

'Keep still while I dry your finger and put some arnica on. Can you move it?'

I was sorely tempted to show him how flexible my middle finger actually was but decided against it.

He reached up to the cupboard above the chipped white sink and pulled out the cream.

'Is it in date?'

He rolled his blue eyes. 'Of course it is. I only bought it the other week. I use it a lot when I'm working. A professional hazard.'

A lump of something collected at the base of my throat as he gently wiped my hand dry with a fresh towel from a nearby shelf and then proceeded to massage in the cream.

I flicked a quick glance up at his face, expecting him to be looking down with those spidery dark lashes of his, concentrating on the task in hand. He was studying me instead, his black hair sweeping over his shoulders.

'That's a lot better, thank you,' I coughed, pulling away. 'The pain is easing off now, but I'll probably have a nice bruise there by morning.'

Vaughan's soft expression vanished. 'Yes, probably.'

I reached down for my bag and briskly marched out of the dimly lit room.

Twenty-two

I swung my Cleo into the parking area at the side of the house and gripped the steering wheel for much longer than was necessary. It was very early but I needed to get a head start for opening day.

I perched my sunglasses on top of my head and checked out my reflection in the visor mirror. What with a chronic lack of sleep last night, my eyes were staring out of my face like two poached eggs. A chorus of wood pigeons serenaded me as I stepped out in a white T-shirt, black jeans and trainers—what with all the baking that had to be done, I needed to be comfortable. I grabbed my handbag from the back seat and locked the car.

The lawns were layered by the first rays of sunshine, and a fresh, crisp breeze weaved its way through the avenues of trees and the flowerbeds, where the scalloped camellias raised their heads to the sky. Glenlovatt Manor had the ability to wind its way around your heart and steal your affections without you even realising it. No wonder Hugo and Lydia had loved the place so much. I glanced at the mausoleum, nestled peacefully further down the grounds. I just knew Hugo was willing me to succeed.

I headed for the tea room's patio doors, praying that a certain dark-haired sculptor was still in bed. Firmly pushing away images of Vaughan lying there all sinewy under his covers, I marched inside, to be met by Gordon coming through the door to the great hall. 'My goodness, aren't you a sight for sore eyes on a Monday morning!'

I smiled back, pointing at his sharp navy suit, blue shirt and pale gold tie. 'You do know you're going to be swooned over by the ladies of Fairview if you insist on wearing that?'

Two streaks of colour trailed across Gordon's cheeks. 'Oh, don't say that!' Then he folded his arms. 'I was a bit surprised you didn't stay over after the ball, as Morven did, but Travis said you were a bit under the weather . . . ?'

I concealed a fond smile at the thought of Travis. What would I do without him?

'That's right. I just felt a bit off colour.'

Gordon's brows furrowed. 'What a shame. Well, I'll let you get to it, but I just came in to say thank you, Lara.'

I could feel a blush steadily rising on my cheeks. 'I should be thanking you.'

'Oh, but that's not so,' he corrected me kindly. 'You've taken on this challenge and you really didn't have to do that.'

'I did. I have to show you and Hugo that he hasn't made a mistake by putting so much faith in me.'

As Gordon left for his study, I headed into the kitchen.

There were still a few hours until we were due to open, so I whisked on one of our new Thistles aprons and got to work on some cherry pie cupcakes. Next I'd have to do the coconut and lime cake, and then a chocolate Guinness cake. Jess would be arriving in half an hour and Morven would be joining us just before opening.

Excitement shot through me like a bullet as I added sugared roast almonds to my baking mix. I watched the glacé cherries bob up and down as my mixer folded them in. They looked like little crimson boats negotiating a creamy sea. I dipped in a teaspoon to taste my mixture, closing my eyes. The tangy cherries merged with the toasted taste of the almonds. Perfection.

'So, that's tea for two, one slice of gin and tonic loaf, and one frangipane tart.'

I'd delivered the order to the table with a satisfied smile. Thistles had been open for only a couple of hours but business was steady.

Our two inaugural cakes of the day—a pear and ginger cake with whipped cream and rum-caramel glaze, and a more traditional orange layer cake—sat like two vain ladies on top of their respective cake stands. Our cake display was a cornucopia of colour; waves of snowy icing atop slabs of fruit-studded cakes jostled deep pink cupcake cases that were filled with swathes of golden baking. Jess had placed her latest batch of sourdough focaccia on a glass platter at the far end of the counter. They were just out of the oven, their specks of green olives and plum tomato glowing like jewels in the crusty mounds of bread. In a twist on the traditional date and oat slice, I'd laced caramel through the mix and then speckled the top with dark chocolate shavings as a finishing touch.

Jess eyed my slice with relish. 'I know what I'm having with my cuppa at break time.'

'That's if I don't get there first,' grinned Morven. 'Blimey, ladies, if I keep working here, I'm going to have to go up a size or two!'

Earlier that morning, Gordon had come back in to 'test' a slice of my chocolate Guinness cake and quench his thirst with an Americano. Now Mrs Baylis, a retired local librarian turned Glenlovatt tour guide, popped in. Decked out in tweed and pearls, her powdered face was wreathed in joy as she looked around Thistles for the first time.

'This is wonderful,' she gasped, clasping my hand, 'the late lady laird would have loved this.'

With her passion for local history, Mrs Baylis had jumped at Gordon's offer to be the official tour guide at Glenlovatt. It had been decided that she would undertake two tours a day, three times a week, to begin with, to monitor public demand. Then, if there was an appetite for them, the number of tours could be increased.

Mrs Baylis glanced down at her dainty watch. 'The first coach party of tourists should be here soon.'

'Are visitors allowed to see the entire house?'

She shook her head. 'No, only the great hall, the dining room and drawing room, and then the guest bedrooms upstairs. The grounds too, of course.' With a smile, she added, 'I'll make sure we end the tours at the tea room.'

'That suits us!' I said. 'I'm sure we'll not have many issues recruiting additional staff in here, should the tours really take off.'

The metallic rear of a coach slid into view. Mrs Baylis smiled again as she headed for the great hall. 'That's the spirit, Lara.'

An elderly couple dressed in walking gear popped their ruddy faces around the patio doors. 'Excuse me. Are you open?' asked the man hopefully.

'Yes, of course. Please come in.'

They nodded polite greetings to the other tables, a few of which were now occupied, and began to openly admire the cakes.

Over the hum of conversation and muted music (I'd selected an array of classical pieces and Scottish reels that were on my iPod) I scooped up two plates from behind the counter, ready to serve the walkers.

The morning passed in a whirl of hungry holiday-makers, and even a small group of primary school children who had come for a short visit to the grounds. Lunchtime came around with Morven having spent the latter part of the morning clearing up the children's debris and keeping them occupied with tales of Gary, the Glenlovatt pirate. My satisfaction at seeing our kitchen return to some semblance of order after the lunchtime rush was abruptly interrupted by a voice behind me.

'Lara?' Vaughan stood by the kitchen entrance, pushing a lock of hair off his face. Excitement was quickly extinguished by irritation, more at myself than anything else.

Behind him, Morven's eyes swivelled between Vaughan and me. Then she popped her blonde head around the kitchen door. 'Jess, I just need a hand behind the counter for a sec.'

Jess replied, 'Ah. Got you. Okay.'

I took a steadying breath and flicked a tea towel over my shoulder. 'Hi,' I declared, indicating some sticky toffee muffins, two slices of raspberry and coconut loaf and a single wedge of lemon meringue pie. 'Leftovers from this morning. Anything you fancy?'

Oh, for heaven's sake! Why hadn't I just given him an icy stare instead of resorting to suggestive chitchat?

Vaughan's lips twitched. 'Do you really want me to answer that?'

I folded my arms across my chest. 'You know what I mean.'

He grinned. 'I do. The place looks great.'

'So not like something out of a snowglobe then.'

'No, it's great. Very classy. Just like its new owner.'

Okay, unexpected. My face tingled with sparks of heat. 'Thank you.'

He leaned closer, his blue eyes intense in a way that made me step backwards. 'I need to speak to you about Petra.'

'You do?' I replied cautiously.

He came further into the kitchen, his spidery lashes fluttering against his cheeks. 'Well, the thing is, I'm not exactly engaged.'

Now seemed like a good time to wipe the already clean work top again. 'Not exactly engaged?' I asked, wishing I wasn't so bloody interested. 'What does that mean?'

Vaughan cleared his throat. 'Petra and I have been dating on and off for several months. Her family and mine have been close since we were kids.'

I put down the tea towel. 'You don't have to tell me any of this. In fact, I'm not sure why you are. It's none of my business.'

Vaughan watched me stack a pile of plates in the dishwasher. 'I just wanted to explain, that's all. She's desperate to get married. She drops hints like two-ton bricks every chance she gets. But we're not engaged.'

I raised my eyes to his. Why did he have to stare like that?

'So why don't you tell her that?' I replied.

Vaughan pulled a hand through his hair and it fell down around his face. 'Believe me, I have.'

The conversation paused while I closed a couple of cupboard doors.

'Petra seems to think if she mentions marriage often enough, it will happen.' He leaned across the work top towards me, tilting his slightly stubbled angular jaw. 'But I am not engaged to her,' he repeated. 'And I never will be.'

Silence fell between us, and before I knew what was happening our lips were inches apart and I found myself staring at the dark stubble snaking around his jaw.

'Vaughan?' came a high-pitched voice from somewhere behind him. 'When are you coming back?'

A young blonde woman had draped herself in the kitchen doorway, a cream bedsheet wrapped around her from which a golden shoulder protruded. Lingering lunchtime customers stared incredulously at the half-dressed blonde. Was Vaughan Carmichael for real?

I sprang backwards, as if jolted by an electric shock. 'You'd better get back to it,' I ground out. 'She'll catch her death in that.'

'This isn't what it looks like,' protested Vaughan.

'It never is, is it?'

Vaughan blinked a few times. 'You're determined to think the worst of me, aren't you?' With a dry laugh, he added, 'Well, you think what you like, Lara. Maybe I should start living up to your high expectations of me.'

He turned and draped one arm across the shoulders of the sheet-clad blonde before sauntering nonchalantly out of the tea room.

Twenty-three

'I don't think I can do this.'

Morven's emerald green eyes widened over the rim of her coffee cup. 'Don't be a daft cow!'

'I'm not,' I bleated, tugging at my frayed socks. 'I think I've just underestimated all the work Thistles would take and I don't think I'm up to it.'

A month had whipped by since the tea room opened and also since Vaughan's and my argument. From that day, on the very rare occasions I spotted him prowling around Glenlovatt, we'd only acknowledged each other with a curt 'Hello'. This week Gordon had mentioned that Vaughan was away in London, showcasing his latest sculptures at some poncy arts event.

I was relieved. It was for the best under the circumstances.

Morven banged down her cup, dragging me back to reality. 'There's no way I'm letting you quit now. You're doing really well with Thistles, and you owe it to the memory of that sweet old man. He believed in you and so do I.'

'That's not fair bringing Hugo into this.'

Morven nodded. 'No, you're right. I shouldn't have mentioned Hugo. But I know it's nothing to do with you not being up for the task. It's that bloody sculptor!'

My coffee cup froze as it reached my mouth. 'What?'

Morven folded her arms. 'Your low mood has got nothing to do with the workload of Thistles. It's because of Vaughan Carmichael, isn't it?'

I didn't reply. I didn't need to. The guilty expression clouding my eyes answered her question.

'I don't mean to bring it up again,' said Morven gently, 'but have you forgotten that a half-naked blonde appeared at the tea room only a few weeks back?'

I swung my head sharply to look at her. 'No, I hadn't forgotten.'

Morven tucked her knees tighter under her on the sofa, leaning over to squeeze my arm tenderly. 'You can't let your feelings for Mr Grouchy impact your judgement.'

Morven was right. Of course she was. I would only be letting myself down if I walked away now, not to mention Hugo, Gordon and Glenlovatt.

'But Petra,' I muttered. 'What if they actually are engaged?'

Morven sighed. 'Well, if it was true, it'd be your lucky escape.' She turned her heavily lashed gaze to mine. 'But that guy is never seen with the same woman twice, so I think the chances of him being engaged to Petra Whatsit are slim to none. You probably guessed this already but the world of the so-called landed gentry is very incestuous.'

I pulled a face.

'No, not like that, you silly mare. I mean that everyone tends to know everyone else, which means if Tabitha Tits-Biggles gets engaged to Timothy Todger-Reeves, it's round the houses faster than you can say Bollinger.'

'I feel really sorry for the children, with names like that,' I joked.

Morven sighed, exasperated. 'Clearly they are a figment of my very creative imagination. Look, if Petra was engaged to Vaughan, believe me, I would have heard about it.' She sidled a little closer. 'Yes, he's gorgeous but he's also a bastard. His reputation with women precedes him. For your own sake, keep him at arm's length, okay?'

I forced myself to smile at my best friend. I knew I had no option but to take Morven's advice, even though I secretly didn't want to. My mood plunged further when my mobile rang. It was Babs, the cleaner at Thistles.

Morven watched me carefully as I answered the call mono-syllabically. She clearly got the gist of the conversation because when I rang off, she momentarily closed her eyes.

'Don't tell me. Babs has just quit.'

'It's not her fault and she was so apologetic,' I explained with a defeated sigh. 'Her daughter's returning to work after having her little girl and she needs help with childcare. She had warned me from the start that this might happen but I was desperate for good help.' I stared into my mug. 'So now I have to find a new cleaner, and Babs was so thorough and reliable, she's going to be a hard act to follow.'

I put my tea back on the coaster and picked up my pen and to-do list, which never seemed to get much shorter. 'I don't like asking you, Morvs, but would you be able to draft a job advert for a new cleaner, please?'

Morven nodded. 'Don't be silly. Of course I can.'

'Babs said she can only work till the end of the week, so the sooner we get someone else, the better.'

Morven suddenly sat up beside me. 'Hang on. I don't think we'll need to place a job advert.' A bright smile lit up her face.

'You remember my Aunt Bea? Well, she's decided to return to domestic recruitment consultancy work.'

I put down my pen. 'Do you think she'll be able to get us someone?'

'Of course she will. She's got a lot of contacts. Leave it with me. I'll give her a ring now.'

I watched my dynamic friend explain the situation over the phone. When she hung up, she was positively frothing. 'One of her friends, Connie Hunter, has cleaned for the Barwood-Symes up at Tyndell.'

I grinned at her. 'You sound like you're speaking in code.'

Morven rolled her eyes good-naturedly. 'Take it from me, that family are fussy with a capital F. Anyway, Connie is fed up with the commuting and had asked Bea to look for a cleaning job in the central belt.'

'And her references?' I asked, pushing myself straighter.

'Glowing, apparently. Bea will send through some of them now.'

As we waited, I took a mouthful of coffee. 'Are you still happy being involved with me and Thistles, Morvs?'

Morven's brow creased. 'What sort of silly question is that?'

I shrugged. 'I just wondered. I mean, you've been so invaluable to me and I know that hasn't left you much time to help your dad out with his business.'

'Listen,' said Morven, 'as long as you're happy to have me around helping you with whatever needs doing, then that's more than fine by me.'

She propped her head back against the sofa. 'I know Thistles belongs to you but I feel like I've got a vested interest in her as well and it's so lovely doing something that's not connected to my family name.'

'Well, as long as you're sure . . .'

She patted me on the leg. 'Quite sure. And I can't leave you and Jess to eat all those delicious cakes on your own, can I?'

There was a sudden ping from Morven's mobile and a text message shot up. We scrolled through an impressive list of references for Connie and Morven texted her aunt back to say we'd love to meet her and have an informal chat.

'See?' beamed Morven, closing her mobile phone case shut. 'Things have a habit of sorting themselves out.'

I grinned back. 'You need to write a motivational book. It would sell shedloads.'

'Nah,' giggled Morven, taking a gulp from her mug. 'I don't think I'm motivated enough.'

September sunshine wrapped itself around me like a golden blanket as I threw open the patio doors to Thistles.

Even though we'd been open for almost two months now, the sight of the high-backed chairs and tables, waiting for the latest batch of visitors, and Lydia's artwork in gold and wood frames never failed to make my heart lift with satisfaction. If it hadn't been for dear old Hugo, none of this would have been possible. A sudden image of him seated in the corner, his silvery moustache twitching with mischief, came to mind and I smiled.

Outside the floor-to-ceiling windows, the lawns winked beneath a mild dusting of dew. I was growing to love Glenlovatt more and more, but on early autumn mornings like this, when the tea rooms and house were in a quiet slumber, it really stole my heart.

I fired up the coffee machine and then headed straight for the kitchen, intending to put some chocolate flapjacks and cookies and cream muffins I'd brought from home out on display after getting started on an ultimate indulgence mirror glaze cake. It had been one of my great-aunt's favourite recipes—an orange flavoured genoise, covered in a chocolate glaze and layered with salted caramel cream; utterly decadent. As the music from my iPod wafted around me in the kitchen, I stirred the orange zest and salt together and poured the melted butter down the side of the glass bowl so that it folded in neatly. Sleepy sunlight tiptoed across the tea room's kitchen floor as I scooped in some double cream.

It was at times like this, that I couldn't thank Hugo enough.

Business had been so good at Thistles that we'd had to advertise for an additional member of staff. Despite only placing a small ad online, I was amazed by the response. Morven and I had managed to whittle it down to four applicants to interview and in the end Becky Taylor, with her pink hair, air of positivity and previous Glasgow tea room experience, was the perfect addition. She was also an aspiring baker, bringing her own sensational lemon drizzle cake to the interview.

'Morning!' Becky skipped into the kitchen, where I was checking on the cake's progress in the oven, her shoulder-length raspberry-ripple hair in a ponytail. She took one look at the chocolate flapjacks and her face fell. 'Oh blimey. I don't think my date slices can compete with that.'

'You're too modest,' I laughed.

Becky feigned shock. 'I am not!'

'Yes, you are. Remember how fast your cherry and coconut scones got snapped up yesterday?'

Her pretty pointed face beamed. 'Yeah, they did go down rather well, didn't they?'

At that moment, Jess arrived, her ballet flats tapping on the wooden floor. 'Morning, both,' she eyed Becky's Tupperware expectantly. 'Ooh, spill. What's in the box?'

Becky thrust it towards us. 'Here, have a look. And please be honest. I won't be offended.'

I gently placed the large container on the kitchen top and pulled off the lid. The inside of the box was separated into four compartments. Red velvet cupcakes topped with swirls of vanilla cream and shiny Empire biscuits studded with glazed cherries occupied the first two slots. Mixed berry meringues sat in the second two like crimson teardrops alongside triangles of lemon chiffon cake.

'Wow,' I exclaimed in admiration. 'You're putting me to shame.'

Becky shrugged off her black leather jacket and smiled at me. 'I want you guys and Morven to tell me honestly what you think. Now that Jack and I have called it a day, I'll have more time on my hands for baking.'

'Oh no. What happened?'

Becky turned around, smudges of tiredness just visible under her make-up. 'Things haven't been going well for a while now. What with Jack and the problems I'm having with this ruddy red velvet cake, it was some night.'

Jess and I gave her sympathetic looks but she just smiled and turned around to unpack her box of goodies.

Morven breezed into the kitchen, her shiny curtain of blonde hair swinging down her back. 'Morning, ladies! Tell me I'm crazy but I've been thinking all night about us throwing something like "The Great Glenlovatt Bake-off".'

'That sounds like a fabulous idea,' I said, leaving the cake to cool and handing her some trays of goodies.

We headed out to arrange the cake counter. 'While we're on the subject of promo stuff, am I right in remembering that you studied web design at some point, Morvs?'

Morven gave Jess's avocado and fetta tartlets a come-hither look of appreciation. 'That's right, before I saw the error of my ways. Why?'

I asked to borrow Becky's iPad, and pulled up Glenlovatt's website and turned the screen round. 'What do you think of this?'

Morven sat down at a nearby table for a closer look, while I continued arranging the day's treats. 'I like the snowy Glenlovatt scene,' she replied, 'but the general look of the site is a bit old-fashioned.'

'That's what I thought. Gordon was telling me that Lydia set up the site years ago but when she passed away, no one bothered to keep it updated. It just looks so neglected, and there's no mention of Thistles, obviously.'

Morven smiled. 'Is this a subtle way of saying you'd like me to take a look at updating it?'

'Am I that transparent?'

'Yes.'

'I'd be very grateful if you did,' I laughed. 'I don't need you to reinvent the wheel, but if you could suggest some improvements and include the tea room on it, that would be great.'

Morven tapped on the screen idly. 'Have you mentioned this to the Carmichaels yet?'

I shook my head. 'No, I haven't. I thought if we could go to them with some suggestions for improvements, that might be the way to go. As Lydia started the site, I don't want to upset them in any way.'

Morven raised an eyebrow. 'Okay. I'll have another look at it and jot down some ideas.' She leaned forwards again, taking in the staid-looking web pages. 'All it really needs is a bit of updating and rearranging,' she said, scrolling through the content. 'A website should be easy to navigate but some of this text is a bit all over the place.' She looked back up at me. 'We'll have to create a new section for the tea room, where we can link our Instagram and Facebook pages, and maybe take it in turns to write blogs? We could promote the baking, give tips, run competitions, have a Thistles customer of the week, that kind of thing.'

'That's a great idea.'

Morven tapped away, reading out snatches of information about Glenlovatt from the website.

'What about setting up a Facebook page for Glenlovatt itself?' I suggested. 'Like the one you did for Thistles? To be fair, Gordon doesn't seem to have the time or the inclination to wade into that world.'

Morven nodded. 'If you don't have some sort of social media presence nowadays, it can have a negative impact on your business. And the house has to be a business to survive. Sad but true.'

I leaned in beside her to look at the paragraphs of information about Glenlovatt and its weird and wonderful characters from the past. It was hard to glean much at a glance from the cramped text.

As if reading my thoughts, Morven said, 'I think changing the font would make the text much easier to read. And the colour scheme needs updating too. Leave it with me and I'll create a mock-up for us to show Gordon.' She jumped to her feet. 'I just had a thought. My cousin Aidan is into photography; he's got a real talent for it. I could ask him to come down and take some photos of Glenlovatt and of us here. We could use on both the site and social media.'

I clapped my hands. 'That sounds great. I love it when a plan comes together.'

At that very moment a platinum blonde helium balloon waltzed in from the great hall. A diaphanous leopard-print dress hung from expanses of brown skin and the feet were encased in bright red platform shoes.

Morven and I swapped terrified glances.

'Oooh, how retro!' exclaimed the balloon in a high-pitched squeak. 'Not my choice of colour scheme but that can be easily rectified.'

She pouted and prodded her way around the tea room, picking up the laminated menu. 'Marble cake,' she read aloud. 'Do you have any coconut water or spinach and kale smoothies?'

Not giving us time to respond, she oozed between the tables and chairs like a snake. 'Brave choices,' she observed, bending down to examine the quilted cushions on the chairs. 'But vintage is so 2017, isn't it?'

My face turned the colour of my hair. 'I'm sorry, you are . . . ?'

The woman's eyes slid from left to right before resting on us again. 'Rhiannon Kincaid,' she answered with a bored air.

'Rhiannon!' interrupted Gordon desperately, almost running in from the hall. 'There you are. I wondered where you had got to.' He placed his arm around her waist with little enthusiasm. 'There's plenty of time for a proper tour later.' With an apologetic grimace, he steered Leopard Lady out of Thistles.

'What was all that about?' I asked Morven, whose carefully plucked eyebrows had arched almost into her hairline. 'Rhiannon Kincaid, did she say?'

'Yeah,' confirmed Morven darkly. 'Haven't you heard of her?'

'No. Should I have?'

'You'd know her if you read all the celebrity magazines. She's the daughter of Royston Kincaid of the Kincaid Shoes empire.'

'She's never out of the gossip pages. The sort that would go to the opening of an envelope, you know?'

I nodded absently. Morven had just got back to her idea about staging a bake-off contest when a tall, thin man in a crisp navy suit knocked on the patio doors, a briefcase under his arm.

Oh for pity's sake. It was like a shopping centre on Christmas Eve and the day hadn't even properly started yet.

'I'm looking for Lara McDonald.'

'That's me,' I smiled, from behind the counter. 'What can I do for you?'

The man's slicked-back dark hair reminded me of a crow's feathers. 'I'm Fraser Doyle from Environmental Health.' He swung a laminated badge in front of me. 'We've had a complaint about the cleanliness of your establishment that needs to be investigated.'

Twenty-four

Morven and I swapped more confused stares.

'Environmental Health?' repeated Morven in an incredulous tone. 'This place is spotless.'

My mind reeled. Who on earth could have done such a thing? And why? I looked around at the swept floorboards, polished tables and sparkling cutlery. We were fastidious about cleanliness. This didn't make sense.

'Who complained?' I bit out, not really expecting him to divulge such information.

Back in the kitchen, the mixer's whirring stopped. Perhaps noticing the sharp edge in my voice, Becky and Jess popped their heads round the kitchen door.

Mr Doyle's lips rose officiously. 'I'm afraid I can't say.'

I gritted my teeth. 'We're due to open soon but, please, do what you need to do. Becky, Jess—take a minute while Mr Doyle has a look at our kitchen.' My fingers gripped the edge of the counter as I turned back to him. 'I'm sure you'll find everything in order.'

Mr Doyle simply cocked a challenging eyebrow.

Becky stepped in, 'Would you like a coffee, Mr Doyle? And perhaps a slice of cake?'

The man took a step forwards and peered into the cake display. 'A cappuccino would be very nice. Oh, and a slice of your Persian tea loaf, please.' He made his way past us and into the kitchen.

'He obviously isn't worried about food poisoning from our cakes then,' I muttered as I came out from behind the counter. 'Who the hell has reported us to Environmental Health?'

Morven raised her hands helplessly, her neatly manicured nails flashing. 'Some malicious bugger with too much time on their hands.' She sidled closer. 'Don't worry. This place is like a palace. You've got nothing to worry about.'

'Yoo-hoo! Surprise, darling!'

No way. No way. It couldn't be.

I turned my head in slow motion, away from Morven's open, confident expression.

'Mum,' I whispered in a papery voice.

'Your mum reported us?' blinked Becky.

'No. I mean that's my mum,' I replied, jabbing a disbelieving finger at my mother where she stood framed in the patio doors, arm in arm with a young hipster bloke.

I stood, rigid with shock as she swept towards me in a cloud of orange and red fringed kaftan, her silvery hair snaking down her back. She planted two theatrical kisses airily on either side of my face before rewarding Morven with an excited squeal and two identical 'mwah!'s and taking a step backwards in a pair of elaborately jewelled sandals.

'You've filled out,' she said to me in her fruity burr. 'Must be all those cakes.'

Becky and Jess appeared hypnotised by the bizarre scene unfolding in front of them.

'Mum,' I said, 'what are you doing here? You said you might come over at Christmas.'

My panic zoomed into overdrive when I spied a pile of luggage channelling the height of Mount Vesuvius perched precariously in the doorway.

Mum's green eyes danced with mischief. 'Wolf and I decided to surprise you!'

'Oh, you've done that, alright—sorry, did you just say "Wolf"?' I studied the young man beside her, all tie-dyed blue T-shirt, beige combats and cropped brown hair. 'I thought you said his name was Alvar?'

Going by the narrow-eyed glare my mother was shooting me from her sun-tanned face, that was obviously a faux pas. 'No,' she growled through gritted teeth. 'This is Wolf. My new partner.'

'Another one bites the dust then,' I muttered to a bemused Morven.

As Wolf wandered over to inspect Lydia's artwork, Mum squared her shoulders. 'Alvar never understood me.'

'He's not the only one.'

Before Mum could reply, Wolf strode back up and extended a heavily ringed hand. 'Nice place you have here. Chrissie has told me all about your new venture, yeah?'

His accent rang with heavy overtones of English public school. Only my mother could go to South America and hook up with someone as British as rainy weather and cream teas.

'Yes, I just own this tea room,' I explained carefully, 'not the whole house.' I didn't want this lumberjack look-a-like with his leather wrist bracelets to think he'd fallen on his feet. If Wolf was dating my mum (and I tried not to imagine anything more graphic than them holding hands), I wanted him to do it for all the right reasons.

He nodded his head casually. 'Cool.'

After a few more moments of charged silence, Mum clapped her hands. 'So, any chance of a cuppa and a slice of cake seeing we've travelled all this way to see you?'

'Of course. Becky, Jess, this is my mother, Christine.'

While my two bakers took charge of the situation behind the counter, I stood aside like a moody teenager. Not only did I have Environmental Health snooping around my kitchen, I now had my hippie–feminist mother and her bearded new toy boy to contend with. And judging by the assorted luggage, they weren't here just for a long weekend.

While Becky brewed the tea and Jess slid two banoffee muffins onto plates, Christine regaled Morven with the 'awful' taxi ride they had from the airport to Glenlovatt. 'It seemed to take forever,' she exclaimed, her tanned fingers fluttering about her throat.

'Mum, the airport is only twenty-five minutes from here.'

Emerging out of the kitchen, Mr Doyle moved to inspect the toilet, giving Mum and Wolf a quick appraisal as he did so. Thankfully Mum was too busy perusing Jess's blackboard specials of courgette and roast pepper quiche and chorizo and rocket rolls to notice—I didn't think I could take one of her anti-establishment rants right now.

My good fortune was only to last for a few more moments. Mr Doyle marched up to me with his clipboard, 'Everything appears to be in order, Ms McDonald.' He thrust a piece of paper at me. 'I apologise for this intrusion but, as I'm sure you will appreciate, we have an obligation to check out environmental health complaints.'

Oh shit.

Mum's head whirled round. 'You're from the council? Environmental Health, did you say?' Mr Doyle seemed to pale slightly under Mum's cat-like stare. 'Am I right in assuming that someone has made a complaint about my daughter's cleanliness?'

'Not my personal habits, Mum,' I laughed nervously. *Oh please, wooden floor. Open up your gaping jaws. Take me now. I won't object.*

Mr Doyle licked his thin lips. 'Madam, we are obliged to investigate any such complaints, but your daughter's premises are more than satisfactory.'

Christine's full mouth twisted in disbelief. 'Satisfactory?' She flung her tanned arms out. 'This place is immaculate. Immaculate, I tell you!'

She snatched Mr Doyle by the arm and spun him round so fast I'm surprised he didn't have motion sickness. 'Look at this gorgeous cake display. Look at it! It's a place of baking heaven. And you have the audacity to come in here and throw your authoritarian weight around?' Ignoring the fact she'd only seen the tea room for the first time five minutes ago, she carried on. 'I'll grant you it's rather unfortunate that it's located in some elitist ancestral pile, probably acquired through the ill-gotten gains of a bunch of inbred aristos . . .'

Morven spluttered beside me, the colour of my face again rising to matching the shade of my hair.

'But nonetheless,' Mum carried on breathlessly, 'my Lara's making the best of a bad job.'

Wolf nodded at Mum's shoulder as he devoured a mouthful of muffin and spluttered, 'Up the workers!'

Time froze at this point as Gordon's voice travelled from where he was standing in the doorway to the great hall.

'Good morning, Lara. When you've got a moment, could this land-stealing, inbred aristo possibly have one of your delicious coffees, please?'

Twenty-five

Anger and embarrassment bubbled in my chest but I managed to contain myself until a bemused-looking Gordon had returned to his study.

'Out!' I barked, alarming Mr Doyle. 'Go on!'

He paled even further and scrabbled about for his paperwork.

'No, not you! I'm talking to these two.'

Morven stifled a giggle while Mum looked crestfallen. 'What?'

'I'm trying to run a business here, in case that has escaped your attention. Any moment now I hope to have hordes of cake-obsessed visitors through that door.'

'We won't be in the way,' protested Mum, folding her caramel arms.

'Yes, you will. You've managed to offend not only the laird but also most of the people in this room and it isn't even lunchtime.'

I snatched up my blue leather handbag from behind the counter and fished out my door key, handing it to Mum, a large silver L dangling from it in mid-air. 'Here. Go back to my flat and make yourselves comfortable. I'll call a taxi for you.'

Mum's golden jaw hardened. 'Well, that is lovely. We've come all this way and you're not going to spend time with your own mother? What happened to supporting the sisterhood?'

I supressed an eye roll. 'I just told you. I'm working.'

Mum put on a show of rooting around in her stripy beach bag. 'A taxi, you say? I think I've spent most of my cash already.'

Wolf mirrored her theatrics, delving into his trouser pockets, then producing a sad face that any mime artist would have been impressed by.

I blew out some air and fetched a twenty-pound note from my purse. 'Pay for your taxi with this.'

'Thank you, darling. I'll pay you back later, of course.'

'Up the workers!' repeated Wolf over his shoulder as they sauntered past a sheepish Mr Doyle, who had retreated to the safety of a corner table, their hands skittering over each other's backsides. Luckily our patrons had yet to arrive or they'd have been turned right off their salmon and cream cheese bagels.

'Can you hold the fort for a few minutes, you guys?' I asked, 'I've got a couple of apologies to make.'

'Don't worry about it, I'll get back to the bagels,' Jess said.

Becky handed me Gordon's cappuccino, which she'd decorated with a chocolate thistle stencil. 'It wasn't you who said it.'

I took the cup and shook my head before walking stiffly over to where Mr Doyle had retreated to a corner table. 'I'm so sorry for that. Can I get you something? On the house.'

Mr Doyle cast a fearful look towards the door. 'She won't be coming back, will she?'

'You mean my mother? No. At least, I hope not.'

Mr Doyle nodded hesitantly. 'Alright then. I've got some paperwork to finish off. It should only take five minutes but an Earl Grey tea would be very nice.'

Becky smiled from over behind the counter and busied herself with a teapot.

Travis was out in the hall. 'Is Mr Carmichael back in his study?' I asked.

He nodded and gestured towards the large coffee cup I was cradling. 'I could be doing with one of those this morning.'

'Go and see Becky,' I answered. 'Tell her it's on the house.'

I clutched the ceramic coffee cup tighter. I wouldn't be making much of a profit if I kept dishing out free drinks.

Gordon had been so understanding and welcoming, he didn't deserve to be slagged off by my mother. Suitable words of apology raced through my mind. All I needed was for her anti-establishment rant to colour his view of me or what we were trying to do for Glenlovatt.

I passed a stony-faced bust of one of their ancestors and arrived at Gordon's study door. Straightening my shirt collar, I lifted my hand to knock but a pool of pale light showed it was slightly ajar, and I could now hear Gordon's voice as he spoke on the phone.

'Well, what else can I do?' His voice sounded desperate. 'That Petra Montgomery-Carlton . . .'

My ears swivelled onto high alert. I knew I shouldn't be lurking there, clasping Gordon's coffee and awash with guilt for listening in. But nevertheless, my trainers remained stuck to the tiled floor. I leaned in a little closer to the gap in the door.

Gordon uttered some grunts and mumbles before his voice became clear again. 'Oh, I met Rhiannon at a recent charity event. No, not that one. This was the one to raise money for the homeless.' There was a pause before he spoke again. 'The funny thing is, she said at first she couldn't attend as she didn't know which of her four homes she'd be in at the time. Yes, I know, ironic, isn't it?' Gordon mumbled a few more words and then he said, 'I know Vaughan thinks he's doing this for all the right reasons but, well . . .'

There was silence as the person at the other end spoke.

Gordon continued, 'I don't want him sacrificing his happiness just so Glenlovatt can carry on.' There was another pause before he said, 'I know, I can't see Petra being the easiest of wives, can you?'

What was Gordon saying? Like a jigsaw, the pieces began to shuffle together. Did he mean Vaughan was contemplating marriage to Petra in order to protect Glenlovatt? After the Ladies and Rogues Ball I'd rushed home in true Cinderella style, fired up my laptop and googled Petra. The internet threw up all sorts of information about the Montgomery-Carlton clan, who'd made their fortune in bespoke bridal gowns.

Gordon's concerned voice went on, 'Yes, the tea room is doing well, as are the guided tours, but, Alistair, we've got another problem, which has only just come to light.'

Another pause, interrupted only by the odd squeak from Gordon's chair. 'Oh, Lara's a sweet girl. Hard-working and enthusiastic too. But you know that Glenlovatt is a money pit.'

There was a long silence before he spoke again. 'It's not just the blasted heating being on the blink. Our landscape gardeners have hiked up their charges and what with this latest problem to hit the house . . .'

What was he talking about?

I steadied Gordon's coffee in my hands. Any moment now I'd drop the bloody thing.

His resigned sigh made my shoulders slump. 'I know, I know,' he agreed, tapping his pen on the desk. Then he dropped his voice. 'But there's no way I'm allowing my son to ruin the rest of his life by marrying someone he doesn't love, even if it does mean losing Glenlovatt.'

Gordon murmured a few things and then spoke again. 'No, Vaughan doesn't know about this latest bloody issue. If I tell him, he could well do something impulsive and I'm not prepared to risk it.'

I'd heard more than enough and had spun on my heel to leave when Gordon's next words held me fixed to the spot. 'I can't see any other way,' he added with an air of finality. 'I wasn't going to tell you this, Alistair, but I owe it to my father, to Vaughan and to Lydia to keep Glenlovatt in the family.'

There was a thud as he banged something on the desk. 'I've been so lucky in my life to fall in love and marry the woman of my dreams. I won't allow Vaughan to sacrifice any chance he has of that.'

With a resigned sigh he added, 'So that's why I've decided to ask Rhiannon Kincaid to marry me.'

I lurched back to the tea room.

'Are you alright?' asked Becky.

I clattered the cold cappuccino onto the cake counter. 'Yes. Yes, I'm fine.'

She narrowed her smoky shadowed eyes. I asked, 'Could you make a fresh coffee for Gordon and take it to him, please?'

'Sure, no problem. Morven's gone to speak to the local paper. They rang with costs for an advertising feature.' Becky gave me one more sidelong glance before picking up Gordon's fresh coffee and walking towards the door.

'Okay. Right. Thanks,' I replied.

By that time, customers had started to arrive and Jess was clearing a table for an American couple. I tried to take in what I'd heard. Surely Gordon wasn't serious—marrying someone so he could hang on to the estate? Anyone could see he was still in love with his late wife.

I fetched my mobile and searched for the name 'Rhiannon Kincaid'. I half-expected spicy pictures to pop up but it was mostly photos of her in slit dresses and towering heels. She seemed to lurch from one man to the next, and when she wasn't decorating some rich guy's arm she was peddling the tacky shoe emporium founded by her late father.

Dejection overtook me. There must be other things Gordon could do to generate more income for Glenlovatt besides allowing this red-taloned socialite to get her claws into the estate.

Gordon marrying Rhiannon and Vaughan marrying Petra? Crikey. Glenlovatt and the Carmichael family would never recover.

Twenty-six

Driving home that evening I cranked up my car radio, but I still couldn't concentrate on anything except the last proper conversation I'd had with Vaughan.

What a judgemental cow I had been! He'd stood there, looking all dark and deep, wanting to explain about Petra, and instead I'd jumped to the wrong conclusions, hanging onto the prior evidence that he was a bit of a philanderer. And as for that blonde girl in the bedsheet . . . Vaughan had wanted to explain about her too, but I'd made up my mind and wouldn't listen. She could have been one of his art models. I inwardly cringed as I thought about it.

Through the windscreen the autumn sky was contorting its pale blue into tangerine. I gripped the steering wheel tighter. Thistles and the tours were all going well but obviously not well enough to sustain an estate like Glenlovatt, if Gordon and Vaughan were both contemplating marrying sugar mummies.

Poor Hugo would be spinning in his grave. And as for Lydia . . .

There must be something that could be done to prevent two car-crash marriages and keep Glenlovatt afloat. I just couldn't envisage that gorgeous house redecorated in leopard skin.

My despondency was soon replaced by irritation when I stumbled, exhausted, into my flat.

Wolf was stretched out in a tangle of limbs on the sofa, hugging one of my stripy nautical cushions. Seated comfortably in my armchair was Mum, her gold half-moon spectacles perched on her face, reading a hardback entitled *Empowering Your Lady Garden: A Definitive Guide*. The cover was all swirls of pink and purple, with a very suggestive silhouette. As I wanted to be able to eat dinner, I decided to avert my eyes.

'Good day, lovey?' she called.

I swiped my sunglasses off the top of my head. 'I've had better.'

Mum snapped her book shut. 'I hope that awful official didn't give you any more trouble.'

'No, Mum, he didn't. The poor sod was terrified after the tongue-lashing you gave him.'

Mum's lips tightened. 'I was just defending my daughter.'

'Well, I don't need defending. I'm more than capable.'

I've had to stand on my own two feet for long enough without you around.

'I won't defend you again then, if that's how you feel,' bristled Mum.

Wolf's closely cropped head had been jerking between the two of us, as if he had a prime seat at Wimbledon.

I retreated without another word into the kitchen. All I wanted to do was slop around in my pyjamas and pummel my frustrations into some unsuspecting dough.

As I clattered about, I heard Wolf call out from the sitting room, 'What's all this about some mysterious letter, Lara?'

'Sorry?'

'That old guy who died left a letter in his will to be opened on some specific date, yeah?'

As I shot up straight like a rocket, I distinctly heard Mum award Wolf a swift slap. 'Ow, Chris! What the hell was that for?'

I sauntered back into the sitting room. 'Have you been going through my things, Mum?'

'No, indeed I have not! What do you take me for?'

I folded my arms and chose not to answer that particular question. 'Well, how do you know about the letter? I didn't tell you about it.'

Mum coloured slightly under her Latin American tan. 'I might have spoken to that chauffeur chappie at Glenlovatt on the way out of the house. Curtis, is it?'

'Travis.' My eyes narrowed further at her. 'What exactly did you ask him?'

'I wouldn't say Chris asked him,' sniggered Wolf, picking a lump of fluff from his sock. 'She interrogated him, more like. The poor guy looked petrified.'

Mum prickled. 'I did no such thing. I simply asked him why some old laird would leave my daughter a tea room and he said that wasn't clear as yet. Then he mentioned this letter.'

I could imagine Mum virtually pinning poor Travis against one of the ancestral busts and shining the light from her mobile into his terror-stricken eyes. 'That's right,' I answered after a beat, deciding it was going to be easier just to get this over with. 'The family solicitor said Hugo's instructions were that this letter was not to be opened until the twenty-seventh of October.'

I returned to the kitchen and filled the kettle, watching the silvery water in a daze. I made a mental note to go and apologise to poor Travis tomorrow.

'Don't you have any idea at all what this letter is about?'

I jumped. 'For pity's sake, Mum! Have you been taking stealth lessons?'

She raised an apologetic hand.

'No,' I replied, once my heart rate had settled down. 'In answer to your question, I have no idea why Hugo left me the tea room.' I snatched some teaspoons out of the drawer. 'Once October twenty-seventh rolls around, hopefully Hugo's letter will provide all the answers.'

'Well, just you make sure you look out for yourself,' Mum advised. 'These sorts of families can be very manipulative. They are all out for themselves. Just look at the Highland Clearances.'

'"These sorts of families"?' I repeated incredulously, heading back to the sitting room. 'And what on earth have the Highland Clearances got to do with anything?'

To my surprise, Wolf piped up, 'You can't bracket everyone the same, Chris.'

My mum's eyes popped. 'Since when did you become a defender of the establishment?'

Wolf rubbed his beard. 'I'm not defending anyone. I'm just saying that not all aristocratic families are a waste of space, yeah?' He untangled his legs from the sofa. 'They very often have the same worries and family conflicts as the rest of us.'

Mum opened her mouth to speak but Wolf had already loped off to the spare bedroom.

That night, I lay in bed trying to ignore the squeaking bedsprings coming from my spare room. Bloody hell! It was like living next door to Edinburgh Zoo. Mum and Wolf had obviously called a truce after their earlier exchange.

But this problem paled into insignificance when I thought about Gordon and Vaughan. The prospect of Gordon marrying that awful Rhiannon woman while still pining for Lydia made my heart sink. And as for Vaughan . . .

I shifted uncomfortably under the covers. Images crowded my mind, of him and Petra walking down the aisle; clusters of confetti gathering in Vaughan's dark hair; their wedding reception at Glenlovatt; her in pools of satin, being photographed against the banks of majestic trees.

I thumped my pillow and sat bolt upright. Through the chink in my navy curtains I could just make out the inky silhouette of the Fairview Hills and a patch of sky studded with stars. I had to concentrate on sensible business decisions and Hugo's faith in me. The last thing I needed after Malta and the Anton fiasco was having my heart broken all over again.

I slowly slid under the covers again, resolved to let this turmoil go and try to relax for the first time all day.

Twenty-seven

 Monday morning swung around, delivering an autumn day of heavy rain.

I weaved round Mum in the kitchen, scooping up a final mouthful of cereal. Christine and her young lover had been in residence in my flat for only a few nights but it seemed more like three months. When they weren't cavorting around the place or feeling each other's bottoms, they were engaged in heated discussions about politics, gender equality or climate change. Tiredness crawled over me like a rash.

As I grabbed my navy leather jacket, Wolf emerged from the bathroom shrouded in a grey dressing gown.

'Morning,' he grinned lazily. 'No rest for the wicked, yeah?'

I plastered a tight smile on my face. 'Yes, something like that.'

He was a bit of an enigma, was Wolf. I still hadn't been able to find out exactly what he did for a living and he skirted deftly around the issue whenever it was raised. From where I stood it was spouting philosophical statements while sounding like a high-school student with too many marbles in his mouth. That was when he wasn't totally absorbed in his mobile phone.

Scrambling around in my handbag, looking for car keys, I resolved to speak to Mum privately when I got home. I sincerely hoped she wasn't giving Wolf money. As a college lecturer she'd never earned a fortune and had squirrelled away whatever savings she could after Dad died, so the prospect of her handing over her hard-earned cash to a layabout filled me with horror.

Mum suddenly appeared from behind him, tugging her belted cream dressing gown tighter. Her grey hair was pulled back off her face in a low ponytail. She appraised my outfit of dark blue jeans, pale pink T-shirt and trainers. 'Don't allow yourself to be exploited by multinationals, darling. And watch you aren't unknowingly pulled into their world of capitalist propaganda.'

My eyes followed her gaze. 'What? Because I'm wearing an outfit from a chain store?'

Mum's mouth contorted. 'That's how these things start. One minute you are your own woman, unrestrained by the shackles of convention. The next you're—'

'Shopping for avocados, walking a labrador and carrying a Dior bag?'

Mum's eyes glinted at my sarcastic reply. 'There's no talking to you when you're like this, Lara.'

I picked up my car keys from the hall table. 'Must dash,' I called. 'There's only so many hours in the day for me to doff my cap at the landed gentry.'

Becky had already started setting things up and was giving the floor a sweep when I arrived. Jess was in the kitchen, shovelling a fresh batch of pecan croissants into the oven, and Morven was at a nearby table, chattering into her mobile and scribbling in an expensive-looking notebook. She mouthed the words 'free publicity' before sticking her thumb up.

The coffee machine burbled behind the counter, and the soft strains of a violin piece nicely complemented the scent of freshly baked scones. The rain had eased for the moment, leaving pearly remnants sliding off the windows. It made Thistles seem even cosier.

An army of ideas to bring more revenue to the estate had been cartwheeling through my mind on the drive to work. It was just a case of getting Vaughan to agree. Trepidation settled in my stomach. I dragged myself back to the present. 'I'll be back in two minutes.'

Becky smiled. 'No problem.'

Taking a steadying breath, I left the tea room and negotiated the snaking great hall staircase. The dark green walls slid past me as I climbed the stairs past paintings of muscular horses, ancestors with elaborate hats, and stippled landscapes, silent witnesses to my furtive ascension. Travis didn't seem to be around and I hadn't spotted Gordon yet either. My fingers raked along the dark, embellished bannister. Gordon had said something yesterday about Vaughan being in Edinburgh, so I hoped now would be a good time. I knew what I was doing was risky but it was for the good of Glenlovatt.

I remembered Gordon taking me on a brief tour of the house and leading me through the right-hand wing. I was sure he'd said the door at the end was Vaughan's studio.

'He's very protective of it,' he'd smiled. 'I've only been in there twice and both times he couldn't hustle me out quickly enough. Artists, eh?'

My heart zipped in my chest. Vaughan would have me thrown out of the house if he had any idea where I was going.

My legs shook slightly but I propelled myself on. A couple of other doors lay ajar, revealing glimpses of a small library carpeted in red velvet, and a box room that housed a canopied single bed with crisp blue linen, satin curtains tumbling to the floor and framing a view of heather-laden hills.

I reached out for the handle on the last door, a heavy, dark-panelled affair. The gold handle rattled in my hand. At first, it seemed to be locked, but the door definitely wasn't entirely secure. It let out a faint protest as I turned the handle for a second time.

I paused for a moment. All I could hear was the sharp tick of a clock further down in the hall. I steeled myself and turned the handle more forcefully. It appeared that while Vaughan had closed the door, he'd forgotten to lock it—presumably, because he was in a bit of a hurry.

I took another deep breath and pushed.

A set of dark curtains covered one very large window at the end of the room. They were tightly drawn, so I could only make out the odd curve and sharp angle of Vaughan's sculptures. I edged my way around a couple of trestle tables, stationed at angles in the centre of the room. My fingers searched for the light switch. Damn. It didn't work.

The room was eerily quiet, apart from an insistent banging. I realised the noise was my heart ricocheting around my ribcage like a stray firework. What was I doing?

Squashing my doubts, I moved towards the curtains and pulled them apart. Pale morning light flooded the studio and I let out an involuntary gasp.

The vaulted ceiling, a dramatic combination of a snowflake design combined with inquisitive-looking cherubs, stared down at an astounding collection of figures, from traditional bust sculptures in various stages of development to a couple of modern installations moulded out of shards of glass. Everywhere I looked, milky faces gazed back. A statue of a naked woman, arms flung wide open, looked to be formed from the purest marble and made me think of a ballerina, all tight limbed in her sinewy grace.

My nostrils breathed in the mix of metal, ceramic and stone that weighted the air, while my mind raced with admiration at the variety and skill of Vaughan's work. I had no idea he was so talented. The sensual thrust of his figures made a lump form in my throat.

Even a contemporary installation of cut glass, occupying one corner of a nearby table, had a strange effect on me. I tentatively reached out to touch it. It was like a glinting star, plucked from the far reaches of the galaxy. What I knew about art could be comfortably written on the back of an envelope but I would have defied anyone not to be impressed by Vaughan's work. My fingers tingled on contact with the star-like creation. The thought of Vaughan's fingers delicately piecing this together and shaping it into life triggered a hot flush on my cheeks.

For goodness sake, Lara, get a grip on yourself!

Ideas started to assemble in my mind. Yes, he could be rather secretive at times about his work, but if I could make him see that his sculptures could benefit Glenlovatt, then maybe he'd be receptive to some suggestions. And he and Gordon wouldn't have to contemplate marrying two rich airheads.

I tugged the curtains closed again. It seemed such a pity to plunge all these graceful sculptures and bold pieces of modern art back into darkness. It was as if Vaughan's studio heaved a melancholy sigh as the velvet drapes swished together again.

Deep in thought, I turned towards the door, but my attention was caught by something in the corner that was covered by a dark blue velvet cloth. Why had Vaughan placed a piece of his work over there out of sight, when everything else was proudly stationed in the centre of the room?

I tried to fight my nosiness but it was no good.

I took tentative steps towards the mysterious object, then slid the cloth away. Underneath the folds of material was a half-finished marble bust of a woman. Part of her head was complete, displaying fine features and waves of hair. There was a serene smile beginning to blossom across her partly completed mouth. The other side of her face was blank, as if Vaughan had pulled away in a hurry. When I leaned in to look more closely at the high cheekbones and partially sculpted jaw, recognition dawned.

This was Lydia.

Awash with guilt for intruding, I pulled the cloth back over the bust and scurried back to the still slightly open door—only to barrel into a tall, silhouetted figure.

How long had he been standing there?

The solidity of his jaw confirmed that it had been long enough.

Vaughan's shoulders stiffened. 'What the hell are you doing in my studio?'

Twenty-eight

His blue eyes flashed in the semi-darkness, making me step backwards. 'I just wanted to see,' I stammered, the words tripping out of my mouth.

'See what?'

Steadying my voice as much as I could, I looked him in the eye. 'Your artwork?'

'What for?'

'What is this, the Spanish Inquisition?' I followed up my idiotic wisecrack with a papery laugh.

Vaughan didn't join in. He merely crossed his arms.

I cleared my throat and scrambled for something to distract him from me having trespassed in his sacred studio. 'Why is that piece of artwork hidden in the corner?'

Vaughan's brow furrowed. 'What artwork?'

'The one covered in the blue cloth.'

'It isn't hidden.'

'Then why is it pushed back over there away from all the others? Is it because it's of your mum?'

Well done, Sherlock. As soon as the words fell from my mouth with all the subtlety of a sledgehammer, I willed them back.

'My work is none of your business and you've got no right to come into my studio.'

He had a point there. *Okay, confession time.* Before I could think better of it, I opened my mouth and said, 'Look, I know about Petra.'

Vaughan's mouth adopted a grim line. 'Know what?'

How long was he going to keep up this two-word-question thing? My words tumbled over each other. 'I know you're thinking of marrying her—for all the wrong reasons.'

His eyes hardened. 'I don't know what you're talking about. And what has my private life got to do with you, anyway?'

Floundering, I knew I had no option but to carry on. I was making a spectacular tits-up of it all anyway, so why stop now?

'I know it's absolutely none of my business, but don't throw your life away just to secure the future of this place. There are other options.'

'Oh, really? And why do you care?'

I stared at Vaughan's cocked eyebrow. 'Sorry?'

He moved into the room, making me take several more nervous steps backwards. He was dressed in a white cotton shirt, dark jeans and a beige waistcoat. Oh bollocks. He looked utterly irresistible.

'Are you jealous, perhaps?' he said with a sneer.

A high-pitched laugh shot out of me. 'Jealous? Why would I be jealous?'

'You tell me.'

The vast blackness of the room, the at works' silhouettes and Vaughan's proximity were unnerving. I tossed my ponytail back over my shoulder. 'I am not jealous,' I replied tightly. 'I was only trying to point out that your father and grandfather wouldn't want you to get married for the wrong reasons.'

The temptation to tell him his father was considering doing exactly the same thing gnawed at me, but finding me in his studio was probably enough for Vaughn to contend with right now. Add to that his thunderous expression and I definitely knew I was not prepared to say any more for the moment.

I wished he would open up the curtains and allow the morning light to swallow up the gloom; it was like being confronted by Dracula in his crypt.

'I think you have an ulterior motive,' he growled, leaning in a little closer.

My legs remained rooted to the floor.

'I think,' he stage-whispered, 'that you're using Glenlovatt as an excuse.'

'Excuse for what?' I said falteringly.

'For this,' he answered, seizing my mouth with his. Shock gave way to excitement at the taste of his lips, as my body moulded effortlessly into his.

Vaughan slipped a hand against my back, the heat of his skin searing through my T-shirt. His tongue danced with mine and a sigh whispered from my chest. His breathing quickened and the sound of my own ragged gasps propelled me out of his arms.

What the hell was I doing?

I pulled back and examined his angular face, a smirk shifting across his mouth.

'I thought so.'

The sight of him judging me was too much. 'Now who's the one leaping to conclusions?' I blustered. The imprint of his lips still tingled. 'I came up here because I wanted to get more of an idea about what you do. I was going to suggest using your sculptures to raise money for the estate.' Tears gathered in my eyes and I pushed past him before he could see them. 'Tell you what, just carry on with your plan to marry that blonde, okay?'

'Lara, wait,' he began.

'You're right, Vaughan,' I called over my shoulder, the tears threatening to spill down my face as I dashed blindly towards the staircase, 'it is none of my business.'

Twenty-nine

Thankfully, Thistles had just welcomed a small group of tourists, so at least I would be occupied for a while. They'd disgorged from a flashy beige minibus, their admiring faces turned up towards Glenlovatt like flowers seeking out sunshine.

As Becky served an Italian couple, their enthusiasm for our cakes was matched by her infectious smile and blushing appreciation of their fervour.

Dashing my tears with the back of my hand, I managed a cheery 'How are things?' to her and Morven.

Becky's nose crinkled. 'Are you alright? You look upset.'

I brushed aside her concern. 'Oh, I'm just a bit tired, that's all.'

'You didn't look like that when you came in here this morning.'

'Look like what?' I muttered, busying myself with a pile of napkins.

Morven folded her arms. 'Like you've just ridden a roller-coaster but not been strapped in.'

My mind still clung to the sensation of Vaughan's mouth against mine. With a hollow laugh, I said, 'Don't be daft,' and fled into the kitchen. I sank against the cool work top and snapped my eyes shut. What an arrogant git! That kiss was his way of letting me know I was one in a long line.

Well, if he wanted to marry Petra Double-Barrel-Whatsit and throw away his happiness on a marriage of convenience, that was his problem. But Gordon was another matter.

Shoving aside furious thoughts about Vaughan, I resolved to speak to Gordon about what I had overheard. If Vaughan wouldn't listen, at least I might be able to make his father see sense.

To my relief, Vaughan had failed to make an appearance anywhere near the tea room.

The lunch rush was over, Jess had left for the day and I was clearing another table when I felt someone approach behind me. It was Gordon.

'We've got a problem, Lara.'

'Well, that doesn't sound promising.'

Gordon smiled. 'Do you remember the *Fairview Herald* competition for a family of four to win a guided tour and afternoon tea here?'

'Vaguely,' I confessed. 'There's been so much going on, I forgot about it.'

'Well, the winners, a local family by the name of McNaughton, are arriving just before 2pm.' He paused.

'Mrs Baylis will be here to take them on the tour, though.'

Gordon frowned. 'Ah. That's precisely the problem. She's been called to collect her granddaughter from school. She's got a heavy cold.'

'Right,' I managed, guessing where this conversation was leading but hoping I was wrong.

'And I've got a long-standing appointment with my accountant,' added Gordon apologetically, 'otherwise I would have been more than happy to do it.' He cupped his hands together in a begging action.

Uh-oh.

'I don't suppose you could take them on a tour of the house? I would be so grateful to you.'

'Me?'

'Yes. That is, if Morven and Becky can manage here.'

Becky shrugged her shoulders accommodatingly. 'We're quiet at the moment.' Morven agreed enthusiastically.

I flailed around for an acceptable excuse. 'But I'm not knowledgeable enough about Glenlovatt. I mean, I know the basic facts but I'm not clued up on it anywhere near as much as Mrs Baylis.'

Gordon brushed aside my concerns with a tanned hand. 'There's plenty of historical background on the internet you can use, and you've got such great communication skills and enthusiasm.'

The words 'laying' and 'trowel' sprang into my mind.

Becky began fishing around inside her purple rucksack. 'Here,' she grinned, 'you can use my tablet. It's fully charged and will make you look the part.'

'Oh, thank you so much,' I said through gritted teeth. 'What on earth would I do without you?'

She poked out her tongue as she handed it over. 'Glad to be of service.'

'Couldn't Vaughan do the tour?' I asked, looking up from Becky's rainbow screensaver, but Gordon had gone in a blur of navy suit. 'I'll take that as a no then.'

Morven directed me to one of the empty tables. 'Here. Sit down, grab some lunch and study up on the history of this place.'

Becky gathered up a tea set and plates from another table. 'How does a slice of tomato and mozzarella quiche sound? Jess rustled some up before she finished for the day.'

'Brilliant, thanks,' I sighed, tapping away on Becky's tablet. I tried to make my eyes two giant pools of irresistibility. 'Morvs, couldn't you do it?'

'Sorry, sweetie, but I've got to go soon. Meeting in town with printers about some fliers. She gave me an encouraging smile. 'You've worked in PR, Lara. This should be a walk in the park for you.'

Shaking my head, I continued pulling up information on the internet about Glenlovatt, and an image of the great house laced in snow like spun sugar appeared on the screen. I started to read aloud: '"Glenlovatt Manor, situated on the outskirts of Fairview, Scotland, is a majestic stately home built in 1760".'

Becky brought over my lunch. 'If this house could talk, I bet it would have a hell of a lot of juicy stories to tell.'

I tapped again on the screen but was interrupted by a shrill voice.

'Business can't be booming when the owner's sitting around on a computer.'

My skin prickled. I'd know that voice anywhere.

I eased myself around in my chair to see Kitty Walker framed in the Thistles doorway, and she wasn't alone. Peering around behind her was her fellow gossip, Moira Kendrick.

'Oh, great,' I hissed to Becky under my breath. 'Just what we need right now—a visit from Cruella de Vil and Bellatrix Lestrange.' I configured my expression into one of fake friendliness and called out, 'So, True Brew not open today then?'

Kitty patted her concrete curls. 'My sister and niece are in charge this afternoon. It's a relief to be able to leave my business in such reliable hands.'

Ouch.

They'd at least made an effort for their visit to Glenlovatt, if their voluminous floral frocks and mismatched hats were anything to go by. They looked as if they'd raided an ancient dressing-up box in the dark.

Becky's mouth tightened with recognition. 'Your old boss and her bodyguard,' she whispered. 'Nice.'

'All ready for the McNaughtons to claim their prize?' asked Kitty with her best great white shark smile.

'Yes,' I lied, 'but how did you know they were coming today?'

Kitty raised her sparkly shadowed eyelids.

'We hear everything in True Brew,' piped up Moira, finding her voice at last.

They clopped across the tea room, snootily eyeing Lydia's artwork.

'You haven't heard of the McNaughtons then?' asked Moira lightly.

Becky folded her arms across her Thistles apron. 'No, should we have? They're not related to some major crime syndicate, by any chance?'

'Are they?' asked Kitty as she pursed her lips. 'I wouldn't be surprised.'

For goodness' sake.

'Anyway,' announced Kitty, squeezing herself into one of my poor high-backed chairs, 'the McNaughton clan are incomers.' She dropped her voice. 'They're from the east.'

'Are they really?' gasped Becky, clutching a heavily ringed hand to her chest. 'Quick, Lara, inform the police immediately.'

Kitty eyed her frostily. 'You may mock, young lady, but I've heard all about that lot.'

Here we go.

'Heard what?' I asked, irritated.

Kitty's frosted pink lips smacked together like an applauding seal's flippers. 'The father's been done for theft, the mother looks permanently harassed, and as for their two teenagers—'

'They look ready to mug elderly people at a moment's notice,' interjected Moira with all the subtlety of a brick.

Kitty nestled back in her chair. 'Two teas when you're ready, waitress. Oh, and we'll have two slices of that Guinness cake while you're at it.'

'Looks slightly dry to me,' murmured Moira.

'We're only being polite,' replied Kitty without a trace of irony.

I swung my head back to Becky's tablet. Time was running out for my crash course.

'Did I hear you say you're conducting the McNaughtons' tour, Lara?'

What a nosy old crone. She and Moira must have been listening outside.

I pasted on a smile. 'Yes, that's right. If I don't return after an hour,' I said, 'search Fairview Loch. I might be swimming with the fishes at the hands of the McNaughtons.' I took a savage bite of my quiche.

'Ahem.' Travis was standing uncertainly by the door, accompanied by four granite-hard faces.

'Lara,' he grimaced. 'I'd like to introduce you to the McNaughton family. They're here for their guided tour.'

I picked up the tablet, praying to the Patron Saint of Gobby Mouths that they hadn't heard my stupid remark.

Mrs McNaughton introduced herself first, as Claire, and I also shook hands with her husband, Eddie. Their son, Robbie, and daughter, Flora, reminded me of hollow-faced models in a flashy clothes advert.

Kitty eyed them over the rim of her teacup.

'Don't feel you've got to hang around,' I said to her pointedly.

Kitty and Moira nestled even further into their chairs, like two old ducks. Which they were.

'No rush,' quacked Moira, 'we've got all afternoon.'

Becky sauntered over and gave the laminated menus a cursory wipe with a cloth. 'Don't worry,' she whispered. 'I can handle these two.'

I indicated to great hall and started to lead the way for the McNaughtons.

I knew some facts about Glenlovatt but I certainly wasn't the encyclopaedia Mrs Baylis was. I'd just have to use Becky's tablet discreetly and rely on my own genuine admiration of the old house to carry me through. Hopefully, they wouldn't be too disappointed with my efforts. I sighed to myself. I was very fond of Gordon but at that moment I could happily have lynched him with one of his Silkworm ties.

'Keep an eye on the family silver,' barked Kitty to our retreating backs.

I bristled with anger. 'After your tour,' I smiled, addressing the family, 'we'll be delighted to serve you a delicious afternoon tea in Thistles. Congratulations on winning the competition, by the way.'

Robbie didn't even look up. He continued jabbing texts into his mobile. Flora was examining her nails.

'Thank you,' smiled Claire awkwardly. 'We're looking forward to it.' She nudged Eddie, who was coaxed into a silent nod.

Oh, someone, help.

We ascended the staircase, shafts of light seeping in through the mullioned window. 'Glenlovatt was built in 1760 by Christopher Carmichael, a successful merchant of fine wines,' I gabbled.

'This is so lame,' groaned Flora under her breath. Robbie, under his crown of blond hair, remained oblivious, seemingly far more interested in videos of farting dogs.

'Don't be so rude,' muttered her father. 'It won't be long till we get our grub.'

My heart ached for Claire McNaughton. There she was in her Sunday best, eager to make the most of the day and instil some culture into her family's heads.

I led them along to the first turret and cleared my throat, remembering a story that had always fascinated me. It was worth a try.

'I particularly love this part of the house,' I explained, sneakily looking at the tablet once more to make sure of my facts, 'and it exists because Christopher Carmichael said his beloved wife, Charity, reminded him of a golden-haired princess.'

Flora's steely grey eyes flickered with the smallest hint of interest. With another glance at Becky's tablet, I carried on. 'He had Glenlovatt built as a token of his love for her.'

'How romantic,' gasped Claire wistfully. 'Isn't that romantic, Eddie?'

Eddie let out a short grunt. He was a bit like a burly mountain bear in his brown suit.

We passed down a short set of steps at the end of the corridor, which led into an alcove with a side door.

'Now, this area,' I explained, 'is where, it is rumoured, two young lads perished while Glenlovatt was being built.'

At the mention of a sinister event, Robbie lost interest in a dancing pig. 'What happened? Were they crushed? Did someone murder them?'

I tried to disguise my pleasure at finally securing his attention. 'The story goes that their boss was eager to impress Christopher Carmichael, so he insisted on the lads working late into the night. There was no such thing as health and safety laws in those days.'

'So what happened next?' pressed Robbie.

I slid my eyes to the tablet for confirmation. 'The two young labourers were careless with some brickwork. It's said they were exhausted from working such long hours and the wall they were building was not up to the standard it should have been.'

I glanced up from Becky's tablet. 'The whole thing collapsed, striking one and then the other.'

Flora clutched the strap of her fringed shoulder bag. 'That's awful. Do their ghosts haunt this place then?'

'Not that I've seen,' I answered, picking up on Robbie's obvious disappointment. 'But it is said that when one of the young men was about to pass away, he insisted they plant two rowan trees in the gardens of Glenlovatt to commemorate their lives.'

'And are the trees still here?' asked Eddie.

'Yes, they are. I'll show you them later.'

Flora's brow creased. 'Why did they choose rowan trees?'

'Well,' I began, repeating what I'd just read on the tablet, 'in old folklore, rowan trees were said to be magical and prevent those on a long journey from getting lost.'

There was a thrilled hush. As I suspected, this family wasn't interested in the design of the buttresses or how many flowers bloomed in the gardens. They wanted to know about the lives Glenlovatt had touched, about the fortunate souls who woke up every day under its roof, and the romances, sacrifices and tears it had witnessed in its two and a half centuries.

'Can you tell us any more, Lara?' asked Flora, when we were towards the end of the tour. 'Any stories of handsome princes?'

'Has anybody ever been executed in the grounds?' piped up Robbie with glee.

'Not yet,' I smiled thinly, thinking of the two unwelcome guests in the tea room, 'but there's still time.'

It was as if I was escorting a completely different family back to Thistles. We filed into the tea room in a gaggle of laughter and chatter.

'Those rowan trees are so cool,' said Robbie, 'but I still think this house is haunted.'

'You could well be right,' I replied, surprised to see Kitty and Moira still in residence.

'They're on their third pot of tea,' complained Becky, whipping a tea towel over her shoulder.

'As long as they're paying; that's all that matters.'

I moved behind the cake counter to help Becky prepare afternoon tea for the McNaughtons. We'd reserved a table for them by the patio doors and they sank down gratefully.

Kitty and Moira examined them like lab specimens, as the two women noisily sipped their Earl Grey.

'Everything still as it should be?' asked Kitty loudly. 'You'd better suggest to the laird he do a stocktake.'

Eddie's bullish head swung round.

'Don't, love,' advised Claire, placing a hand on his jacket sleeve. 'They're not worth bothering with.'

Undeterred, Kitty carried on. 'We're not used to that kind of people moving into Fairview.' She stabbed her slice of double chocolate cake, having already polished off her Guinness cake, and forked a chunk into her mouth.

I was considering asking them both to leave when I was distracted by a strange gurgling sound. Initially I thought the kitchen sink drainage was playing up again.

'She's choking!' screamed Moira. 'Kitty's choking!'

I turned to see Kitty's face was scarlet and her eyes bulging terrifyingly.

Before I could even move, Claire was behind Kitty and pulling her to her feet, performing sharp thrusts to her abdominen that had us all wincing. On the fourth attempt, a piece of double chocolate cake shot out of Kitty's mouth.

'Oh my goodness, Claire,' I said, still in shock at the speed of events. 'Well done!'

Claire scooped her bobbed brown hair behind her ears. 'I used to be a nurse.'

All eyes swivelled to Kitty, now looking like a discarded duvet cover from the 1970s. I continued scooping fresh cream into a small pot and arranged several fat scones for the McNaughtons. 'Kitty, I think you need to say something to Claire.'

Kitty gasped a couple more times. 'Thank you. Thank you very much.'

Claire resumed her seat and sipped her tea before finally acknowledging Kitty with a curt 'You're welcome.'

Thirty

I had never been so grateful to fall through my front door as I was that evening. That was until I remembered I had two noisy and uninhibited houseguests.

I kicked off my trainers and watched them skitter across the mat. Things seemed unusually quiet tonight. The faintest traces of music seeped through the closed spare room door and a note from Mum was propped up on the breakfast bar.

Just gone to a local exhibition on The Power of The Vagina in 21st Century Scotland. Will be back soon! Love Mum xx

I squeezed my eyes shut. Great.

I let the note flutter out of my hand and tugged today's newspaper out of my bag. If Wolf was happy to wallow in his room to the creative strains of some folk band, that suited me. I clicked on the kettle and made myself a hot chocolate, before flopping onto the sofa with the paper and scanning the articles. Headlines swam in front of my tired eyes: stories about philandering MPs, the never-ending struggle to achieve work-life balance, a husky that could sing opera.

I turned a couple more pages, trying to absorb the words, before a large black-and-white photo made me stop. There was something vaguely familiar about the pointed jaw and hooded eyes of this man, a lock of hair tumbling onto his brow. He was attractive in a public schoolboy kind of way. A throng of trees loomed up behind him and his face possessed an intense quality. Considering he was wearing a dinner suit, the whole effect was dramatic. Above the photograph a headline screamed, 'Young Heir Search Goes On'.

My eyes turned back to the man's image. What was it about him that made me think I recognised him? Apart from the Carmichaels, I didn't spend much time with the landed gentry.

I turned my attention to the accompanying article and read that the photo was of Brodie Fairbairn, heir to the well-known Fairbairn Stationery empire. The story recounted how the thirty-two-year-old had suddenly disappeared, citing family pressures as his reason for absconding from the ancestral pile overlooking the moody beauty of Loch Ness. He'd been missing for several months after having a series of heated arguments with his parents over his future.

As I read on, my attention switched repeatedly between the article and the man's face. According to the report, Brodie Fairbairn had made it abundantly clear to his family that he wanted to pursue a writing career. This had not been warmly welcomed by his parents, which led to him vanishing into the Inverness night. Details of his whereabouts and confirmation of his safety were still being sought. His parents had spent a fortune on private detectives but there had been no conclusive sightings of him.

My brows knitted. I was sure there was something familiar about him. Had he visited Thistles or been at Glenlovatt, perhaps? Surely not.

The creak of the spare room door interrupted my thoughts and I glanced over my shoulder. Wolf ambled out in a haze of dark brown beard, and stone grey combat trousers slung loosely on his frame, teamed with a pale blue T-shirt. He was clutching a novel with something resembling a phoenix on the cover.

His head jerked up. 'Oh, hi there, Lara. Didn't hear you come in. Good day, yeah?'

Was it the angle of his face, perhaps? Or the slant of his slate grey eyes? Whatever it was, realisation dawned as I alternated my eyes between the dapper guy in the paper and the hipster dude in my flat.

I scrambled up from the sofa, thrusting the newspaper article in front of him.

'Wolf. This is you, isn't it?'

Alarm spread across his face. 'What are you talking about?'

'This,' I repeated, offering the open newspaper page to him. 'You're Brodie Fairbairn, aren't you?'

Wolf inclined his head towards the article. Silence sandwiched itself between us.

He gingerly took the newspaper in one hand, gripping his novel in the other. A kaleidoscope of emotions travelled through his eyes. 'Shit.' His chest heaved and he reluctantly muttered, 'Yes, that's me.' Before I could comment, he took a step forwards. 'Please, Lara. Don't tell Christine.'

'Are you serious? You're in the national press. People are looking for you—your family, friends, even private detectives!'

Wolf dashed a hand over his cropped head. 'Well, what if I don't want to be found, yeah? What if I'm happy as I am? You know your mother's views on the so-called privileged.'

'But, Wolf, er, Brodie—'

'Wolf,' he said quickly.

'Okay,' I sighed. 'Wolf. You have to tell my mum who you really are. What if she finds out like that?' I pointed an accusing finger at the newspaper.

Wolf stroked his beard. 'Do you know this is the happiest I've been for a long, long time?' I flopped back onto the sofa and watched him sink dejectedly into the armchair opposite. 'That bloody Fairbairn name has clung to me for years like a curse. Everybody just assumed I'd take over the reins of the family business.' He let out a weary laugh. 'The thought of overseeing some sodding stationery factory, marrying a jumped-up posh girl who only wanted me for my money . . .' His voice vanished into a whisper. 'I felt like the walls were closing in.' He leaned forwards slightly. 'You have no idea how many times I tried to speak to my parents about it all. They know I want to be a writer.'

'But they don't approve?'

Wolf snorted, raising his eyebrows. 'That's the understatement of the year. Even when I had a top literary agent interested in me they still kicked off with all the duty and tradition crap, yeah?' He shuffled his feet across the carpet. 'If they weren't giving me the silent treatment I was being frog-marched into Dad's office.'

'So you took off abroad?'

Wolf nodded. 'Yep. Grew a beard, roped in a few favours from a couple of close friends and kept my head down.' A warm spark ignited his grey eyes. 'Then I met your mum.' His expression slid into a soppy smile. 'I've never met anyone like Chris before.'

'And you're highly unlikely ever to again.'

Wolf laughed briefly, showing off a slash of even teeth.

'So do your parents know you're safe?'

'Of course they do. I couldn't leave them hanging like that.' He raised his hands in the air. 'I sent them a postcard when I was in Europe. At least it was something.'

Wolf went on to explain how he'd met Mum at an arts festival in South America. By then he'd well and truly shrugged off the debonair, floppy-haired persona, turning himself into a trendy hipster.

'I've written my first novel,' he added, 'and that got me an agent.' Wolf carried on. 'It's a black comedy. My agent has got it out to publishers at the moment.'

We both turned to look at the newspaper article, now lying in a crumpled heap on my coffee table.

'But what about your passport?' I puzzled. 'That's pretty risky, travelling in your circumstances.'

Wolf's mouth twitched at the recollection. 'Let's just say I have one or two friends who Mum and Dad most certainly didn't approve of. Their "connections" were invaluable, if you know what I mean.'

Visualising Wolf engaging the services of passport fraudsters wasn't so difficult. Conjuring up his alter ego, the sharp-suited heir, was proving trickier.

By the time Wolf had finished telling me his story he looked exhausted, so I offered to make us some coffee. 'You have to tell Mum,' I repeated, more forcefully this time. 'She'd want to know.'

Wolf's pleading eyes reminded me of a puppy's. 'But what if she can't accept me for who I really am? I can't lose her.'

Crikey. He really was in love with my mum. I gulped and steadied myself against the kitchen doorframe. 'From what you've told me, Wolf is really who you are, not Brodie Fairbairn.'

Wolf's mouth split into a grateful smile.

'But you have to tell her,' I called over the clatter of cups. 'I don't want Special Forces breaking down my door. Even worse, I don't want Mum finding out from the papers.'

I'd rather face balaclava-clad soldiers any day of the week.

Thirty-one

My little chat with Wolf resulted in a sleepless night. Mum had returned with enough material on the powerful vagina to paper my bathroom twice over. As she and Wolf vanished into the spare room, I'd directed a stiff nod of encouragement to him and retreated to my bed.

More secrets. It just made me feel even more certain that this marriage debacle had to be out in the open up at Glenlovatt. Gordon was obviously carrying the weight of the estate's financial woes and, more than likely, he felt he couldn't speak to Vaughan about it, for obvious reasons. Hugo was gone. Perhaps I could step into the breach.

In the morning, unable to eat, I scooped up my bag after a quick coffee. Mum and Wolf were probably still asleep, their door tightly closed. As I examined my lipstick in the hall mirror I guessed that Wolf hadn't yet revealed to Mum who he really was: there had been no theatrics from my mother, no rants about the 'pillaging upper classes', not so much as a raised voice during my wakeful night.

I drove to Glenlovatt beneath a canopy of russet and beige leaves, negotiating the country lanes in a haze and unable to appreciate the song of blackbirds and the curves of the Fairview Hills the way I normally did. Because of last night's insomnia I'd been motivated to get to Thistles even earlier than normal and do some baking. Images of mini chocolate and vanilla cupcakes, maple and pecan slices and a banana loaf danced in my head.

I eased my car into Glenlovatt's snaking grounds. What would Gordon think of my latest idea to earn some extra money for the estate—and more importantly, what would he think of my impertinent advice against marriage to the toxic Rhiannon?

'I know what you're thinking of doing, Gordon.'

Bugger!

I had planned to broach the subject with some tact, not charge in there like a bull in a tea shop. Obviously, my mouth again wasn't communicating with my brain.

Gordon paused in front of me with his morning coffee. 'Oh?' he smiled. 'And what might that be?'

I moved closer, out of earshot of the occupied tables. A family of four, decked out in expensive walking gear, were tucking into their Americanos and slices of crumb cake with gusto.

Gordon's curious expression sent my stomach into an impressive somersault. Last night and this morning I'd been all fired up about raising Rhiannon with him. Now, as he stood there, reminding me of Vaughan with his thick eyebrows and broad shoulders, my resolve shook.

'What is it?' he pressed. 'What's wrong, Lara?'

'Could we go to your study for a moment, please?'

Gordon took a big glug of his coffee. 'Of course.'

We were silent as we walked along the cool black-and-white tiled hall. Everywhere I looked, Vaughan's talents were evident. A spiralling acrobat shone within the confines of an antique cabinet, and an ivory white horse's head, its mane bristling in an imaginary wind, was set on a nearby plinth.

Until I had ventured into Vaughan's studio—until I had seen firsthand what beauty he was capable of making—I hadn't really taken much notice of his work dotted around the house. Now it screamed out at me, demanding my attention and causing a weird flipping sensation in my chest.

Gordon swung open his study door and slid it shut behind me.

'I know about Rhiannon Kincaid,' I blurted. There I went again. Miss Tactful.

I waited for Gordon to erupt, to vent his anger or blame me for snooping. Instead he slowly turned to face the window behind his desk and gazed at the nodding flowers bursting from their beds. Guilt welled up inside me. What a bloody clumsy way to raise the subject with him! I couldn't have been any less tactful if I'd been waving a placard with the words 'Don't Marry That Bleached Bitch!'.

I wanted Gordon to say something. Anything. Finally, he spoke. 'I don't think I have any other option.' His voice was laden with resignation. 'How do you know about it?'

I sank into a chair. 'I accidentally overheard you on the phone the other day.' This time, I rallied my reason before I spoke again. 'Please don't do anything rash. Things can't be that bad, can they?' I put my hands up defensively. 'You don't have to tell me. It's none of my business but you've been so good to me. I just want to help.'

Gordon's silvery grey eyes looked resigned. 'You are helping. Really you are. You're doing such a great job with the tea room but this place . . .' He cast his gaze around the study helplessly. 'It swallows up money fast.' He placed his white coffee cup on the desk. 'Things are a lot worse than we feared.'

I didn't know whether I wanted Gordon to continue. 'In what way?'

He sat down behind his desk, the curtains casting shadows across his face. 'We've discovered Glenlovatt has developed dry rot in her masonry.'

'How bad is it?'

Gordon plucked his spectacles out of a nearby leather case and slid them on. Then he reached across, pulling a leaflet from the top of a pile of papers. 'Bad,' he answered shortly. He gave the paper an aggressive shake. 'According to the builders it's been developing slowly over a long period of time.'

I shuffled in my seat. 'Well, what can be done about it?'

Gordon examined me through the glint of his half-moon spectacles. 'They've told me dry rot can spread under, over and through masonry walls, effectively hiding in any nook or cranny.' He slapped down the builder's leaflet and picked up his coffee. 'Because it can spread like that, we've been advised to have additional measures, such as masonry sterilisation, so we don't miss anything.'

Gordon leaned forward and steepled his hands. 'This sort of thing can cause widespread structural damage, which is exactly what we don't want. If we find that even some of the timber and brickwork has been affected by this dry rot fungus, then, the builders said, they would have to apply a fungicidal paste to act as some sort of protective chemical barrier.'

I really didn't like the way this conversation was going. 'The cost?'

Gordon announced a figure that more closely resembled an international telephone number.

'Bloody hell!'

'Apparently it's a good long-term investment, as it can prevent attacks from wood boring insects for years to come.' Gordon smiled ruefully. 'Added to that, we also have a colony of bats living up in the eves, so I want to make sure they don't come to any harm either.'

My eyes widened. 'Really?'

Gordon noticed my horrified expression and gave a short laugh. 'Don't worry, we occasionally hear them but hardly ever see them, just the odd ones soaring across the gardens at nightfall.'

'That's a relief.'

Gordon's chest heaved under his red checked shirt. 'I can't let this place go under, Lara. It's our family home.'

I ferociously shook my head. 'But you can't marry that woman because of it. You still love Lydia. Anyone can see that.'

Judging by Gordon's stricken face, I knew I'd put my size sixes well and truly in it—again.

'I'm so sorry,' I gushed, 'that was tactless of me.'

'No, it wasn't. You were just speaking the truth.'

He turned his silver head away, lost in thought for a few moments. Lydia's portrait looked down on both of us from the wall.

'You must think I'm terrible,' he said on the crest of a sigh. 'Contemplating marriage to someone for money.'

I gathered myself. 'No, I don't think you're terrible. You just seem to think you've got no other option—but you have.'

Gordon's shoulders sank further. 'I can't see it.'

With no coherent plan to base the statement on, I blurted, 'Yes you have. You're looking at her.' I smiled manically, jumping to my feet. 'Leave it with me. And, please, promise me, Gordon, that you won't do anything rash for now.'

He looked as if he was a drowning man who had suddenly been thrown a rubber ring. 'But what are you going to do?'

'I'll get back to you with the details soon, trust me.'

I hurried out of the study before slumping against the hallway wall. Shit! Now I really *did* have to come up with a plan to help

Glenlovatt—and it would have to involve Vaughan, whether I liked it or not.

During the lunchtime lull, I moped about, lost in thought.

I had to think of something—and quickly. If there was any way at all I could help Glenlovatt I would do it without hesitation.

'Tada! Well, what do you think?'

I jumped as Morven thrust her iPad in front of me. I dropped my brie and grape salad sandwich back on plate. As promised, she'd pulled together a mock-up of the new Glenlovatt website.

'If Gordon gives it the go-ahead, Aidan said he can pop round tomorrow morning to take the photos.'

'It looks amazing!' I grinned. 'Gordon is going to be seriously impressed.'

'Do you think so?' she blushed. 'Are you sure?'

'Of course!'

I loved the cream and gold colour scheme, and the text rolling across the screen in a more readable and attractive font, with a side column promoting Thistles in mint green, was a vast improvement. It was subtle and attractive, far more in keeping with an ancestral home. In its former incarnation it had been more like an advert for an undertaker. 'Let's finish our lunch and then take this to him. We might as well while it's quiet in here.'

'What about Vaughan?' Morven asked with a hint of apprehension.

I arched my eyebrows. 'I wouldn't worry about him if I were you. If it's not something he can use his chisel on, he's not interested.'

Becky poured a fresh bag of coffee beans into the machine. 'You like him, don't you?'

I almost dropped the iPad in shock at her question. 'Don't be daft!'

She swung round, sending her pink ponytail shooting back over her shoulder. 'He's dangerously attractive, you've got to admit.'

'That's why he should be wearing a "Keep out" sign around his neck.'

Becky's burgundy lips slipped into a wry smile. 'I find they're the ones that tend to be the most fun.'

A fleeting image of Anton shimmered into my memory. 'Yes, well, I've had enough of the bad-boy variety to last me a lifetime, thanks very much.'

Becky placed one hand on her hip. 'Oh, you can never have too many bad boys.'

Morven rolled her eyes. 'Stop encouraging her.'

I laughed a little too loudly as I took a further bite of my sandwich. 'If you're so interested in our resident grump, why don't you make a play for him then?'

Becky fixed me with a meaningful stare. 'Lara, it's not me he's interested in.'

Thirty-two

 The next morning arrived bright and crisp with sunshine fingering its way across the Fairview hillsides.

Gordon was extremely enthusiastic about Morven's suggestions for the Glenlovatt website. He'd given the mock-up the go-ahead, as well as awarding her a tidy little extra sum for all her efforts. Buzzing with enthusiasm, Morven had rung Aidan, who had agreed to come over first thing to take new photographs of Glenlovatt, and of us and Thistles.

I'd only just pulled up in my Cleo and hitched my sunglasses on top of my head when Becky swung into the space beside me in her acid green Polo. She waved enthusiastically from the driver's seat and snatched up her bags before jumping out. She looked lovely in her navy blue floral tea dress, splashed with yellow and orange roses. Teamed with dark platform shoes and her pink hair piled in a chignon, it was like she'd stepped out of a forties musical.

Morven, who was already hovering by the side entrance, had opted for a dress too, but hers was a long red lace number. She had tied her hair back and added cream wedges to her outfit.

I glanced down at my mint-coloured shift dress and stacked heels. I'd washed my hair and let it dry naturally, partly because

I'd felt too knackered to give it the full blow-dry treatment. My corkscrew curls fell over my shoulders. Just as long as it didn't rain, I was quietly optimistic they would behave themselves for the day. And, of course, I was wearing my charm bracelet too. I did hope the good fortune I believed it was bringing me would continue.

'I love your outfit,' Becky beamed, 'but I tell you what. As soon as Aidan is finished with us, I'm taking all this lot off.' She waggled a carrier bag.

'I'm with you on that one,' I smiled, pointing at my shoes. 'If I had to totter around in these all day I'd end up falling on someone.' I pulled my own change of clothes, which were folded up in a holdall, from the passenger seat.

'Talk about instruments of torture,' muttered Becky, lifting one leg to give her right foot an ineffectual wiggle.

A squeal of tyres sending gravel spurting in all directions made us spin round in alarm.

'He's prompt,' said Morven, squinting in the morning light.

Out of a black Porsche stepped a pair of long, muscular legs. The driver was blond, with broad shoulders and a wide grin, attractive in an American jock kind of way, dressed in a lilac T-shirt and jeans.

Aidan swung a bag and tripod out of the boot of his car and strode towards us. 'Morven,' he exclaimed, planting a theatrical kiss on each cheek.

'Hi, Aidan. This is my boss and best friend, Lara McDonald. Lara, meet my cousin Aidan Docherty.'

'I'm not Morven's boss,' I corrected. 'She's my colleague.'

Aidan's hazel eyes flicked over me and he smiled charmingly. 'Hi there.' We introduced him to Becky, who eyed him appreciatively from under her kohl-lined lids.

'We're just waiting for our other colleague, Jess, to arrive. She should be here any minute. Let me take you to the tea room,' smiled Morven, before engaging her cousin in some general chat. She guided him towards the patio doors.

While Aidan set up his equipment, Morven, Becky and I got busy ensuring the tea room was at its best for photos.

'Sorry I'm late,' called an exasperated Jess. 'I couldn't prise Harry away from the telly.'

She had caught her hair up in a glossy ponytail and was wearing a pretty rose pink and white striped dress. 'Just dropped him off at his grandma's.'

We introduced a blushing Jess to Aidan, and then all got involved, setting out the cake counter with today's choices, which included raspberry pavlova; chocolate marble cake, and a marzipan, ricotta and fruit cake. We'd all had to bake late the night before to get ready for the shoot.

'I don't just have bags under my eyes,' muttered Becky near my ear, 'they look more like bloody suitcases.'

'You look great,' I assured her, 'although I do know what you mean. I was still standing in that kitchen at one o'clock this morning, beating egg whites and folding almonds.'

Becky rolled her eyes. 'Think I ended up almost falling asleep over my melted chocolate mix at home.'

Jess carefully arranged on a cake stand the rose and macademia cupcakes I'd made, before scribbling her lunch options onto the blackboard behind the counter.

'I'm glad you couldn't hear my language this morning when I was up making the venison pie,' she said, going a fetching shade of pink at the memory. 'Thank goodness Harry was still asleep.'

'Why, what went wrong?' asked Morven. She leaned over Jess's shoulder, her green eyes dancing with approval at the venison pie nestled in a large ceramic bowl. 'It looks irresistible to me.'

'Oh, that one is fine,' explained Jess. 'It was my first effort that didn't go so well. My hairdryer packed it in and I was so busy trying to fix it, I forgot about the pie being in the oven.'

'Well, venison version two is a huge success,' I encouraged her, silently promising to reserve a slice for myself for lunch. 'What else does Aidan do for a living?' I said quietly to Morven.

'He's a fitness trainer.' She dropped her voice further and tagged on, 'a *personal* fitness trainer,' with heavy emphasis.

'You've not mentioned him much before.'

Morven tilted an eyebrow. 'Bit of a black sheep in the family.'

I clocked Aidan sending me a cheeky grin from across the room as he set up a tripod. 'Lara, how do you manage to keep in shape when there are all these wicked treats around?' he asked.

'A good girdle,' I joked, poker-faced. 'And it's amazing what a pair of big knickers can do.'

Becky tittered.

Aidan was momentarily thrown, judging by the confused knit of his fair brows. Then he regrouped his charm offensive as he adjusted the focus on his camera. 'Maybe I could give you a one-on-one training session and set you up with a routine? Not that you need it, by the looks.' He flashed his eyes at me again.

Oh, for pity's sake.

'He's quite the mover, isn't he?' I asked Morven with amusement.

'He certainly is,' growled a familiar voice from the great hall doorway.

My stomach dropped. Vaughan.

He was leaning against the doorframe in a loose white shirt and navy jeans. He must have only just come out of the shower because his hair hung in slightly damp clumps around his shoulders.

Vaughan gave me a cool smile. 'Good morning, ladies. So what's happening here then?'

Becky lowered her tea cup. 'Uh-oh,' she muttered dryly. 'It's testosterone at dawn.'

'Do you mind?' I asked Vaughan, irritated. 'Aidan has come to take photos for our social media and the new site.' I tried to ignore the way the shirt clung to his biceps.

Vaughan tilted one eyebrow. 'Oh, is that what he's supposed to be doing?'

'He's only just got here.'

'Yes, I think I may have heard his understated arrival,' said Vaughan.

Aidan smiled frostily at him, before sending another shark-like grin my way.

'Vaughan Carmichael,' said Vaughan smoothly, striding over to Aidan and extending one hand. Aidan shook it in return.

'So you're here to photograph the ladies . . . ?'

'That's right, though I think it's going to be a struggle even for me to do them justice.'

Vaughan gave the merest ghost of a smile. 'So what magazines do you work for? *Scottish Society*? *Landed Gentry*? Or perhaps *Social Scene*?'

Aidan concealed his irritation but only just. 'I'm freelance.'

There was an awkward pause.

Morven's cousin snatched a glance at the windows. 'If you'll excuse me,' he said to Vaughan, 'I'd better press on. I'd like to make the most of this natural light.'

'Of course,' replied Vaughan, catching my eye for an instant. 'My apologies.'

He stalked past us, only stopping as he was about to pass me. 'Enjoy your photo session with Action Man,' he grinned, before disappearing out the tea room door.

Irritation gnawed at me and I opened my mouth to answer him, but he'd already gone.

What was all that macho posturing about?

I jumped when I suddenly felt Morven sidle up behind me and sigh. 'You know what? I give in. Why don't you two go to bed together and put us all out of our bloody misery?'

'Time to rock'n'roll, ladies,' called Aidan.

The remainder of the morning rolled past in a sea of chattering customers. The four of us barely paused, weaving in and out of the tables.

Aidan had taken an array of new photographs of Glenlovatt. He'd captured the regal old beauty of the house so well, as we saw when he showed us some of the results on his laptop, having harnessed the golden specks of light bouncing off the windows and the majestic turrets soaring into the autumn clouds. He'd also taken some more 'arty' shots, closing in on the butterscotch stone and the intricate details of the thistle-carved buttresses, blurring the tangles of trees and capturing Glenlovatt in a dreamy haze.

Inside, Aidan had photographed Morven, Becky, Jess and me holding up some of the cakes, and set up others of our cakes and pies artistically placed on one of the tables. Lastly, he'd taken a couple of photos of each of us on our own. When it was my turn to be photographed, I felt like his camera lingered on me slightly longer than was necessary, and as he was leaving, he pressed his business card into my palm. 'Call me,' he breathed with a theatrical wink.

I thanked him politely for all his efforts, and then Morven and I watched him screech off in a flash of shiny black. Back inside, I filed his number in the waste paper bin. Not really what I needed right now.

'That lady's in again,' commented Becky at lunch, fetching two clean cups from the shelf. 'The one in the purple coat.'

I glanced round from pouring fresh milk into one of the miniature milk bottles we used as jugs, glad of a reason to shake Morven's earlier words from my head. *'Why don't you two go to bed together and put us all out of our bloody misery?'* I was still confused by Vaughan's odd behaviour that morning. If I didn't know any better, I might start to think he was actually jealous!

I looked over at the elderly lady Becky was pointing out. 'I thought she seemed familiar,' I agreed. 'She's been here a few times now, hasn't she?'

'More than a few,' said Becky, carefully slicing a portion of frangipane tart and transferring it onto a plate. 'If I remember rightly she's been in here almost every day for the past week.'

I snapped open a bag of fresh coffee. The woman was sitting at one of the window seats towards the back of the tea room, from where you could gaze out onto a wilder section of the gardens. Purple heather sprouted from the edges of the flowerbeds and there was the faintest glimpse of the silvery Fairview Burn much further down the grounds. On a sunny day it sparkled like a glossy, watery ribbon, splashing over the rocks.

'I'll go and take her order,' I said, collecting my pad and pen from the top of the counter.

Her pinched, freckled face was turned towards the gardens when I approached her table. I felt as though I was intruding on her thoughts. 'Good morning. What can I get you?'

She swung around, my voice pulling her away from wherever she had mentally travelled to. 'Oh. Hello, sorry. Could I have a pot of tea and a fruit scone, please? No jam, thank you.'

'Yes, certainly.'

I hovered a moment, unsure whether to initiate any more conversation. 'It's a lovely view,' I attempted. 'On a clear day like this, the burn really is pretty.'

Her hooded eyes moved downwards towards the water. 'Yes, it really is.' She paused, her speckled hands idly fingering the menu. 'I'm so glad Glenlovatt is open again to the public after all these years.'

'So you know the estate well then?'

The question appeared to startle her. 'Yes, something like that.'

'Have you been on a tour of the house yet?' I smiled.

The woman protectively tugged her coat tighter. 'No, I haven't.'

'It's great,' I encouraged. 'Mrs Baylis, the local librarian, conducts the tours and what she doesn't know —'

'I'm not really interested in the house,' the woman said. 'It's the gardens that hold memories for me.'

She stopped short of elaborating, deciding to snatch up the patent black handbag at her feet instead. 'I've changed my mind about the tea and scone. I must go.' She noisily pushed back her chair and offered me a hurried apology from under a crown of salt-and-pepper layered hair.

Then she was gone.

A couple of other occupied tables eyed the woman curiously as she disappeared out of Thistles, the tail of her coat flapping in her hurry.

'What was all that about?' asked Becky, as I walked back to the counter. 'What did you say to her?'

'I haven't a clue. I only asked her if she'd been on a tour of the house, and then she got all touchy and left. She seemed really interested in the gardens. She said something about them holding memories for her.'

Becky shook her head slightly. 'I wouldn't worry about it. I'm sure she'll be back.'

Lunchtime was quieter than the morning, so I devoured a tuna sandwich before telling Becky I wouldn't be long. Thank goodness she was reliable!

I freshened up my deep pink lipstick, straightened my simple blue cotton T-shirt and tied my ponytail before negotiating the staircase, one apprehensive foot in front of the other. I propelled myself forwards until I reached the closed door, odd taps and thumps penetrating slightly between snatches of music from the other side. I raised a trembling hand to rap on the door. No response. I tried again—nothing. 'Sod knocking,' I muttered angrily, opening the door.

'Hey!'

Vaughan was standing over a workbench, a hunk of stone positioned in front of him. He was wearing a pair of old black jeans—and nothing else. His hair hung about his sweaty shoulders, and dust clung to his fingers. The black curtains were now pulled right back, accentuating his angular profile. A volley of birdsong flooded into the room from the open window.

My power of speech momentarily ebbed away.

He tossed his chisel onto the bench. 'What the hell do you think you're doing?' Then the appearance of a mischievous grin threw me off kilter for a moment. 'I take it your heartthrob photographer has gone now?'

I banged the door shut behind me and gathered my resolve. 'Now you listen to me,' I barked, 'your dad is carrying the weight of Glenlovatt on his shoulders and it's time we did something about it.'

Vaughan slid his hands into his pockets. I tried very hard to ignore the smattering of wiry black hair that trailed down his chest to the waist of his jeans. 'Oh yes?'

Hold your nerve, Lara. He's like an animal. Don't show fear.

I straightened my spine. 'He's told me about the dry rot problem and how much it's going to cost.'

Vaughan's muscles tightened under his skin. 'What dry rot problem? What are you talking about?'

Oh shit. Me and my big mouth. Not content with offending an elderly customer earlier, I'd gone and put my foot in it again.

Thirty-three

Vaughan pulled on a white cotton shirt, thrown over a nearby chair. 'I don't believe this,' he muttered under his breath. 'Dad is always telling me that one day Glenlovatt will be mine and yet he keeps something like this from me?'

I watched his fingers deftly fasten his shirt buttons. 'It's not just the dry rot you should know about,' I stumbled. 'That's only part of the problem.'

Vaughan's eyes glittered. 'What else?'

I fiddled with my bracelet. 'It's going to be really expensive to fix. The tours and Thistles are doing well, but this dry rot thing has major financial implications.'

Vaughan moved towards me. 'Lara, you're waffling. Just tell me.'

'I guess Gordon didn't want to concern you with it all, especially as you've been working so hard on your art.' I blew out a cloud of air.

'If you're going to do it, just spit it out, Lara.'

'Your dad is considering marrying Rhiannon Kincaid.'

A silence louder than any bellow seemed to echo around the art studio.

'Is this some sort of sick joke? What the hell for?' he gasped, before the answer registered in his eyes.

'Look, I know it's none of my business but you can hardly pass judgement,' I replied in Gordon's defence. 'You're considering marriage to Petra for the same reason.'

Vaughan's face darkened. 'Don't be ridiculous.'

'You mean you're not?' I asked in a thin voice.

He dragged a dusty hand across the top of his head. 'No, I am not.'

I felt my heart thud in my chest.

'Or, at least, I'm not anymore.'

Confusion rained down on me. 'What do you mean?'

Vaughan stepped in front of me and took both my arms. 'Do you honestly think I could marry that vacuous woman when I can't stop thinking about you?'

His fingers burned my into my bare arms. 'What?'

'You heard,' he croaked, pressing his mouth hard against mine. I moulded my body into his, revelling in the sensation of muscles sliding under his skin. His tongue teased mine and I responded, making him groan.

Despite all my protestations, Vaughan had slowly worn down my resistance.

'Why didn't you tell me?' I murmured after a few moments.

'Because I'm not used to feeling like this. I'm usually the one in control.' He lifted a thumb and traced it slowly down the contour of my cheek. 'You're like some force of nature. Everything was quiet here until you came and . . .'

'And?'

'Left my head spinning.'

His eyes rose to my hair, which he entwined in his fingers. He pulled my mouth towards his again and I selfishly kissed him back, revelling in the taste and smell of this gorgeous, complicated man.

'There's got to be something we can do,' Vaughan said finally.

'There will be,' I assured him breathlessly. 'We'll think of something.'

Vaughan looked down at me again hungrily before seizing another kiss. Ribbons of electricity fired through every part of me. Eventually, we pulled ourselves apart. 'There's no way my father is marrying that woman.'

I lifted my hand and traced it down the angular lines of his face. 'He's worried. Very worried. The only reason he's contemplating it is to secure this place and your future.'

Vaughan closed his eyes momentarily as my fingers slid under his jaw. His shadowy eyelids had me momentarily spellbound.

'He still loves Mum,' he murmured, revelling in the touch of my hands. 'He always will.' He turned and walked back over to the sculpture he had been working on and caressed the forming features with his fingertips. It was such an intimate gesture, I bit my lip.

'Your dad will not be marrying her,' I reassured him.

'And I certainly won't be getting married to Petra,' he growled, moving back to take me in his arms again. 'Because of you, Lara, I can't. No matter what happens.'

Arriving home in the late afternoon, I flicked between emotions like a faulty light switch.

Falling for Vaughan had been a rollercoaster experience.

He'd made a couple of appearances in Thistles during the afternoon, grinning at me as he'd taken away his tea and a large slice of coffee and walnut cake. Then his smile would falter, and I knew the whole situation with Glenlovatt and his father was crowding in on him again.

I headed to the kitchen, planning ot take it all in while trying out a new pineapple and carrot loaf recipe. I knew I should eat something but every time Vaughan strode into my thoughts my stomach rose and fell like a tsunami. Still, Wolf could eat for Scotland, so I knew it wouldn't go to waste.

Right on cue, Wolf walked into the kitchen and closed the door behind him.

'Hi,' I smiled. 'Everything okay?'

Wolf looked shaken. 'Not really.'

He shuffled from foot to foot in a pair of battered blue and white baseball boots.

'Have you told Mum?' I whispered over the hiss of boiling water. 'Not yet.'

His words hung in the air between us. 'Oh, for pity's sake,' I sighed. 'You really don't have an option here, you know.'

Our exchange was interrupted by the entry buzzer.

'Don't answer it!' snapped Wolf, lunging at me with an outstretched hand.

I switched off the hob. 'Blimey, calm down.'

His face was stricken. 'Please ignore it.'

I folded my arms. 'Why do I get the distinct impression you're hiding something?'

Wolf drew a hand over his beard. 'I feel bloody awful dragging you into all of this, Lara.'

I stared him down. 'Into all of what, exactly?'

Again, the buzzer sent its scream across my hall.

'I'll get it, shall I?' called Mum's disembodied voice.

'No, Chris, don't answer it!' Wolf bolted from the kitchen in a blur.

'Hello?' asked Mum, leaning towards the intercom.

A gruff voice crackled out. 'Hi there. Could I speak to Brodie Fairbairn, please?'

Wolf and I swapped anxious stares behind Mum as she pressed the intercom button to reply.

'Sorry, there's no one here by that name.' A flicker of recognition appeared on her face as she turned to us. 'Isn't that the young man from that rich family who did a runner months ago?' she asked us over her shoulder. 'Why on earth is somebody asking about him here?'

Wolf looked haunted. 'Christine,' he begged. 'I can explain.'

Mum continued to engage with the rusty-sounding voice downstairs. 'Sorry we can't help.'

'Are you sure about that, madam?' the male voice probed. 'I think you may know this gentleman under another name.'

Mum was perplexed. 'Who is this?'

There was another crackle. 'My name's Charlie Ronald. I'm a journalist with *The Informer* newspaper.'

Mum aimed a confused look at us from over her shoulder and pulled a face before pressing the button again. 'I think you've got the wrong address.'

Wolf risked a couple of steps towards Mum. 'Chris,' he said quietly. 'Please listen.'

'His name is Brodie Fairbairn,' announced the reporter, 'but you probably know him as Wolf Skyjack.'

I turned to Wolf and repeated, '"Skyjack"?'

Wolf simply shrugged his shoulders. 'What can I say? I just liked it, yeah?'

Mum turned her head away from the intercom. Her face was tight. 'What is he talking about, Wolf?'

Thirty-four

Mum's head swivelled between us and the raspy voice. 'You must have heard of Brodie Fairbairn,' continued Charlie Ronald from downstairs.

Mum pulled her finger off the intercom button, plunging my flat into silence.

Wolf tried to take her arm but she shook him off.

'I told you to tell her, didn't I?' I shot out at him. 'I warned you this could happen and that she'd find out from someone else.'

Mum's mouth fell open. 'You knew about this? My own daughter and you didn't think to tell me?'

The buzzer erupted again and a flush rose in my cheeks Enough. 'You two need to talk,' I called as I swung open my front door and clattered down the communal staircase. 'I'll get rid of this journalist.'

A fresh breeze hit my face as I opened the main entry door. Charlie Ronald was leaning against a wall, a dictaphone in his hand. He had receding black hair, a ruddy complexion and dubious taste in leather jackets. On seeing me he sprang forwards like a kangaroo on caffeine.

My mind was in turmoil about what to do or say, but right now Mum was my main priority.

'Hi,' I said crisply. 'How can I help you?'

The evening light illuminated a greasy sweat on Charlie Ronald's brow. 'Sorry to disturb you. I'd really appreciate any information you can give me. I understand Brodie Fairbairn in staying with you.'

Who the hell had Wolf been talking to?

I tried for an innocent smile. 'Sorry, Mr Ronald, but there's no one of that name staying in my flat.'

Charlie Ronald's ragged brows fenced like two warring caterpillars. 'My source was very convincing. Reliable, too. They were adamant Brodie Fairbairn is staying with you.'

I pressed my lips together. I didn't expect him for one minute to tell me but I thought I'd ask anyway. 'Who gave you this false information? Who is this supposedly reliable source?'

Charlie Ronald smirked. 'Now you know I can't tell you that, Ms McDonald.' Damn, he knew my name. 'I've got to protect my contacts.' He dug a hand into his trouser pocket. 'I'm sure I heard a bloke's voice in your flat just now.'

I dismissed his observation with a tinkly laugh. 'Oh, that was just my boyfriend.' I leaned in slightly towards him and immediately wished I hadn't, my senses confronted by a tidal wave of cheap citrus aftershave. 'If you really want to know what's going on, your best bet would be Kitty Walker. She owns the True Brew tea room in town.' Summoning all the acting skill I had, I carried on. 'If there is any truth in what you've said about this Brodie guy staying locally, Kitty would know, trust me.'

Charlie surveyed me for a few moments. Then he pulled a notepad from inside his jacket pocket to scribble down Kitty's details.

'Sorry you've had your time wasted here,' I smiled sweetly, 'but I'm sure Kitty will be more than happy to help.'

Charlie continued to hover on the spot, delivering suspicious glances upwards at my sitting room window.

'If you're interested in a story about my new tea room I'd be more than happy for you to interview me.'

As I'd hoped, a glazed expression took over his features. 'Thanks, but my newspaper isn't into twee,' he said pompously. 'We're more about the truth, you know?'

Yeah, that's when you're not getting your arses sued off, I thought.

Casting a final sidelong look at my petrol blue curtains, Charlie Ronald walked over to his car. 'I'll be back.'

How long I'd be able to stall him was anybody's guess. I trudged back up to my flat on reluctant legs.

I stepped through my front door to be met with Mum and Wolf engaged in a shouting match in the hall. Well, to be fair, Mum was doing most of the shouting. Her face was almost as crimson as her kaftan. Wolf, on the other hand, looked positively anaemic.

I was hoping to scuttle past into my room unseen. So much for that.

Mum swished her hair back over her shoulder, like a silver whip. 'And as for you,' she snapped, hands planted firmly on her hips, 'my own daughter! Why didn't you tell me as soon as you found out?'

Exasperation took over. 'Mum, Wolf's—er, Brodie's—family is in stationery, not nuclear weapons.'

Mum's jaw jutted further. 'Don't be so flippant. That's not the point and you know it.'

Wolf rubbed his face helplessly. 'Chris, I love you. I'm a prat for not telling you about my background but I was terrified I'd lose you.'

Mum's mouth tightened. 'Am I that much of an ogre?'

I transmitted a telepathic message to Wolf to not answer that, which, thankfully, he seemed to receive.

'You've got to admit, Mum, you are intimidating when you go all political,' I said.

She looked stung. 'I thought you were Wolf Skyjack, struggling writer and visionary, not Brodie Fairbairn, stationery empire heir.'

Wolf's leather bracelets slid down his tanned arms as he lifted them in the air in surrender. 'Don't you get it, Chris? Wolf Skyjack is who I really am. He's the person I've wanted to be all along.' He stretched out his hands towards her. 'Thanks to you, these past few months I've been able to be the real me.'

Shock rippled through me when I noticed tears clinging to Mum's lashes. She never cried. Not since the Fairview branch of 'I'm A Woman, So Get Over It' closed down in 2004. She used to say that crying was an indulgence she couldn't afford.

Her voice crackled like tissue paper. 'Right now, Wolf, I don't know who you are.' She then swung around to me. 'And as for you, Lara, where was your loyalty?'

She dashed into the spare room and banged the door.

Wolf started after Mum but I pulled him back. Despair was carved into every detail of his face—well, what you could see of it under his brown beard.

'Let me talk to her,' I suggested.

Wolf heaved a heavy sigh and nodded. 'I can't lose her, Lara,' he said in desperation. 'She means everything to me.'

'I know she does.' I patted his shoulder. 'Go and make yourself some tea.'

He sloped off into the kitchen while I scrambled together some words to say to Mum.

From the other side of the spare room door I could hear random thumps and bangs. I rapped gently and entered, not waiting for Mum to tell me to clear off. She was moving erratically around the bed, snatching up clothes and throwing them into a case.

I almost didn't recognise my spare room. Like the rest of my flat it had a nautical theme, with a navy and sky blue bedspread and sea green satin cushions. Mum had put her own stamp on things already, though. Her fabulous collection of necklaces was draped over the oval mirror on the dressing table opposite the bed. They hung there like raindrops, in shots of vibrant colour. Every time she barged past, throwing and thrusting her belongings into her case, they rattled and jiggled ominously. Across the top of the white scalloped headboard, Mum had casually tossed one of her pale green shawls. The room even seemed to carry a different scent than usual, the apple-scented oil diffuser I kept on the windowsill obliterated by Mum's lavender candles.

I smiled to myself. She made her presence felt wherever she went.

I clicked the door shut behind me and hovered. 'Mum, please. What are you doing?'

She glanced up at me and then rammed a loose red shirt into the depths of her case. 'What does it look like I'm doing?'

'Don't you think this is a bit of a knee-jerk reaction?'

She swung round sharply to face me. 'No, I don't. He's not who he said he was. Worse than that, you knew about it.'

'Only in the last couple of days. It wasn't a major conspiracy.' I took a step towards her. 'I'm so sorry you found out like this. I did tell him to tell you as soon as I found out about it but I honestly think he panicked. He was terrified of losing you.'

Mum's eyes shone as she pushed a pair of canvas flats on top of a fringed shirt. 'I feel like I don't really know him now.'

I extended my hand and took her wrist gently. 'Yes, you do. You heard what Wolf said. You've helped him become the person he is right now.' With Vaughan lurking in my thoughts, I went on, 'You are so lucky to have someone like Wolf. He's risked so much to be with you.'

Mum started to reply but clamped her mouth shut.

'He knew he'd probably be discovered once he returned to the UK, but thought that what he feels for you was worth the risk.' I pulled her down to sit beside me on the bed. 'And look at what has happened now. Some greedy cretin, probably a so-called friend of his, has dropped him right in it. They've gone to the press to make a few measly quid.' I forced her to look at me before continuing. 'And was that the first thing he was bothered about? That someone he knows and trusted went behind his back to the papers? No, it wasn't.' I cupped both her hands in mine. 'The first person he was worried about was you, Mum. Wolf can't help coming from a privileged background, can he? But he can help who he chooses to be with—and that's you.'

Mum's lashes were laced with tears again. 'Did Wolf really say all that?'

Blimey! I'd only ever seen my mum like this once before over a man and that was when my dad died.

'Yes,' I replied. 'Yes, he did.'

She picked up a pale pink scarf from the case and played with it absent-mindedly. 'He's not that much older than you. What if he tires of me?'

I studied her, admiring her angular cheekbones and unblemished skin. 'This isn't like you, Mum. Your confidence levels are normally stratospheric. It's far more likely the poor sod will struggle to keep up with you.' I playfully nudged her shoulder. 'After we lost Dad, what did you tell me?'

She looked at me thoughtfully for a moment. 'I told you that we're only here once and to always grab happiness whenever and wherever it comes.'

I arched an eyebrow. 'I think you need to listen to your own advice.' I stood up and moved towards the door. 'Oh, and when you two make up, can you do it quietly, please? I've got a carrot and pineapple loaf to get back to.'

Thirty-five

My kitchen resembled a war zone.

Flour decorated the black marble work top and a trail of mixing bowls wound its way towards the sink. It was like somebody had picked up one of those snow globes, given it a wild shake and then emptied the contents across every conceivable surface. My frenzied bout of baking had been therapeutic—up to a point. Now all I had to do was tidy up the debris.

After I'd restored order, Mum offered to rustle up a quick pasta for dinner—that was once Wolf and she managed to peel themselves apart.

While she got started, I poured us all a glass of wine and slumped down on the sofa beside Wolf.

'Thanks for whatever you said,' he grinned through a tangle of beard. 'I really appreciate it.'

'Don't mention it,' I yawned. 'I just wish I was as good at sorting out my own love life.'

'Oh?' asked Wolf, clearly interested. 'Is it anything to do with that Vaughan guy, by any chance?'

Geez, was there anyone who had missed our clearly less-than-subtle attraction to each other? Mum had most definitely noticed. Whenever his name happened to pop up, she'd narrow her eyes. After the revelation that Wolf was from a well-known, moneyed family, the discovery that her daughter had also locked lips with a member of the Scottish establishment might send her right over the edge.

My feelings for Vaughan pricked at my heart. Anton and the foaming waves of Malta seemed so distant now. It was as if that entire trauma had been experienced by someone else.

'Lara? Earth to Lara?'

Wolf's voice woke me from my daydreaming. 'Sorry.'

He wiggled his eyebrows. 'You don't have to tell me, but it might help, yeah?'

I scooped my feet up underneath me and proceeded to show symptoms of a severe bout of verbal diarrhoea. I found myself telling Wolf everything: how I was desperate to make Thistles a successful business, Glenlovatt swallowing money, Gordon considering marriage to a woman he didn't love, Vaughan's dilemma about saving the house and helping his dad, and how I felt about the gorgeous, moody artist. Wolf listened carefully, nodding occasionally and offering murmured support at times. When I finally finished talking, I threw my head back against the sofa.

'Your mum told me a few bits and pieces but I had no idea things were that bad—or that you were so crazy about this guy.' He sat forward, all lean angles under his orange T-shirt. 'But I can sympathise with Vaughan. It's not all expensive clothes and Land Rovers, yeah?' Wolf laced his fingers together. 'Of course, being part of a family with inherited money does have its advantages, but when you feel you're not cut out for all that crap . . .' He heaved a long sigh.

'My dad used to say that things have a habit of working themselves out,' I said, 'but what with this letter from Hugo's will hanging over us all, I just can't help but wonder what's still round the corner.'

We sat in silence for a few moments, within only the occasional noise from Mum as she worked in the kitchen. Every so often, she'd emit a happy hum of some unrecognisable tune. Wolf acknowledged her singing with a grin.

I pushed a stray curl back from my face. 'So who do you think went to the press about you staying here?'

Wolf's mouth curled downwards. 'I've got one or two ideas. There are a couple of so-called "friends" who might value money more than our relationship.'

'What are you going to do now?' I asked. 'Although of course you're both welcome to stay here for as long as you want.' Surprise registered as I heard myself say the words. I must be mellowing. Not having Mum's clattering jewellery or Wolf's trainers abandoned in the hall was a strangely sad prospect.

There was determination in Wolf's stare. 'I've decided to take Chris to Edinburgh for a few days to meet my parents.'

'Are you sure? Don't you think you ought to re-establish your relationship with your parents first before dropping a bombshell like Mum on them?'

Wolf smiled, displaying a row of even white teeth. 'And a gorgeous bombshell she is too.' He stretched his arms lazily above his head. 'My folks are going to have to accept things have changed. I've changed. Chris is part of my life now.'

How I wished I could be there when my mother, with her forthright opinions and boisterous laugh, catapulted into the Fairbairns' world of charity dinners and horseracing.

'And anyway,' he carried on cryptically, 'I have some business propositions to suggest to them.'

'Oh?'

Wolf started to say something but fell silent when Mum swept in on a cloud of lavender.

'Time to set the table?' I asked her, uncoiling from the sofa.

She gazed at Wolf and nodded. 'Yes, please.'

I went into the kitchen, unaware that Wolf had followed me. 'Crikey! You made me jump.'

Wolf placed a finger to his lips and looked furtively over his shoulder to where Mum was placing the pot on the kitchen table. 'Don't worry about all that Glenlovatt stuff, yeah?' he said quietly. 'Things will be okay.' He pulled open the cutlery drawer.

'I wish I had your optimism.'

Wolf awarded me a wink. 'I owe you one.'

I blushed. 'Don't be daft. I didn't do anything.'

'You've given me a bolthole here, and you got me and your mum back together. I appreciate it.' He took out the forks. 'Leave it with me. I'll repay you for all your help.'

My brow creased. 'What do you mean?' I asked, but he'd wandered back to join Mum at the table, leaving me with a pile of plates and a confused expression.

Thirty-six

 My flat felt empty without Mum and Wolf crashing about in it.

Wolf had contacted his parents to say he would see them at their weekender in Edinburgh. There had apparently been joyous wailing down the phone from his mother and a series of gruff but welcome sentiments from his father. It was at this point he'd informed them that he was bringing his new 'partner' with him.

What the Fairbairns would make of my fifty-two-year-old mother with her voluminous kaftans, anti-capitalist philosophies and vaginal empowerment speeches was anyone's guess, I thought. I hoped they wouldn't choke on their foie gras.

Still, Wolf and Mum were deliriously happy. Wolf seemed to be more accepting of himself and a lot of that I attributed to Mum. She was like a whirlwind of positivity. Their future plans, however, seemed to be a bit hazy. And, while I missed them, I also wasn't sure how I felt about the prospect of having them as lodgers on a permanent basis. In any case, they were due back from Edinburgh that evening and I was eagerly anticipating Mum's review of Wolf's family.

As I pulled into the parking area, the Monday morning sky was carrying puffs of cloud behind the buttery façade of Glenlovatt, the contrast accentuating its grandeur and beauty. I snatched up the large, square plastic container from the back seat, having undertaken some additional baking at home last night to get ahead. The weight of my latest batch of raspberry and white chocolate fudge, cherry and coconut scones and vanilla cupcakes was heavy in my hands. A crisp breeze weaved its way through the treetops and a chubby wood pigeon cooed noisy greetings.

I carefully negotiated my way across the gravel with my awkward load. Tiredness crept over me. Not only had I been furiously baking until late into the night, I'd also been jotting down a scramble of ideas to generate more income for the place. My suggestions were a bit random, to say the least, but having to get this expensive dry rot treatment meant anything was worth a try. Glenlovatt had snuck her way into my heart (as had a grumpy sculptor, I acknowledged) and I refused to entertain any thoughts of the place going to rack and ruin. As I unlocked the patio doors I inwardly promised Hugo I wouldn't give up.

Gordon and Vaughan's raised voices were coming through the door to the great hall. 'Why didn't you tell me, Dad? Why did I have to find out from Lara?'

Oh no. Why would I have expected Vaughan to approach any subject with a degree of tact? He was such a hot-headed, passionate man. *And that's why you are so attracted to him,* singsonged a voice in my mind.

Dumping the container on a nearby table, I nervously left the tea room and approached them in the hall. They both swivelled round.

'Bloody dry rot or Rhiannon Kincaid,' grunted Vaughan to no one in particular. 'I don't know which is worse.'

Gordon raised his hands helplessly. 'I didn't want to worry you, son.'

'But that's the whole point, Dad. I don't want you shouldering the burden of this place on your own.'

Gordon visibly tensed. 'Glenlovatt isn't a burden. It's our home.' He turned and offered the spiralling staircase a fond smile. 'Everywhere I look, your mother is there.'

Vaughan's expression softened. 'I know she is.' He rubbed a hand down his face. 'Look, Dad, I know how this place eats up money and that it has its problems, and that's why I considered marrying Petra. I couldn't bear the thought of Glenlovatt failing.' He let out a sigh. 'I mean, the existing issues you told me about were bad enough . . . I just wish you had told me the full story before now.'

'I didn't want you worrying about that as well as everything else. Things were problematic enough as it was.' Gordon gave his son a soft smile. 'When I heard you were thinking about marrying her, I hoped you'd come to your senses. Then when I found out about the dry rot, I just knew that if I told you, you would be even more tempted to rush into something.'

'But you were prepared to marry Rhiannon Kincaid for the same reason?' questioned Vaughan. 'How does that work?'

'I had the most wonderful marriage to your mother and I cherish every day I had with her. But you're only thirty-two and the last thing I want is you throwing your life away like that.'

I looked at the father and son, and bit my lip. 'Sorry, Gordon, but I had to tell him. Both of you were thinking the same thing and about to make the same stupid mistake.' I came closer and reached out, touching Vaughan's arm. Under the ice blue wool of his V-neck, I could feel his warm skin.

Gordon watched us with dawning recognition before a smile twitched at the corners of his mouth. I moved further forwards, almost placing myself between them. They towered over me, their similar heights and broad shoulders casting shadows on the chequered floor.

'I've got twenty minutes before opening up,' I said. 'Why don't we go to Gordon's study and look over some ideas I've had for this place?' Their enquiring expressions encouraged me to speak again. 'I'm not saying Glenlovatt will be rolling in money because of my suggestions, but I'm hopeful one or two of them might help a bit.'

Gordon and Vaughan exchanged glances before nodding. 'Pity we can't offer the grounds to some A-lister for a concert,' Vaughan said with a short laugh.

'You won't need an A-lister.'

A familiar male voice had travelled from the entrance.

'Sorry, sir,' blurted Travis to Gordon, 'but this lady and gentleman insisted on speaking with you and Master Vaughan.'

My eyes threatened to roll out of their sockets.

'Mum! Wolf!'

Thirty-seven

Vaughan's attention shot between me and the pair standing inside the door. 'Did you just say "Wolf"?' he muttered under his breath.

'Long story,' I replied, my mouth suspended open at the sight of my mother and her young beau.

They were almost unrecognisable. Wolf was rocking a sharp navy suit teamed with a white shirt and crimson satin tie. He'd got rid of the scraggly beard and in its place was a neat peppering of brown stubble. Not to be outdone, Mum was decked out in a pretty maxi dress in slate grey. The fluted material fell in deep pleats and enhanced the colour of her hair, which she'd gathered to one side with a sheaf of white ribbon. She'd teamed her outfit with a deep blue jacket and carried a leather case, giving her an air of Grecian goddess ready to do business.

'If you remember,' I finally croaked, 'this is my mum, Christine, and this is her partner, Wolf. Sorry, I mean Brodie. Or . . .'

Wolf stepped forwards to put me out of my misery, and shook hands enthusiastically with Gordon and Vaughan. 'Just call me Wolf,' he smiled. 'Oh and, Lara, you can close your mouth now.'

Mum handed the leather case to Wolf. I tried to grab her attention with a series of imploring 'What the hell is going on?' looks, but she chose to avert her eyes and ignore me. Why had they turned up at Glenlovatt dressed like two marketing executives?

'If you have a moment, Mr Carmichael, I'd like to discuss a business proposition with you and your son.' Wolf winked at me, seeing my shocked expression.

'I think, right at this moment, we're open to any suggestions,' admitted Vaughan ruefully.

We all moved to Gordon's study, where Travis furnished us with tea and shortbread. Extra chairs were placed in a semicircle around Gordon's desk.

'What's going on, Mum?' I implored.

'Patience, darling.'

Wolf reached into the leather case and handed a glossy leaflet to Gordon. 'Have you heard of the Aspirations Arts Festival, by any chance?'

Vaughan nodded. 'Of course. It's a huge event.' I knew that this festival had been going on for years and drew large crowds, as well as lots of publicity.

'Isn't it held in Edinburgh?' added Gordon.

'Yes,' confirmed Wolf, loosening his tie a little. 'It usually is. At the Longleavie Estate.'

Gordon smiled. 'Ah yes. That's right. The home of the Curnow family, isn't it?'

I presumed this was another aristocratic dynasty, and risked a sly glance at Mum. She raised her eyebrows slightly but, thankfully, refrained from one of her rants.

'Well,' explained Wolf, cutting through my relief, 'the Curnows are good friends of my parents. They've known each other for years.' He took a sip of tea and leaned forwards. 'The Aspirations Arts Festival is the Curnow's baby but now they've got a new and lucrative business that they want to concentrate on. They feel that if they continue with the festival, it would just all be too much.'

At Wolf's pregnant pause, my stomach rolled with butterflies. Was this conversation going where I thought it was?

'I've spoken to the events company they always use for the festival and they think it would be a great idea if Glenlovatt took over the mantle. That is, if you're interested?'

I couldn't prevent a thrilled gasp. Mum smiled at my very public reaction.

'But we've never done anything like this before,' admitted Gordon nervously, 'at least, not on that scale.'

Wolf leaned back confidently in his chair. It was hard to believe that just a week ago he was slouching around my flat in faded clothes and sporting a beard a dormouse could nest in. 'But that's the thing,' he grinned, 'Glenlovatt would simply be the new location for the festival. The event itself would be overseen by a professional events team.' He leaned forwards again, his face alive with enthusiasm. 'This is a gorgeous venue and you certainly have the grounds to accommodate the festival.'

Seeing Gordon's and Vaughan's hopeful but uncertain expressions, Wolf carried on. 'If you agree to be the venue for the Aspirations Arts Festival, we are talking publicity that money simply can't buy. You'll have artists and bands clamouring to use your grounds. This festival can guarantee you and your family home a secure future.' He straightened his shoulders and added temptingly, 'You're looking at profits stretching into six figures.'

'Almost all the festival participants for this year are signed up already,' interjected Mum. 'It's just a case of notifying them of the change in venue . . . which we took the liberty of running by them earlier in the week.' She laughed at my expression. 'Please close your mouth, Lara.'

Gordon and Vaughan simply stared at each other.

'When is it on?' I asked finally, as both the Carmichael men seemed incapable of stringing a coherent sentence together.

'October twenty-seventh to twenty-ninth; a long weekend of activities,' confirmed Wolf, enjoying a bite of buttery shortbread.

'The twenty-seventh of October,' repeated Vaughan. 'That's when we open Grandfather's letter.'

It was also, I realised, my late great-aunt Hettie's birthday. Another strange coincidence! Goodness knows what Hugo would have thought of it all.

Gordon threw his hands in the air with uncharacteristic exuberance. 'That seems like an excellent omen to me!'

'Great!' beamed Wolf, reaching for Mum's hand. He gave it an affectionate squeeze. 'I'll email you all the details and then you can speak to the Curnow family. They've said they are more than happy to give you any advice or help you might need.'

Handshakes were exchanged all round and we exited Gordon's study in a bubble of chatter. Mum lingered beside me. 'I probably should tell you this more often, but I am so proud of you, Lara. You're such a strong and determined young woman!'

'I wonder where I get that from?'

Mum grinned. 'When Wolf told me his plans about bringing the festival to Glenlovatt, I thought it was a wonderful idea.'

Then she sighed. 'When I lost your dad, I was so preoccupied with being both a mother and a father to you, that I lost my way a bit.'

'Mum, don't be silly.'

She stared into the middle distance for a moment, before turning her attention back to me. 'I should have lectured you less and mothered you more . . .'

'Mum,' I argued, 'you were, and still are, terrific.'

She smiled. 'Thank you, but I'd like to start fresh, in any case. What do you say?'

I threw my arms around her, inhaling her chemical-free shampoo. 'I'd like that.'

We pulled back and grinned at one another 'Thank you so much for doing this,' I said.

She brushed off my appreciation. 'It's not me you should be thanking.'

Wolf was exchanging pleasantries with Gordon when I marched up and planted a huge kiss on his cheek. 'What was that for?' he blushed.

'You know very well what for,' I choked. 'You really didn't have to do this.'

He shrugged his shoulders. 'I wanted to.' He glanced at Mum, then back to me. 'Could we have a quick word?'

Mum and Wolf guided me away from the others. Wrapping his arm around my mum's shoulders, he announced, 'We're moving in together.'

I blinked. 'You're leaving me?'

They grinned. 'I'm afraid so,' Wolf said, 'I hope you won't be too heartbroken not hearing my meditation CDs on a continuous loop.'

'Where are you going to live?'

'In a flat on the outskirts of Edinburgh, so not that far away.'

'And Wolf's just heard that a publisher has made a generous offer for his book,' Mum added. 'I think all the publicity about the "discovery" hasn't done him any harm.'

Sporting a wide smile, Wolf explained, 'My book is about a tormented heir to a fortune, who decides to take off and then meets the woman of his dreams.'

'That sounds vaguely familiar. Can I get a signed copy when it's published?'

'I think that could be arranged.'

'Well, I'm really pleased for both of you,' I grinned at the two of them. 'And I will miss the sounds of those meditation mantras—at least to begin with.'

I hugged and kissed them both. 'And please remember, if your book is turned into a film, I'd really appreciate an invite to the premiere.'

Wolf performed a playful salute. 'I'm sure that wouldn't be a problem either.'

Travis was instructed to drive Mum and Wolf back to my flat and, as I watched them glide away in the glossy Daimler, Vaughan appeared by my side. Gordon had vanished and we were alone by the granite front steps.

'Careful,' he growled into my shoulder. 'I get jealous when you kiss other men.'

His teasing words trickled over me like warm honey. A lock of his hair was falling forwards and I so wanted to brush it back.

'I wondered if I could take you out to dinner this Saturday?'

I glanced up, burying squeals of excitement. 'That would be lovely.'

Try to play a bit hard to get, McDonald!

A wide grin lit up his whole face, sending butterflies through my stomach.

I knew I was playing with fire, but I was more than willing to risk getting burned—or at least slightly singed.

For the remainder of the day I drifted around in a daze. I got several orders wrong, poured milk instead of water into three pots of peppermint tea, and gave six customers the wrong change—and that was just in the morning.

Lunchtime rolled around and my head was still dancing with thoughts of what I should wear for my dinner date with Vaughan. I was putting together an order for an elderly couple of salmon and cream cheese bagels and two pots of Assam tea when I was interrupted by a sharp poke in the ribs from Becky.

'Take a look outside.' She led me over to the far window.

The sky was delivering patches of grey cloud and Glenlovatt's trees stirred gently. In the distance, ghostly rain was approaching. And over by one of the less formal flowerbeds strolled an elderly lady in a purple coat.

Morven, who'd been casting her eye over the accounts, appeared at my shoulder. 'I've seen her here a couple of times in the last week. Do you think she's alright?'

'She's going to get soaked in a minute if she doesn't come in.'

Jess appeared from the kitchen, wiping a delicate smear of flour from her right cheek. 'Is that the same lady again? I wonder what the attraction is up here, that she keeps coming back.'

I weaved between the empty tables, heading for the patio doors on the other side of the tea room. 'I'll go out there. See if she's okay.'

There was an edge to the breeze as I closed the patio door behind me and walked down the few steps to the lawns. Blades of grass waved like green fingers and there was the occasional noise from the burn when the water made its force known to the rocks and boulders. The woman was pacing down a narrow path, her head bowed.

'Excuse me?' I called, waving slightly. 'Are you alright over there?'

She stopped and jerked her head around. I saw she had a rather distressed expression on her face.

I moved tentatively towards her. 'Rain is on the way and, believe me, if my hair gets wet, I look like a radioactive explosion.'

A shadow of a smile crossed her mouth. 'I suppose you're right,' she admitted after a pause and began walking with me back up the path towards the warm haven of Thistles.

'You sit there,' I encouraged her, 'and I'll bring over some tea. How about an almond slice to go with that?'

'Please don't go to any trouble.'

'It isn't,' I insisted. 'Honestly.'

As the woman self-consciously removed her coat, I set about preparing a tea tray. 'Seems like something has upset her,' I explained quietly to Morven, who had abandoned the accountancy paperwork for the time being.

Morven's brow furrowed. 'Poor woman. Do you think she's a bit . . . confused?'

I scooped an almond slice onto a plate for her. 'I don't think so. I mean, she's elderly but she's very sprightly. Something is clearly bothering her, though.'

I angled myself between a couple of tables, and set the slice and tea down in front of her. She was lost in her own thoughts again, drinking in every detail of the gardens that spread out in front of her.

'Here you are,' I said brightly. 'That should warm you up a bit.'

'Thank you.'

I poured the tea for her and she cradled the thistle-sprigged cup in her papery hands, taking grateful sips.

'I'm sorry,' I apologised, 'I hope you don't think I'm being nosy, but in this job I find myself chatting to people all the time.'

The lady dismissed my words with a shake of her grey hair. 'Please don't apologise. You must have thought I looked a silly old woman, wandering about out there.' She placed her cup carefully back on the saucer. 'I expect you're wondering why I've been coming here as often as I have.'

'Well, I was hoping it was our irresistible baking but I'm starting to suspect it's not,' I joked.

She laughed briefly, crinkling her nose. 'This house,' she said falteringly after a few moments, 'and especially those gardens hold a lot of memories for me. I hadn't been here for years and then when he died, I knew I had to come back.'

'Was it your husband?' I smiled softly. 'Did he love coming here?'

'It wasn't my husband,' she answered swiftly, fixing her doleful eyes on my face. 'I was in love with Hugo Carmichael.'

Thirty-eight

 Shock registered in my voice. 'Hugo?' I sank into the chair beside her.

A deep sigh escaped the lady. 'When I was just a young woman, he gave me a job here, assisting the gardeners. I was a tomboy as a girl, you see. Loved the fresh air and helping my father in his allotment.' She took another sip of tea. 'He taught me all about the plants and the soil, how to grow vegetables, and I became more and more interested in horticulture. One day, my girlfriend and I thought we'd come to Glenlovatt for a wander.'

Recollection warmed her blue eyes. 'I was only about twenty at the time. It was a gorgeous spring day in April 1959. There were snowdrops bursting out of the ground and the sky was ocean blue.' She swallowed, but carried on. 'Enid and I were walking near the edge of the formal gardens when I heard two men talking.' She raised a wobbly finger. 'They were just over there, by the clumps of heather.'

My eyes followed to where she was pointing.

Her hand travelled to her chest and sat there against the lavender wool of her jumper. 'I didn't know who Hugo was at the time but it turned out he was asking one of his gardeners for some advice.' Her eyes fluttered closed for a brief moment. 'He was so handsome, with that dash of dark hair and a lovely smile.'

'What happened?' I asked, engrossed.

'Well, he was asking the other chap what he could do to revive a peace lily. His gardener didn't seem to have a clue, though. Before I could stop myself, I politely interrupted their conversation and suggested Hugo saturate the soil if it was dry, then ensure the excess water could drain away from the plant and only give it water when the soil dried out and the plant recovered.' She blushed for a moment. 'Sorry, I'm wittering on.'

'No, you're not. What did Hugo say?'

She gave a little chuckle. 'I could tell he was impressed. I don't think his gardener was too happy, though, being undermined by a young slip of a thing, and a woman at that. Awarded me a right frosty glare, he did.' Her expression became softer. 'Hugo and I had a chat about the gardens and then, before I knew it, he was offering me a job as assistant gardener.'

I rested my chin on my hand. 'Please go on.'

The lady's chest heaved. 'Truth be told, I fell in love with Hugo Carmichael that first moment I set eyes on him. And when I started working for him here at Glenlovatt, my feelings grew.' Oblivious to the rattling cups and murmured conversations taking place around us, the woman continued. 'I never told him, of course. That just wasn't the done thing.'

'Do you think he knew? That you were in love with him?'

'No,' she said, clearly shocked by the suggestion. 'I hid it well—or, at least, I tried to.' A wistful look came into her eyes. 'And even if I told him how I felt, we were poles apart.' A darker edge appeared to her voice. 'That father of his, the old laird, would never have allowed it anyway.'

My heart ached for her. 'So what happened then?'

'Nothing,' she replied simply. 'Nothing happened, except about a year after I started working for him, Hugo became engaged.'

'That must have been terrible for you,' I sympathised, the very thought of Vaughan doing the same thing sending a pain jabbing squarely into my heart.

'It was just as awful for him,' she concluded as she sipped the last of her tea. 'Lachlan, Hugo's father, had him married off to Madeleine Tennant.' She contorted her lips at the memory. 'She was a right madam.'

Madeleine Tennant, I repeated to myself silently. *Gordon's mother.*

'When Hugo and Madeleine announced their engagement I left his employment and moved to London. I couldn't bear the thought of staying, seeing them together day after day.' She smiled absently. 'I lived in London for a long time. Got myself a job doing gardening in a couple of city parks.' She laced her fingers together, a pale gold wedding band on her left hand. 'I met my husband, Eric, there. When he passed away six months ago, my niece suggested I move back up to Fairview to be with her.' Sadness clouded her features. 'I did think about coming to see him once I'd returned and got myself settled. Silly, really, I suppose.'

'Not at all.'

'Oh, how I wish I had!' she blurted, rattling her teacup. 'When Janet, my niece, told me about Hugo's passing, I couldn't believe it. Even at our age's you still sometimes believe you have time on your side.' She stared wistfully out at the grey sky. 'I decided then that I had to come back to Glenlovatt, even though I knew the memories would be painful ones.' She looked down at the table. 'I just wish I could let Hugo know that I never forgot him.'

A kernel of an idea began to form. 'Tell you what, I think I might have a suggestion.'

We arranged an informal ceremony for first thing on the Friday morning.

The woman, who had told me her name was Nancy Stewart, requested that her chosen tree, a red oak, be placed close to the mausoleum, and Gordon agreed that was entirely appropriate.

To protect Nancy, I'd massaged the facts a little, saying she was a former gardener on the estate (true) and that she simply wanted to pay her respects to Hugo (also true). Possibly Gordon and Vaughan suspected there was a little more to the story but they were tactful enough not to enquire further.

Hugo would have loved this clear autumn morning on the Glenlovatt estate. There was an orchestra of birdsong as we congregated at Hugo's final resting place.

Morven and I made an executive decision not to open Thistles until later that morning, so that Nancy's tree-planting would happen without interruption. We had organised a little private gathering in the tea room afterwards.

At Gordon's insistence, Travis was despatched in the Daimler to collect Nancy from her niece's house in Fairview. She arrived at Glenlovatt in a black swing coat with red trim on the collar. Dark patent shoes shone on her feet. After meeting Gordon, she nervously glanced around.

'Hello, Nancy. You're looking lovely.'

Her smile was shaky. 'Thank you, Lara. You too.'

Her cloudy eyes examined Morven, Becky and Jess in turn. 'You're all looking so smart.'

I'd opted for a navy blue shift with a slim white belt and had piled my hair up. Becky's pink hair, pulled off her face in a tight ponytail, added a flash of colour to her black cotton dress. Morven stood beside me in a sharp navy trouser suit, her hair pulled tightly into a bun at the nape of her neck, while Jess had opted for an aubergine top and skirt with a dark fitted jacket, her chestnut hair in a neat plait.

Nancy raised her eyes to the sky. Patchy clouds scudded across the turrets of Glenlovatt. 'Did the tree arrive safely?'

'Of course it did,' beamed Gordon. 'We made sure of it.'

Vaughan took Nancy's hand warmly. 'Grandpa would be very honoured you wanted to do this.'

Nancy's mouth quivered but she managed a weak smile.

Travis, also looking dapper in a black suit, directed one of Glenlovatt's gardeners to approach, a small wrought-iron trailer behind him, the wheels clicking and spinning on the cream path. When Nancy saw the tree in the trailer under the dappled rays of watery sunlight, she simply nodded and mouthed, 'Thank you.'

Vaughan's brows knitted and he whispered to me, 'She wasn't just an employee of my grandfather's, was she?'

'What makes you say that?' I asked innocently.

He smoothed his dove grey silk tie. 'Nancy looks every bit as devastated as my dad did when we lost Mum.' He eyed me carefully. 'She was in love with Grandfather, wasn't she?'

'Yes,' I answered. 'Yes, she was.'

'Did they . . ?'

'Oh no! Nothing like that. He never knew how she felt. She never told him.'

Vaughan studied Nancy as she stood nervously, her gaze never straying far from the mausoleum that reared up majestically in front of us.

'After Hugo became engaged to your grandmother,' I explained quietly, 'Nancy was heartbroken and left Fairview altogether. She took herself off to London and only moved back recently.'

Vaughan's blue eyes were thoughtful. 'I see,' he said, gazing into mine. 'You're a real romantic, Lara McDonald.'

'I know,' I sighed.

He moved his mouth closer to my ear, 'I've got to go away on business this afternoon, but I'll be back in time for our dinner tomorrow.' He leaned closer. 'I can't wait.'

Excitement coursed through my body. I pulled myself together when Gordon emitted a polite cough. 'I know this is a small gathering,' he said, 'but the people here are the ones who either knew my father or have been of invaluable help since we lost him.'

He aimed an encouraging smile at me, Morven, Jess, and Becky, who flushed under her strawberry locks. 'Nancy was a valued employee at Glenlovatt and wanted to mark Hugo's passing by planting a special tree to commemorate his life.'

Gordon raised a hand and the gardener tenderly lifted the tree from the trailer onto the carpet of grass in front of us, beside a carefully prepared hole. The tree had smooth and silvery grey bark, and slender branches.

'Nancy's choice of tree is a red oak,' Gordon explained. 'She thought this particular species was suitable not only because of its vibrant colour but also because it takes twenty years to flower, and another twenty years to produce a good crop of acorns.' Nancy bowed her head when Gordon added, 'In a sense, the red oak is like Hugo: it simply gets better with age.'

A murmur of agreement buzzed round our small throng and Travis nodded solemnly. 'Before we plant the tree,' Gordon concluded, 'would you like to say a few words, Nancy?'

She appealed to me silently. 'Go on,' I mouthed.

Nancy pursed her lips and stepped forwards. She stole another glance over her shoulder at Hugo's final resting place, with its proud blue and yellow Carmichael family crest.

'Thank you so much for today,' she faltered. 'Thank you all.' She drew a ragged breath. 'When my niece told me about Hugo passing away, I didn't want to believe it. I knew he was ninety, but when someone like him leaves the world, it really does have an impact.' She raised her jaw a little. 'I was only in his employment for a year, but during that time I came to realise what a kind, positive and intelligent man he was.' Nancy searched the middle distance for a few moments. 'I never forgot him,' she confessed, her forlorn eyes coming to rest on mine, 'and I never will.'

Then she simply lowered her head again.

Gordon cleared his throat. 'Thank you, Nancy, for those lovely words.' Then he bent down and grasped the handle of the spade the gardener had passed him. 'Right, let's get this tree settled in.'

'Then it's back to Thistles for some tea and cake,' Becky confirmed, slipping her arm around Nancy's shoulders.

Vaughan's hand searched out mine and we walked up to Nancy. He towered over the petite woman like he was a huge oak tree himself. 'Nancy, you are welcome to come to Glenlovatt and visit Hugo any time you like.'

She smiled warmly up at him before asking, 'Has anyone ever told you that you're almost as handsome as your grandfather?'

Thirty-nine

 'Oooh what's that?' asked Morven, pulling the colour catalogue across the top of the cake counter later that day.

'A sales rep came in earlier. There's some lovely stuff in there.'

Morven was intrigued. 'Like what?'

'Oh, you know, embroidered table napkins; coasters; printed chiffon scarves; fancy stationery . . .'

Morven flicked through the glossy pages of the catalogue. 'Pity there isn't a gift shop in Glenlovatt,' she mused. 'I think some of these products would sell well here.'

I sprinkled some chocolate on a cappuccino. 'I think you're right.'

The afternoon rolled past on a hectic tide of sugar-starved ramblers and a coachload of elderly holiday-makers from Newcastle. The second group from the coach had just returned from their guided tour of Glenlovatt with Mrs Baylis, eager to be fed and watered.

'Excuse me,' blustered a woman from the group. 'Did you happen to see one of our gentlemen leave the tea room just now?'

Morven, Becky and I shook our heads in unison. 'No, sorry,' I apologised. 'But we have been a bit distracted with customers.'

The woman's wide-set blue eyes registered rising concern. 'Oh dear. He's wearing a blue and green chequered scarf and a black full-length coat. He's got receding grey hair. His name's Mr Stelling. Norman Stelling.'

Morven's face was sympathetic. 'Sorry, no. Is there a problem?'

The woman, presumably the tour organiser, heaved a sigh. 'He gets a bit confused at times,' she admitted. 'Norman has a tendency to wander off if he isn't chaperoned.'

'Would you like me to go and have a look for him with you?' offered Morven. 'If that's okay with you, Lara?'

'Yes, of course. We'll cope in here. I'll let you both know straight away if he comes back.'

The woman gave a smile of gratitude. 'Thank you so much.'

Morven guided the concerned woman towards the door.

'Actually, perhaps I'll pop out into the grounds again,' the woman suggested. 'Norman's a keen gardener at home, so there's a fair chance he'll have wandered back outside.'

'And I'll check round here,' said Morven, her leopard-print pumps turning into the hall. As she left the tea room I could hear her calling out Mr Stelling's name over and over, her voice ringing against the walls.

The tour organiser was soon back with a bemused Mr Stelling in tow. 'I was right about where he was,' she said with a smile. 'Norman was having a lovely time admiring the flowers.'

I gave the man's arm a gentle pat. 'As long as you're alright, sir.'

Norman beamed through a set of yellowing teeth. 'Oh, I'm perfectly fine, thank you. I was having a nice walk before she came and dragged me back in here.'

The woman pushed a strand of white hair back from her face. 'Well, you might not need another cuppa but I most certainly do.' Sliding me a sideways grin, she announced, 'In fact, if you had anything stronger, I could be persuaded.'

I smiled. 'Coming right up—the tea, that is.'

'Thank you so much again for all your help,' said the tour organiser. 'I hope your friend isn't still looking for Norman in the house?'

Where had Morvern got to, anyway? At that very moment she came bustling back in from the hall, a look of pure excitement on her flushed face.

'Ah, there you are,' I exclaimed. 'I was just about to send out the search party. Mr Stelling was in the garden all along.'

'What? Oh, yes, of course,' said Morven distractedly. 'I thought as much. Listen, you won't believe what I just found.' She pulled me aside to the barista station, barely able to contain whatever her news was.

She told me that, searching along the hallway, she had rapped on a couple of doors before popping her head into the rooms to check. One was a storage room, cluttered with spare jackets, discarded wellingtons and assorted hats, but no Mr Stelling. She had moved on to the next door a few feet down. 'It was a second storeroom,' she explained, 'this one with a couple of old grey filing cabinets, and a wooden table and chair.' She'd hurried on and found a third, final, door at the end of the corridor, but the handle on this one wouldn't budge at all. What if the missing man had stumbled in there and had collapsed against the back of the door?

'Now I was really worried,' Morven said, 'especially when I tried the door again and it opened slightly but not all the way.' Silently apologising to the Carmichael family for any damage she might do, Morven had placed one hand on the door and the other on the handle. With a fierce grunt, she pushed the weight of her body against the dark panelled door until it surrendered and swung open, dragging Morven in with it.

She had fallen into the room and dusted down her jeans. At least there was no injured or confused pensioner in need of assistance. 'It was then that I took in the layout of the room and I had an idea,' she grinned excitedly at me. 'I've got to show the room to you after we close up this afternoon.'

Morven led me out of a now empty tea room and down the corridor.

'I don't know what you'll think,' she said, 'but I can definitely see possibilities with it.' Her flats tapped faster as she neared the door. 'It's not huge but it's a decent size, and there's a small window at the end. It looks as though it might have been used at one time to store tools.' Morven beckoned me in. 'And that shelf running down the right-hand side could be used as a counter.'

I stepped in front of her and poked my head into the space. 'This house is like an Aladdin's cave,' I laughed. 'You think you know all there is to know about it and then it produces another surprise.' I looked around, taking in the window view of a side hedge and a couple of apple blossom trees. 'So, are you going to tell me your idea for this room then?'

Morven clasped her hands. 'What would you think if I suggested this room be a gift shop?'

I felt a warm glow. 'I think that sounds a terrific idea. Obviously we'd have to run it past the Carmichaels but I'd be surprised if they didn't go for it.'

'You think?'

'Why not?'

Morven twirled around in the centre of the room, like a ballerina. 'We could start off just stocking a few items and see how it goes.'

I pointed at the shelving. 'The basics are already in here. All it needs is a good clean, some stock and we're ready to go.'

'Now don't get me wrong, Lara. I've got no intention of leaving Thistles, or you, high and dry. I just thought it might bring in a bit more revenue.'

'I'm sure it would,' I agreed. 'And if we recruited one person to work in it, that would be fine.'

Morven shot me a quick look as she ran a hand along one of the shelves. 'Well, what I actually thought was that we could suggest we take, maybe, two part-time staffers and see how things pan out.'

I gave her a playful jab in the ribs. 'Careful! You're beginning to sound like me.'

Morven laughed, examining the empty room again.

'Do I detect that you have two particular people in mind for this job?'

'I might.'

'You're a woman of mystery, Morven Knight. Okay, let's take your idea to Gordon now.'

'Now?'

I linked my arm through hers. 'Why not? No time like the present, as they say.'

Forty

 'He said yes!' cheered Morven, as we spilled out of Gordon's study. 'He said yes!'

'I know. I was there! So come on then,' I teased as we headed back to Thistles, 'don't keep me in suspense.'

'About what?' asked Morven innocently.

'What do you think? About who you have in mind to approach about working in the gift shop.'

Morven smiled. 'They are both lovely ladies who you've already met.'

I furrowed my brow. 'Well, that doesn't narrow it down much.'

She favoured me with a mysterious look. 'I'm going to ring them right now and ask if we can pop round to speak to them. Are you okay with that?'

'You're the boss.'

Once we'd tidied up for the day, I jumped into my car and followed Morven into Fairview for the first of our two appointments. The air now had a distinct chill to it, but even the coming colder months couldn't dampen my spirits.

Soon, I pulled up behind Morven on a side street close to Fairview's train station. Morven gave me a cheeky grin as she led me through a gate to a house covered in white pebble dash that looked clean, if a little tired. A hall light glittered through the front door's frosted glass and there were enthusiastic yelps from a West Highland terrier in the front window. Morven rang the silver doorbell.

Claire McNaughton opened the door, looking flustered. 'Oh, I'm so sorry, ladies,' she gushed. I've only just got back from collecting Flora from choir practice. Please come in.'

She ushered us into the front sitting room, where Eddie was reading a newspaper. We exchanged pleasantries before he removed himself, saying, 'I'll leave you ladies to it then.'

'Would you like a tea or coffee?' Claire asked.

After yet another day of having tea and cake between serving customers at Thistles, we politely declined, and Morven got down to business. 'We've got a job proposition for you. Our new venture won't be up and running for a few weeks but we really wanted to approach you about it.'

Claire's eyes swivelled between us. 'Oh?'

Morven smiled warmly. 'We wondered if you might be interested in working in our new gift shop part-time?'

Claire's expectant expression bloomed into one of delight. 'What, you mean working in that beautiful, big house?'

'Yes, we do,' I grinned.

Morven's enthusiasm was equally infectious. 'It would be great to have someone who can do first aid too. If somebody else should choke, heaven forbid, you're right there.'

Claire smiled with pleasure.

'But we should emphasise,' added Morven, 'that the pay won't be huge and we're planning on keeping things small and simple to begin with, to see if the gift shop takes off.'

Claire rose to shut the sitting room door quietly before resuming her seat on the sofa opposite us. 'As far as I'm concerned, your job offer is perfect. But there's something I want to tell you first, before you hear it from anyone else.'

I glanced at Morven, curious.

Claire looked down at her hands. 'You'll probably remember what that Kitty woman said about us when we came to Glenlovatt for that guided tour we won.'

Morven curled her lip in disgust. 'Everyone knows what a gossiping old witch she is. Don't worry about it.'

Claire half-smiled. 'I did get that impression, but what she said was partly true. We used to live in a lovely part of Stirling. I worked as a senior nurse in a local hospital and Eddie was project manager for a construction company.' She fiddled with her brown bobbed hair nervously. 'Everything was fine until Eddie started gambling.' A flush crept up her neck. 'Our financial situation became a disaster very quickly and things got desperate.'

I followed her gaze out the sitting room window, taking in the small, well-cut patch of grass and two stout rose bushes. A dark cloud scudded past.

'Eddie wasn't thinking straight,' she continued. 'He'd never committed a crime in his life before.'

'What happened?' I asked carefully.

Claire's fingers knotted together. 'He got caught stealing food from our corner shop.' She shuddered as she recalled it. 'Eddie regretted it straight away but by then it was too late.'

'What happened?'' asked Morven.

'He got a caution but, as you can guess, it still hit the local paper and the gossips round our way had a field day. The kids had a hard time of it at school.'

I sighed. 'And so, you moved?'

Claire nodded. 'I gave up my job and we decided to start again elsewhere.' She picked up her tea, clutching the cup in both hands. 'Eddie got help for his gambling and has managed to get a job as a labourer in Glasgow.' She gazed fondly at a photo of Robbie and Flora on the sideboard, their faces bathed in sunshine, and a sapphire blue swimming pool behind them with palm trees dotted around it. 'I did think about returning to nursing but the kids really needed me around when Eddie had his problems.' She smiled gratefully at us. 'I don't want to be away from them for long shifts. Not until they settle in more here and regain some confidence. So your job sounds perfect. Thank you.'

As we left, Morven confirmed to Claire that she'd send her more details and keep her posted on when the gift shop was due to be up and running.

'Now on to prospective employee number two,' smiled Morven mysteriously. 'I just hope you approve and that she's as enthusiastic as Claire was.'

I followed Morven in my car. We swung past the train station and carried on through a roundabout beside the park. The swings moved slightly in the breeze and the surrounding trees reached out into the sky like searching fingers. Morven pulled in to the kerb and I eased the Cleo in behind her.

'It should be over here somewhere,' she explained, glancing down at Google Maps on her mobile. 'We're looking for number thirty-three.'

When we found it, it looked to be a former council house, semi-detached with a newer conservatory jutting into the back garden. Ivy trailed down next to the black front door.

Before we could knock, an attractive woman with enquiring eyes and sharply cut blonde hair answered the door. After warm introductions, she ushered us down the hall. 'Aunt Nancy's just through here. Please come in.'

The hall smelled of cranberry and a small lamp glowed on a side table. As we were led into a sitting room, I saw who was in front of me and broke into a fond smile. There, with her pale pink lipstick carefully applied and a purple cardigan draped around her shoulders, was Nancy Stewart.

'Perfect,' I whispered to Morven, moving towards Nancy, who rose from her seat. She aimed the remote at the TV screen, and the quiz show she had been watching fizzled and died.

'So what's all the mystery?' she asked, tugging off her gold spectacles. My eyes drifted to a photograph on the mantelpiece of Nancy and, I presumed, her late husband on a cliff top, craggy rocks propping up a bank of blue sky. He had a kindly smile, and whispery flaxen hair brushed away from his forehead.

Nancy looked at us with a worried expression. 'Is the red oak alright?'

'Oh yes, don't worry about that,' said Morven. 'That's not why we're here.'

She smiled pointedly at me, so I snatched the opportunity to kick off our discussion. I explained about Morven's idea for the gift shop and that even though it was still in its infancy, we were eager to get things moving.

'So,' Morven exclaimed with an edge of trepidation, 'we wondered if you might be interested in becoming our other part-time assistant in the gift shop?'

Nancy's shocked expression made me raise my hands in concern. 'If you'd rather not, then we completely understand. Or if you feel you may not be up to it, for whatever reason, that's fine too.'

The room was silent apart from the ticking of a clock somewhere. Then, Morven leaned forward, smiling. 'I did tentatively mention it to Janet and she thought it was a wonderful idea.'

I grinned at my best friend. 'Did you, indeed?'

Nancy gave a deep breath. 'I would like that very much.'

We both smiled with relief.

'Then that's settled,' confirmed Morven as she rose to her feet. 'We've got our two members of staff lined up. Now all we have to do is create a gift shop!'

Since Wolf and Mum's momentous visit to Glenlovatt earlier that week, plans and preparations for the arts festival were going full throttle.

Gordon had spoken about the Aspirations festival to the Curnow family, who had been more than happy to help with any enquiries. They had even invited Gordon over to their estate in Edinburgh.

Once I'd had a chance to catch up with them, I'd learned that Wolf and Mum's visit to his family seat had been 'entertaining', by all accounts. Once they'd recovered from getting their only son home again after he'd been missing for several months, they'd turned their attention to my mum, the silver-haired cougar. However, Wolf took great pride in recounting for me how Mum had charmed his parents from the beginning. She had simply been her confident self and they had been heartened by how close she and Wolf were.

As he was regaling me with their visit, Wolf became thoughtful for a moment. 'It was obvious to my parents how I feel about Chris, and they know how much I've changed since I've been away.'

'And the stationery empire?' I asked.

Wolf sank his head back against the sofa. 'We've come to an agreement with that too. I'll concentrate on the family business on a part-time basis for now, as long as my writing comes first.'

The air of contentment swirling around Mum and Wolf was contagious. I'd skipped out of my front door that morning, armed with the most annoying grin on my face and a constant, fizzing sensation in my heart. Vaughan was forever hovering at the corner of my thoughts. The thought of seeing those long legs and tousled hair when he returned late today, and then at our dinner date, caused an excited lump in my throat.

The sun spiralled its way through the clouds and onto Glenlovatt's rolling lawns. As I opened up for the day, I spotted my reflection in one of the windows. I'd chosen a blue Breton top with three-quarter-length sleeves, a quilted navy jacket and tight black trousers. My unruly red curls tumbled down my back in a springy ponytail. Happiness brimmed in my grey eyes. The whole package, from my carefully selected clothes to my glowing skin and expectant eyes, screamed, 'I'm in love and I can't bloody help it!'

Yes, I was behaving like a love-struck fifteen-year-old.

I patted another gingham cushion into place before turning back to setting up before Becky and Jess arrived. Clicking on the iPod, I hummed along as I arranged today's selection of cherry and coconut slice, apple strudel and Viennese whirls. Every time my mind wandered towards this evening I'd grin inanely. I'd barely been able to sleep with thoughts of Vaughan, the new gift shop and the festival churning through my mind.

I finished tweaking the cake counter and decided to treat myself to a cup of steaming tea and a corner of slice. Taking them out onto the patio, I sat down at one of the tables, and admired the view and the faint tinkle from the stone water feature further down the incline. I took a bite of the slice, the sweet taste filling my mouth and teasing my tastebuds.

A noise from inside attracted my attention. 'Jess? Becky?'

No response. I stood and popped my head inside and thought I saw a flash of movement out the door to the great hall. As I turned to go back outside, the light flutter of an open newspaper on the table nearest the patio doors startled me. I didn't recall seeing it there before.

I picked it up and took it back to my breakfast table to flick through as I ate. Lord knows I was unlikely to get another chance to catch up on the news today. I savoured the burst of cherries in my mouth as I glanced down at paper; then almost choked when I saw the photograph on the open page.

Forty-one

I slumped backwards in my chair.

Vaughan was concentrating on something to his right, while the blonde beside him was servicing the camera with a dazzling smile. The photograph had obviously been taken at night, as stars were popping in the inky sky above their heads, and a striped restaurant awning fluttered airily in the background.

Petra's triumphant grin repeatedly stabbed me in the chest. Her long legs were encased in tight black trousers and her hair streamed out behind her like a glossy flag. Vaughan, in his dark suit, resembled a strong-jawed aftershave model far more than the clay-encrusted, furrow-browed sculptor I knew. I really didn't want to read the accompanying gossip column but the words shouted up at me deafeningly.

'Looks like society beauty Petra Montgomery-Carlton has bagged herself a handsome beau. She and dashing sculptor Vaughan Carmichael are set to tie the knot after a whirlwind romance . . .' There was more about how they met and the extortionate price of Petra's trousers, but my mind had raced ahead. Could this be true? Was *this* the mysterious 'business trip'

Vaughan was currently on? It would explain why he'd avoided any specifics of what exactly he was going away for.

I thought back to all the protestations about Petra, the way he'd kissed me . . . Why had I thought I was any different from all those other girls he'd toyed with? Why hadn't I listened to my brain instead of my heart? Vaughan Carmichael had obviously been trouble but, yet again, I'd blundered in, ignoring all the alarm bells. Obviously I hadn't learned a thing since Anton and Malta. Vaughan viewed me as a nice little distraction until he finally married Petra. I struggled with a painful sob, pushing the newspaper angrily back across the table, where it fluttered gently in the autumn sunshine.

What was I going to do?

I looked back in at Thistles, with its white-painted walls, polished tables and Lydia's artwork proudly displayed. Sunlight pooled on the wooden floor in golden puddles. I'd put so much passion and commitment into this project. More importantly, Hugo had made my dream a reality and I felt I owed him so much. Add to that all the support from Morven, Gordon, Becky and Jess. What would this place be like when Ms High-and-Mighty became Vaughan's wife? Imagining her sashaying around Glenlovatt in her Burberry wellies as lady of the manor made more tears congregate on my lashes.

Glenlovatt and Thistles would always mean the world to me. I couldn't and wouldn't leave now, even if Vaughan was about to marry someone else. I dragged a hand down my tear-stained face. I'd just have to throw myself into helping with any arrangements for the festival and keep out of Vaughan's way for good.

Huh. Easier said than done when my business was situated inside his ancestral home.

I motored through the next few hours on autopilot.

Thank goodness Vaughan wasn't due back till later. The very thought of seeing him at that moment made me shudder with pain and embarrassment.

I served an elderly couple their cream teas with an empty smile on my face, then moved robotically back behind the cake counter and fussed unnecessarily with a stand of carrot and banana cupcakes I'd arranged earlier. Pausing to look out on my little kingdom from behind the counter was not a good idea. From the circular wooden tables to the proud high-backed chairs, Lydia's thistle artwork dotted around, the huge windows beckoning in the flowers outside and the little patio laced with a busy hedge of tiny white buds—all of it pressed against my heart. I'd worked so hard and, again, I wasn't prepared to give all this up, even if it meant watching Vaughan and his fiancée playing happy families right under my nose.

'Do you mind if I take a five-minute break, Morvs?'

Morven snapped her head up from her laptop. 'Of course. Are you okay?'

'Yes, fine,' I protested, far too quickly. 'I just need some air.'

I was about to move towards an empty table on the patio when I heard my mobile give the sharp trill of a text message from the depths of my bag. I pulled it free and stepped outside.

The heavy scent of honeysuckle was in the air as I sank down onto a quilted seat and looked at the house. Its grand windows winked from the cream and butter stone like wise old eyes. Trying desperately to compose myself, I looked down at my mobile.

It was a text from Vaughan.

I'll be back this evening. Can't wait to see you. V x

A shocked laugh rumbled up from inside me. Of all the sodding cheek!

I read it again, just to make sure I hadn't imagined it. No, sure enough the arrogant cretin had indeed sent me that message. Had he seen the photo of him and Petra blazoned across the newspaper? It didn't sound like it.

I'd been counting the hours till our date. I'd planned all my beauty treatments and what I was going to wear. I'd not been sleeping or eating properly with all the anticipation. I felt an utter fool.

Maybe he had seen the photo and had decided to try to brazen it out? Perhaps he was banking on the possibility that I hadn't? Or maybe he hadn't seen it at all?

I blinked back the pain. Well, he would receive a homecoming from me that he wouldn't forget in a hurry.

After we'd tidied up at the end of the day and Morven and Becky had gone home—not without sending some sidelong enquiring glances my way—I loitered around in Thistles, angrily awaiting Vaughan's return.

Pain shone in my eyes as I slicked on some fresh pink lipstick in the tea room toilet. My reflection in the oval mirror was ghost-like, despite the fiery colour of my hair escaping from its curly ponytail. I angrily zipped up my glittery make-up pouch and shoved it into my bag, next to the newspaper photo of Vaughan and Petra. I heard Vaughan's rumbly voice talking to Travis in the hall. I turned and walked back into the tea room. Time to face the music.

'Lara!' His deep voice rumbled across the empty room.

I looked up. He was gorgeous in dark jeans, desert boots and a red V-neck T-shirt.

He might look like Christian Bale but he's still a dick.

Before I had a moment to compose myself, he was across the floor and his mouth was on mine. Sparks flashed behind my eyelids but I found the strength to push him away, the feel of his skin lingering on the tips of my fingers.

'I've got something for you,' I said.

Vaughan's lips stretched into a wide grin. 'I like the sound of that.'

'I don't know that you will,' I replied coldly, slapping the page from the newspaper on top of the counter.

Vaughan's smile trickled away. 'What's this?'

'You tell me,' I ground out, trying to steady the shake in my voice, 'although it looks pretty obvious from where I'm standing.'

He pushed the dark hair back off his face. 'I don't understand.'

'Oh, I think I do. Your supposed business trip has made the news. Congratulations.'

Vaughan studied the photo lying in front of him. 'You think I've been sneaking off with her?' he said quietly.

I stared at him accusingly.

Vaughan's eyes hardened. 'For your information, I've been working on a special sculpture. A very special sculpture, in fact.' He jerked his head dismissively at the photograph. 'I don't know where this has come from but it isn't recent.'

I folded my arms protectively across my chest. 'Right.'

Vaughan's face turned to granite. 'You don't believe me? You've seen that photo and you've already made up your mind. What happened to innocent until proven guilty?' I opened my mouth to speak but was silenced by his raised hand. 'Do you know what? Forget it. You don't believe me—or, at least, you don't want to.'

He snatched up his brown holdall, swung it over his shoulder and was gone.

Forty-two

Keeping busy was my only option.

I baked like I was continuously on caffeine, offered to help with any last-minute problems with the imminent arts festival, and ensured all the tea room admin was in order for Morven. Then there was the gift shop to organise, thank goodness.

Every so often I would glance up at the tea room calendar in the kitchen. Circled in thick black pen were the dates of the twenty-seventh to the twenty-ninth of October, marking the arrival of the Aspirations Arts Festival and the reading of Hugo's mysterious letter, when I couldn't avoid Vaughan any longer. The thought of all this sent my stomach into a tailspin.

Morven assured me she was more than capable of dealing with any issues relating to the preparations for the gift shop and I knew that was true. But I also knew that the minute my concentration lapsed, my thoughts would travel to Vaughan. The only way to deal with my shattered emotions was never to have a spare moment to think.

During a mid-morning lull or a relatively quiet lunchtime, Morven and I would sit together over a pot of tea and discuss our progress with the gift shop. Becky's mum, an enthusiastic bargain hunter, managed to source a comfortable old stool for Claire and Nancy to sit on while working there, and I threw myself into assisting Morven with locating and ordering other essentials, including a cash register. I also helped prepare a roster for Claire and Nancy—anything to keep my mind occupied.

We'd homed in on a small number of items to stock: luxurious stationery customised with the Glenlovatt name; coasters featuring delicate reproductions of Scottish artworks; paints and pencils in a range of different packs; some gorgeous ladies' handbags, and leather wallets for gents; a selection of silk scarves and an assortment of silk ties; as well as intricately carved letter openers and a range of scented candles.

'I think we should start with this lot and see how we go,' said Morven. 'What do you think? Lara?'

'Sorry, I was miles away.'

Morven's eyes narrowed. 'Lars, are you really alright?'

'Yes, of course I am. I'm just a bit tired, that's all.'

'Are you sure?' she pushed. 'It hasn't got anything to do with—'

'Honestly, Morvs, I have so much on right now, I just don't even want to go there.'

Morven played with the pages of the catalogue lying on the table in front of us. 'You've been working flat out recently. Don't overdo it, okay?' She glanced down at her rose gold wristwatch. 'It's your turn for lunch now.'

I slipped on my navy leather jacket and headed out to the gardens. The early October air was crisp and a tangle of clouds flurried overhead. Walking steadily along the path, I made my way further down the grounds. I could hear the musical splashes from the Fairview Burn, and intermittent song from birds as they flapped from tree to tree. Branches heavy with orange and red leaves dipped above my head.

I dipped my head, gently pushing a branch out of my way as I crossed down past a bank of high hedgerows. The mausoleum's silhouette, now boasting Nancy's red oak to the right of it, made me fight back a sigh. Sinking down underneath a nearby willow, I rammed my back poker straight against its solid, dark trunk. I pushed my beige flats further into the grass, watching as the emerald blades sprang back up again. They were resilient. Lucky them.

I had rehearsed in my mind what I wanted to say to Hugo, plucking words as though I was selecting flowers for a special bouquet, mixing and matching so they complemented one another. Instead, I opened my mouth and a heavy sob crashed out. 'I'm sorry, Hugo. I'm so, so sorry.'

I half-expected him to answer me, but all I could hear was my own ragged breathing and spurts of birdsong. I dashed tears away with the back of my hand. 'I didn't mean to fall in love with Vaughan.'

I slumped down the tree trunk, tears now running freely down my cheeks. 'I don't know how I'm going to handle being here at Glenlovatt when Vaughan is with someone else.' I rubbed my eyes, making them smart. 'But I promise you, I won't let you down. Even after this.'

I uncoiled myself and stood up. There were bits of leaves and grass clinging to my jeans. I dusted my clothes down sharply. 'I've learned a lot about myself these past few months and that is because of you.' My attention locked onto the Carmichael family crest of gold and blue roses and thistles, decorating the mausoleum entrance. 'All I can do is try to build on the success we've had. Oh, and avoid your grandson. It's for the best.'

Then I put my hand up to my mouth and blew Hugo a kiss.

The October weeks passed, leaving a carpet of read and amber leaves across the Glenlovall grounds. I, meanwhile, continued to avoid Vaughan at all costs. To my irrational irritation, he was doing exactly the same to me. A couple of times I thought I saw a tall, dark shadow hovering by the tea room door, but when I looked closer there was no one.

At other times Gordon would remark in passing that Vaughan was away, working on his 'secret project'. On those few occasions he questioned me directly, his kind eyes would study me enquiringly: 'Have you seen much of my son of late?', I would rearrange my face into a polite smile and assure him that we were both just so busy. I could tell he knew I wasn't being entirely truthful but chose not to press the point.

At home after another long day, I watched clouds of flour travel up to my kitchen ceiling. Goodness knows how this chocolate mud cake will turn out. Probably a bloody disaster, just like my personal life. I shook my head savagely before chopping dark chocolate into wedges with uncharacteristic force.

The Aspirations Arts Festival was a riotous carnival of colour. Rows of tents and strings of red and white bunting weaved their way across and around the Glenlovatt grounds, like dozens of butterflies.

Gordon and I had meandered around beforehand, astonished at how efficiently everything was taking shape. Tarpaulins had been erected near the festival entry, to host a variety of artisans—everyone from woodwork craftsmen to Celtic jewellers, glass blowers and leatherworkers. There were a couple of mobile libraries, packed with everything from Scottish poetry to Tartan Noir. There were child-friendly spaces littered with beanbags, books, and art stations where they could paint, paste and draw.

A puppeteer was making final adjustments to his cast of woodland animals, their glossy painted expressions and wooden limbs ready to come to life.

A bit further down the sweep of lawns was a collection of writers and painters, there to present and sell their work. Some wore pensive expressions as they hovered over their particular creations, positioning their landscapes of shaggy Highland cattle and craggy, sea-soaked harbours, or stacking their piles of novels to attract the crowd who would hopefully be arriving shortly.

A sound check burbled close by, where a pair of stand-up comedians were perched on a small stage. A theatre troupe waved at them cheerily as they sauntered past dressed in bright tights and feathered plumes.

The festival was due to open in an hour and the basket of butterflies I was carrying around in my stomach now threatened to envelop my whole body. I couldn't quite believe it was the twenty-seventh of October already.

'It's going to be quite a day,' grinned Gordon, nodding to a couple of jugglers in top hats. 'And don't forget that Hugo's solicitor is arriving at 6pm to read out that letter.' He raised his eyes to the sky. 'Goodness knows what revelations it will contain. I suppose we'll know soon enough.' He added with a sigh, 'Even in death that old bugger can manage to cause a stir.'

I forced a laugh, but the mention of the opening of Hugo's letter triggered those butterflies into action again. Despite my efforts to bury myself in the business of the tea room and all the festival and gift shop preparations, I couldn't avoid Vaughan Carmichael today. I was dreading it.

Travis appeared. 'Mr Carmichael? Phone call for you, sir.'

'Excuse me,' apologised Gordon, following Travis across the dew-decked grass.

I looked up at the morning sky. The sun was making promising glimpses from behind scudding clouds and the smell of wood smoke lurked in the air. Glenlovatt looked proudly on, like a contented mother admiring her family.

I smiled absently at an elderly gent at a nearby stall who was laying out a selection of carefully crafted and painted snow globes. He adjusted his beige quilted gilet before tipping his cap respectfully at me. Hugo used to do that all the time. It was an old-fashioned mannerism but one that used to make me glow.

Oh no. Not again. The ghost of Hugo shimmered before my eyes, threatening tears.

I spun on my heel and took quick steps back towards the house. One consolation, at least, was that we expected Thistles to be even more busy than usual over the weekend. Hopefully, we'd be swamped with coffee-seeking culture vultures and cake-craving writers and I wouldn't have time to sit down, let alone think about Vaughan and his impending marriage.

I had recruited two temps from a hospitality agency to help us cover the expected long weekend rush and assist in doing some extra baking for the additional customers. They were Greta, an older lady who had worked in a bakery chain, and Logan, a tall, gangly student. Becky protested otherwise, but Logan most definitely fancied her. When he'd come in last week for a chat, his square, freckled face morphed into a tomato when he'd clocked Becky's candy-haired cuteness. When Morven or I asked him a question, he was fine. But when Becky did the talking, he transformed into a gibbering wreck.

'Logan's cute,' I had remarked, after he'd almost given himself concussion walking into the door on his way out. 'He's got that cheeky look going on, hasn't he?'

Becky had sucked in her cheeks. 'You make it sound like he's an eight-week-old puppy.'

'Very funny,' I'd replied, brandishing a cake slice at her. 'There goes your defence mechanism again.'

'And you can talk!' guffawed Becky, piling more cups into the dishwasher.

The atmosphere had assumed a rather tense edge at that point and we'd both dropped the conversation.

A throng of hungry art collectors now spilled into Thistles and Greta's grey head was bowed in concentration, counting out change, while Logan was describing the ingredients of an Eton Mess to a man wrapped in a woven waistcoat.

Each time a new customer came in, I'd deliver a wide smile and a 'Good morning', hoping my cheery smile would keep thoughts of Vaughan at bay.

The morning disappeared in a flurry of customers seeking warm, buttered scones and cups of delicious scented coffee. Once lunchtime arrived, we were subjected to many families with hungry children.

Jess's lunch choices of the day, cod fishcakes or lasagne with crunchy salad for the children, and blue cheese tartlets or steak and ale pie for the adults, received many orders. Business was so busy, it made our heads spin. Tables were occupied, cleared and then occupied again. Festival goers filtered in and out as though on a conveyor belt, many with pieces of artwork or books under their arms, along with goodies in our trademark white and green Thistles bags.

We'd opted for a relay system, so that all of us in the tea room were able to have a quick browse and snatch a breather and a snack. 'Go on, Lara,' urged Greta. 'Get a break. It's a little quieter now.'

A huge part of me didn't want to. Though it was already mid-afternoon, I didn't feel particularly hungry.

Greta frowned at me. 'You need to eat something.' Then she used the tongs to pick up the last of the seeded turkey and cranberry salad rolls. 'Here,' she instructed, wrapping it in one of our green napkins, 'you can nibble on that while you walk.'

I dropped my head. 'Thanks,' I said. 'I won't be long.'

I brushed past a family of four in baseball caps, and strode out into Glenlovatt's majestic hall and darted out of the side entrance. My feet crunched the pink gravel and I found that I must have been hungrier than I'd thought. I polished off the last of the roll Greta had given me and deposited the crumbs in my napkin. I lobbed it into a nearby bin as I walked across to the line of tents, canvas and bunting rippling in the afternoon breeze.

Cars were still gliding into the allotted parking areas, guided in by local volunteers, their neon jackets bright dots in the distance. From somewhere close by, a PA system crackled into life, giving details of a talk that was soon to begin. A handful of students decked out in brightly coloured waistcoats delivered friendly smiles to the arrivals, along with a program and map of the grounds. Over by the oak trees, jugglers were hypnotising some preschool children with their flying batons. The performers' top hats, encrusted in silver mirrors, dazzled as they dipped and weaved in front of their youthful audience.

I stopped at a jewellery stall, for want of something to do. Up ahead I saw Gordon chatting to the man in the beige gilet. When he spotted me, he waved cheerily. I waved back and fingered a pair of rose gold earrings. Vaughan was an open wound that I had to forget about but there would always be reminders of him everywhere I went here. Maybe I should take a short break some-where, like the Lake District. I could rent a little cottage, wander the shores of Coniston Water, take myself on some long walks, recharge my batteries and try to put all this firmly in my past.

My chest heaved. I couldn't take a holiday at the moment, especially while Thistles was still being established, let alone the gift shop. And what would I do on a holiday by myself? I'd probably spend the week wandering around myriad beautiful lakes without even seeing them, moping and feeling sorry for myself.

Making a new resolution not to dwell on the past or things I couldn't control, I drifted away from the jewellery stall—and froze.

Vaughan and Petra were standing by the corner of a red tent brimming with paintings of heather-dotted Scottish landscapes. They were in animated conversation. Vaughan's arms were crossed while Petra toyed with strands of her sunflower yellow hair, her white maxi dress flapping about her heels. She looked like she'd just walked out of a shampoo advert.

I wanted to move but the sight of them together was magnetic.

Vaughan's muscles tensed under his black shirt. His sleeves were rolled up and there were glimpses of his muscular arms. He turned his head sharply in response to something Petra said.

Bugger! I think he saw me.

I turned away and started back towards the tea room, increasing my speed. If I was quick I could lose myself in the crowds. My heart thrashed against my ribcage. The crushing pain at seeing both of them together was speedily replaced by a desperate urgency to get away. I didn't dare look back.

Staring straight ahead, I muttered 'Excuse me' here and there, squeezing through the crush of bodies until I'd almost reached the edge of the lawns, when I felt a tug on my right arm.

I spun around, confused.

Vaughan's hand was clamped on my arm, with a frozen-faced Petra bringing up the rear.

'You can really move when you want to,' he gasped, 'but I'm not letting you run away on this occasion.'

'I'm not running away,' I snapped. 'I have to get back to work.'

The disbelief in his voice was evident. 'Oh yes?'

'Yes,' I said, snatching my arm away. 'Now, if you'll excuse me, I must go.'

Petra's heavily made-up face was hard. Pushing my loose hair back over my shoulder, I turned back towards the tea room before letting out a sharp squeal as I was lifted off my feet, the grass suddenly falling away from me. 'What the?'

Vaughan had swung me cleanly over his shoulder and was now striding purposefully through the bemused crowds. What the hell was he doing and where was he taking me? My bum was pointing upwards for all to see while my red curls tipped down and over my horrified face. At least that was a blessing.

'Put me down now!' I yelled, thumping his back with my fists. 'This is not funny! Put me down, you bastard, or I'll kick you somewhere delicate!'

'Bastard?' laughed Vaughan. 'That's not very ladylike, is it? And I'd like to see you kick me somewhere delicate from up there. Physically impossible.'

I raised my fist and gave his sinewy back another hard clout. To my satisfaction, he let out a lion-like roar. 'Stop hitting me,' he growled, jiggling me as he walked. 'No need to make this worse than it needs to be. This is as embarrassing for me as it is for you.'

I gaped in astonishment while Vaughan proceeded to say a polite 'Hello,' 'Good afternoon' and 'Hi there' to people he obviously recognised.

'I bloody well doubt this is as embarrassing for you as it is for me! I'm the one with my arse up in the air.'

There was a gravelly laugh in response. 'This has to be done,' he explained coolly as I hung on for dear life. 'I'm going to speak and this time you are going to actually listen to what I have to say.'

Forty-three

Despite my incessant wriggling, Vaughan's strong arms kept me in a vice-like grip over his shoulder.

A horrible thought hit me squarely as I was bumped along. People I knew. People I no doubt grew up with. People who knew my mum and dad. People who went to bridge club with my late Great-aunt Hettie. People who were my customers at Thistles. Many of them would be part of this festival crowd and they were probably getting a good eyeful right now.

I gave up wriggling and held on tight, squeezing my eyes shut. 'I don't know what you're playing at, Vaughan, but you wait till I get down from here.'

Vaughan came to a sudden, jolting stop. 'You mean, when I *put* you down.'

With a sweep of his arms I was swung downwards, catching a glimpse of blue sky as the world righted itself and my feet sunk into the grass. I blinked, steadying my feet, and realised he'd carted me near the main throng of stalls. Why had he brought me back down here?

An inquisitive crowd gathered around us, including a thunderous Petra as she caught up. I straightened my dress and belted jacket before pinning Vaughan with a killer stare.

'What the hell are you playing at?' I spluttered, 'you can't just cart me across Glenlovatt, like some serving wench.'

'You said it, darling,' spat Petra.

'You be quiet,' snarled Vaughan at her from over his shoulder. 'This is mostly your fault.'

Petra fell silent.

Vaughan looked at me intensely. 'Lara, if you'd just let me—'

'I've got to get back to the tea room,' I butted in furiously. 'We're flat out and Morven will be scrambling search dogs and helicopters.' I stepped backwards into the growing sea of expectant faces that had decided to wander over and watch. Clearly this looked more interesting than ceramic bowls and watercolours. Just then all the frustration, hurt and anger I'd been holding inside came bubbling to the surface, volcano style. 'You're a self-centred, arrogant arsehole,' I burst out, fighting back tears. 'Why couldn't you have just stayed being a bad-tempered sod and left me alone?'

The pain on Vaughan's face was immediate. 'I couldn't stay a bad-tempered sod because of you, and I most certainly couldn't leave you alone.' He tugged a hand through his hair but it just tumbled back down around his face. 'Don't you understand, Lara? Yes, I admit I was a selfish arsehole when I first met you. But that's the whole point. You've changed me.'

A collective sigh rippled from the female spectators.

'You're this infectious bundle of beauty, kindness and perseverance.' He gave an exasperated laugh. 'Believe me, I tried to ignore my feelings for you for a long time.' He took a step closer, his voice rich with emotion. 'Then, when I realised how much Hugo meant to you, how determined you were to make Thistles a success, and then how stunning you looked at the ball . . .' He issued a wicked grin. 'And how could I forget the sight of those legs at that fashion show?'

Laughter punched the air from a few people in the crowd.

As I tried to conceal my blush with a tear-stained eye roll, Vaughan delivered the killer punch. 'I want to be with you, Lara. I'm in love with you.' He helplessly raked his long fingers through his hair again and I watched it fall back down around his face in an alluring blue-black curtain. 'I fell for you the moment I set eyes on you but I didn't want to admit it.'

This made no sense. I glanced at Petra, who was looking on with a dark expression. She dragged her eyes over me and then made a move to leave.

'Oh no you don't,' said Vaughan, snatching her by the arm. 'You've got some explaining to do yourself.'

Petra's tanned jaw slid open. 'How dare you speak to me like that?' she said huffily, glancing around at the curious crowd.

Vaughan's brows were thunderous as he looked back at me for a moment. 'I need Lara to hear this.' His expression turned grim. 'You're not running away, Petra. For once in your life, you're going to be honest with yourself and with everyone else.'

'I am most certainly not running away,' she barked. 'I've just got more important things to do than take part in this little spectacle.'

'Oh, for goodness sake!' burst Vaughan in frustration. He turned his blazing blue eyes on her even more forcefully than before. 'If you don't tell Lara the truth right now, I'm going to tell everyone here about the fun you had at that exclusive Edinburgh club last month.'

Petra's face froze. 'You wouldn't dare.'

'Wouldn't I?' he hissed back. 'I've got nothing to lose now. I love Lara and that's all that matters to me, whereas you can't live without your daddy's money.'

Petra closed her eyes for a moment.

Vaughan's expression grew darker still. 'I helped you out when you needed it that night. All I want is for you to tell Lara the truth about what's been going on.'

Petra tilted her chin, a look of defiance on her face.

'Tell her!' roared Vaughan, making me and the rest of the onlookers flinch.

Petra's fingers crawled to the pink gold shell swinging around her neck. Two dashes of colour appeared on her cheeks. 'Oh, alright! For goodness sake.' She gave her hair a toss. 'That picture in the paper,' she said finally, 'it's not what it looks like.'

'What?' I asked dumbly, but Vaughan's hot glare persuaded me to listen.

'You really are a bit slow, aren't you?' observed Petra.

'Petra, I'm warning you,' threatened Vaughan. 'Just get on with it.'

'Okay, okay.' She gave the inquisitive festival goers a condescending bat of her eyelashes. 'That newspaper photo of Vaughan and me was probably from about eighteen months ago.'

I wrinkled my brow.

Boredom settled on Petra's fake-tanned features as she examined her nails. 'My family have got a lot of contacts at that paper. I persuaded the diary editor to reprint that picture as a favour, and gave him an exclusive about some possible wedding plans to keep it interesting.' She looked up at me, a tiny smile skirting around the corners of her red-lipped mouth.

'But why?' I puzzled. 'Why would you do that?'

Petra flicked her pale gaze over me incredulously. 'Isn't it obvious?' She inclined her head at Vaughan. 'For some bizarre reason, he's nuts about you.' Her statement was hard and without emotion. 'I was jealous, okay?'

My memory dug deep, recalling the moment I saw the newspaper left open in the tea room, and a flash of someone leaving.

'Hang on. You deliberately left that newspaper in Thistles, didn't you?' I challenged. 'You wanted me to see the photo of you and Vaughan together.'

Biting her lip, Petra tossed her hair back over her shoulders.

Pulling my attention away from Petra wasn't difficult. I wanted to see Vaughan's face. A light-headed sensation stole over me. 'So you're not seeing Petra?'

Petra bored voice chimed in first. 'She catches on fast.'

'No, I'm not,' confirmed Vaughan with a sharp look at his former girlfriend. 'That was what I was trying to tell you. How could I be interested in anyone else when you're around?' He fixed Petra with another stony look. 'Especially someone who tries to wreck all the hard work you've put into the tea room.'

My mind reeled. 'What are you talking about?'

Vaughan jerked his head in Petra's direction. 'I believe you had a visit recently from the council's Environmental Health department.'

'Yes,' I faltered.

Vaughan grimaced. 'Three guesses who arranged that.'

All heads turned to look at the blushing blonde.

'The inspector's business card fell out of her bag the other day when she dropped in uninvited, yet again,' explained Vaughan. He reached into his trouser pocket and brandished the small white card high in the air. 'What a busy girl you've been, Petra.'

She raised her neck as if to launch into some verbal tirade, before thinking better of it.

'So,' Vaughan said to me through a small smile, 'I think I've managed to keep you quiet long enough to explain everything. Any questions?' He reached out and took my hand in his. 'I don't know what you've done to me. Once upon a time the idea of me declaring my undying love in front of a crowd would have brought me out in hives.'

Undying love? My mouth dropped open in another unappealing shape. What an idiot I'd been. But why had it taken so long for him to explain all this to me?

'Go on!' yelled a woman in a floral dress. 'Kiss him, otherwise I will!'

'Oh, sod it!' I cried, throwing my arms around Vaughn's neck and putting my lips on his. A moan escaped from his throat as he pinned me against his chest.

The wolf whistles and ripples of applause continued even after we finally drew apart. Over Vaughan's shoulder I could see Petra's billowing dress as she strode back towards the house, yelling into her mobile. I gazed up at Vaughan, who was grinning down at me.

'I've got something for you.'

He turned me around and led me down an incline, away from now dispersing crowd and in the direction of the mausoleum. I could now see Travis stationed beside a large object, concealed under a draping blue velvet cloth.

'Perhaps you've noticed that I was away a lot recently,' began Vaughan with a tinge of apprehension. 'Well, this is what I was doing.' His fingers tightened around mine as we approached the covered object. 'I just couldn't seem to get the inspiration I needed here to finish this particular piece. A master marble sculptor I really admire agreed to mentor me through it. Only thing is, his studio is way out in the Ayrshire countryside. That's why I've had to disappear of late. That, and,' he added with a chuckle, 'I wasn't going to get anything done with you here distracting me.'

I rolled my eyes at him and then noticed a slight tremor in his hand. 'Are you shaking?' I asked softly.

'Don't be daft,' he laughed, a little too quickly.

I couldn't quite believe it: Vaughan Carmichael, the arrogant artist, was nervous. Smiling, I turned towards Travis.

With a theatrical flourish, he removed the cloth, leaving me gasping.

Forty-four

I was spellbound.

'The bust of your mum, 'I whispered. 'The one you hadn't finished.'

Vaughan's fingers teased mine. 'Do you like it? I mean, I've spent hours holed up finishing it and I've almost lost the woman I love because of it but, you know, no pressure.'

I ignored his joking tone and tentatively moved towards the piece, almost expecting her to open her eyes. The bust had been set on a stone plinth. The sun created a halo-like effect around the white marble face and sculpted shoulders. Vaughan had portrayed his mother perfectly, from the arch of her eyebrows to the slight tilt of her nose. 'She's beautiful,' I murmured, running an appreciative finger down a deep fold of hair and along the silky looking material covering her shoulders.

'*You* are beautiful,' he smiled. 'I don't know what you've done to me, Lara.'

I smiled up at him and took his hand, wandering right around the bust and marvelling at the delicate curve of her shoulders, the intricate waves in her hair and the planes of her face, which Vaughan had captured so hauntingly. An image of him shirtless, toiling over his work as he carved and polished, suddenly came to mind. I could see the muscles sliding under his skin, perfecting every detail, and my skin fizzed at the thought of it.

'So,' I said, 'this is what you've been secretly working on.'

'Yes,' confirmed Vaughan, 'with the emphasis fully on "working". I wasn't out clubbing with Petra, or anyone else, for that matter. I was holed up sculpting this.'

Vaughan lifted his hand to caress the curve of my face. His touch sent bolts of excitement sizzling through my stomach. 'I started that bust of Mum years ago, before she died. I was really happy with how it was coming along and was all set to present it to her on her birthday.' A heavy sigh interrupted his words. 'Then, when we lost her so suddenly, I couldn't bear to look at it, let alone think about finishing it. I stashed it away in the corner. A few times I thought about trying to return to it but the motivation just wasn't there until you came along.'

A few of the festival attendees were now circling the bust and giving compliments. They stood back in admiration, drinking in its ethereal beauty.

'You were my inspiration to finish it, Lara.'

I shook my head in wonder. How could I have been so wrong?

The sound of gravel cracking and spitting under heavy tyres made me look up at the house, where Petra was clambering into a black beast of a car. It squealed off down the drive, sending more gravel flying.

Vaughan's gaze followed mine. 'I knew she could be manipulative, but I had no idea she'd stoop as low as she did.'

'She must have liked you a lot to go to those lengths,' I admitted.

Vaughan tilted a dark eyebrow. 'Petra liked the thought of becoming the lady of Glenlovatt far more.'

We took a few steps away from the art lovers and stood close together, admiring his family home. Its honey toned splendour was breathtaking today under the shifting sky and changing trees.

'If we can keep these festival events going, plus the tours and the tea room . . .' I began.

'We?'

Heat radiated from my face. 'Oh, sorry. That was presumptuous.'

Vaughan tilted his face to mine. He kissed me more hungrily this time, pressing his hard body into me. And this time my mouth and body responded just as eagerly, without fear of a large audience.

'Ahem. Vaughan?'

I pulled away, shocked. Gordon and Travis were loitering nearby on the grass.

Gordon could barely hide his pleasure. 'I'm sorry to disturb you both but Hugo's solicitor will be arriving soon. It's time to hear what the old fellow was up to.'

Forty-five

 I stuck my head into the tea room to be greeted by Morven's harassed expression.

'Where the hell have you been? You were only supposed to be gone for half an hour.'

Greta jerked her head at Morven. 'She's been worried sick. She even thought you might have quit and done a runner.'

'Don't be silly,' I laughed a little awkwardly. 'As if.'

At the counter, Greta and Logan were spinning closed the last bags of scones for lingering customers and turning off the coffee machine for the day, while Becky and Jess were clearing tables and cleaning up the kitchen.

Vaughan's apologetic face leaned around the corner beside mine. 'Please don't blame Lara for going AWOL. It's all my fault.'

Morven answered with a slow smile. 'Oh, I see.'

I tried very hard not to blush. 'So, anyway, we have to go to hear the reading of Hugo's letter. I'm so sorry about this. Will you be okay?'

Greta bustled backwards and forwards behind the cake counter like a silver battleship. 'We can manage here, love—it's almost closing, anyway.' Logan didn't look as convinced but I called out my grateful thanks as we left.

With anticipation hanging in the air, Vaughan, Gordon, Travis and I filed into Gordon's study. A window was open, delivering the animated chatter of the slowly dispersing crowd.

Mr Chalmers, Hugo's solicitor, shook hands with each of us in turn. After exchanging a few pleasantries, we all sat down in a semicircle of chairs that Travis had hurriedly pulled together.

Gordon looked apprehensive as he poured tea for everyone. I had only known Hugo for a short while, but in that time I'd realised what an unpredictable force of nature he was. Goodness knows what was in the thick, creamy envelope that Mr Chalmers had now pulled from his leather briefcase.

Vaughan stretched his long legs out in front of him and reached for my hand. Today had been a rollercoaster of emotions. One minute, I was wandering around with a broken heart; the next, I was being carted across the grass by the man I thought I had lost forever. I was still swimming along on a tide of happy disbelief when Mr Chalmers cleared his throat and began reading Hugo's letter.

"'If you are reading this, dear family, it must be the twenty-seventh of October. I hope you are all well and that Glenlovatt is going from strength to strength. I loved this place with every part of my being. It has the capacity to bewitch and enchant everyone who visits.'"

Mr Chalmers paused slightly before he continued.

"'I have a story I wish to share with you all now that I am gone. You see, many years ago, during my youth, I was bewitched and enchanted by a young lady.'"

Vaughan, Gordon and I exchanged raised eyebrows.

"'I had met her at the Fairview Highland Games. Our family were presenting the prizes and she was wandering around with a young man. When I saw that riot of red curls, I was smitten.

"'I soon made sure her male companion was a thing of the past and we began courting in secret. We lost our hearts to one another, even though we knew our relationship was unlikely to last. Times were different then. Tradition was put on a pedestal and I was young and weak.

'"Eventually, a member of the Glenlovatt staff saw us together and told my father. I allowed myself to be held to ransom by family convention and a marriage was arranged for the benefit of our estate. In doing so I gave up the woman I loved. But before we separated, I gave her a silver bracelet. A bracelet I had made specially in Glasgow in the hope that she would know what she meant to me. I wanted her to know I would always love her."'

Mr Chalmers adjusted his glasses. '"The silver bracelet had four charms. Two of elaborately decorated cakes and the other two—"'

'—of silver spoons,' I interrupted, staring incredulously down at the bracelet hanging from my wrist.

Mr Chalmers paused for a moment. Gordon and Vaughan glanced at each other with obvious confusion. Then Gordon's gaze followed Vaughan's to the silver bracelet draped from my wrist.

'"This lady,"' Mr Chalmers continued to read, '"was Hettie Blackwood."'

My stunned face jerked upwards to look at Vaughan and Gordon. 'My great-aunt. The girl Hugo was in love with . . . She was my great-aunt.'

My mind was freewheeling. Mr Chalmers adjusted his silky gold tie and continued. The three of us exchanged shocked glances but listened intently.

'"I loved Glenlovatt, but even though I loved Hettie more, I allowed a sense of duty to control my destiny. As I grew older I began to resent this house. Sometimes, in melancholy moments, I would view Glenlovatt as the catalyst of my unhappiness."'

Gordon shifted slightly in his chair. 'I always knew he and my mother didn't have the most wonderful of marriages.'

Vaughan gave a short laugh. 'That's an understatement, Dad.'

Mr Chalmers cleared his throat and the room once again descended into respectful silence.

'"That is why I did what I did. When I saw Lara wearing the silver bracelet and realised she was Hettie's great-niece, I saw this as an opportunity to try to correct the wrongs of my past. I should have realised when I first saw her that she was related to Hettie: those red curls, her determined spirit, even their shared love of baking. It brought back all the love I had for Hettie so many years ago."'

Tears clouded my eyes.

Mr Chalmers paused before continuing again. '"Once I got to know Lara and discovered her passion for baking and her desire to have a business of her own, I knew I had to help her. It was the least I could do. In my mind it would go some way to righting the wrong I had done to my beautiful Hettie. I hope this presumption on my part has brought some happiness and satisfaction to you all."'

Mr Chalmers looked up, no doubt taking in our open-mouthed expressions. 'Nearly done now,' he said.

'"So here is my final instruction and request. I have set up the Hettie Blackwood Trust and this trust will, as of today, help to support the running of Glenlovatt Manor."'

Gordon gripped the arms of his chair. 'What on earth have you been up to, Dad?' He then looked squarely at Mr Chalmers. 'How much did Hugo squirrel away, Graeme?'

Mr Chalmers named a figure that drew a chorus of gasps from all of us.

'I always thought Hugo was a bit on the tight side,' admitted Vaughan to no one in particular, 'but he was obviously busy planning this all along.'

Mr Chalmers gave the final page of the letter a crisp shake and read the closing paragraphs. "'To my dear Gordon. You have made me so proud to be your father. You are a son who is selfless and kind, always thinking of others before yourself. Please forgive me for my confession. I always respected and loved your mother but not in the way I should have. She was a faithful wife, and a loving mother to you and, for that, I will always be grateful to her. As for you, I never told you often enough how proud I am of you and that is a mistake I should have rectified long ago. Hopefully this letter will go some way to making amends for that. I know you suffered intolerable pain when you lost Lydia, but you carried on. You were a rock, not only for Glenlovatt but also for your son and for me. I always will be your loving father.

"'To my dear Vaughan. You are far more of a man than I ever was at your age. Chase your dreams and find a love that will endure. Do you remember my words of advice to you that summer when you turned twenty? You had just lost your beloved mother and life was proving to be difficult for you. I told you to make your mother proud and to find someone who you could love. I know in my heart that you will do just that and I am proud of you too. You are a credit to your mother and father.'"

Mr Chalmers smiled and finished reading out the letter.

"'And to Lara, the girl with the fiery red curls. Thank you for having the bravery to take charge of your future. I know what I expected from you was a great deal. You were thrust into Glenlovatt with no knowledge of what lay ahead for you. But I knew you could rise to the challenge. Thank you for allowing me to help you, for you have brought my darling Hettie's memory back to Glenlovatt, where it belonged all along. I know that may sound rather selfish but please understand that the love I had for your great-aunt never died. I saw an opportunity to change your situation, and not to take it would have been a lasting regret.

I did for you what I should have done for Hettie and I hope that, in some small way, this demonstrates how repentant I am for not being the man I should have been.

"'I hope you will always wear the silver bracelet knowing I will watch over you and the rest of my family.

"'Fondest love, Hugo.'"

There was a silence weighted with disbelief.

Finally Gordon's voice, thick with emotion, shattered the quiet. 'Well, trust my father to get the last word.'

Travis spoke quietly—I'd almost forgotten he was there. 'They broke the mould when they made Hugo Carmichael.'

Perth, Scotland, September 1978

Hettie slid a round-tipped knife slick with white icing over the plain dome of cake. As she did so, her eyes strayed to her naked wrist.

Not seeing the dancing silver bracelet there was oddly comforting; much better it stay curled up in the bottom of her leather jewellery box. She had had no other option but to remove it. It was just too much of a reminder of what could have had.

Its absence affirmed that she'd moved on. It proved to her that he was in her past. She put her oven gloves away in the drawer and made a concerted effort not to conjure up the sound of his laugh, or the way his dark hair fell away from his face.

Outside her kitchen window, leaves adorned the trees in riots of bold red, mustard yellow and burnished orange. The variety of autumn colour triggered thoughts of Glenlovatt. She had heard from friends who still frequented Fairview that Hugo and his wife were so proud that their only son, Gordon was starting university. While she eased open the oven door, she smiled at an old school photograph on the windowsill of her two daughters, all gappy smiles and straight brown hair. Their school ties were askew and there was something infectious about their youthful grins.

Placing her mixing bowl in the sink, Hettie then leaned against it, and allowed herself a moment to recall the days of love and laughter she had shared with Hugo. Despite her inward protestations, she knew the truth.

As she looked around her simple kitchen, with its coral-coloured tiles and paisley linoleum flooring, she knew that, despite the anger and hurt she had carried around for so long, Hugo would always be with her.

And, despite everything, she still loved him—that would never change.

Epilogue

 Even in my wildest dreams I couldn't have imagined how beautiful a Christmas wedding at Glenlovatt could be.

The trees looked as if they had been covered with icing sugar and the grounds were carpeted in a thick layer of fresh snow. And despite the chilly December morning, the sky had delivered us beautiful marmalade and vanilla sunshine.

In the great hall, swathes of white tulle decorated the guests' chairs while silvery fairy lights were strung at the entrance, to greet friends and family. Vases of icy blue roses sprung from almost every conceivable surface. Thanks to the combined efforts of friends and family, we had managed to arrange everything in time for our much-wanted winter wedding at Glenlovatt.

Vaughan was something to behold in his dark grey three-piece suit and lavender silk tie. When he unleashed that smile of his as I stood waiting at the entrance to the hall, my heart rippled. There was a look on his face that reminded me of the way Gordon gazed at photographs of Lydia, a deep longing that stole the breath from your throat.

Wolf had been delighted to give me away and I hung on to him desperately as we began that long walk down the aisle, my cream column-style wedding dress suddenly seeming impossible to take a proper step in. As he evaporated into the seat beside Mum, I gave them both a grateful smile. Beside them Morven gave me an encouraging wink from under her fascinator, then turned to Jake with a look that clearly said, 'We're next, matey.' The poor guy doesn't stand a chance.

My fingers clutched nervously at my bouquet, a posy of silver-painted berries, blue heather and snow-dusted pine cones—and, of course, a couple of purple thistles for good measure. Vaughan had also pinned a thistle to his jacket lapel.

As the service began, I caught sight of myself in a mirror on the wall behind the celebrant. I saw a woman with red curls piled up into an elaborate do, who looked a lot like me, but who was exuding a confidence and happiness I'd never felt before.

'Speech! Speech! Come on, Lara! Say something!'

'Yes, you're not normally short of something to say!'

I laughed as our wedding guests encouraged me to get to my feet as they filled the dining room at Glenlovatt with the sound of exuberant happiness.

'Your audience awaits, Mrs Carmichael,' whispered Vaughan beside me. 'Go on, darling.'

I took in a huge breath and rose to my feet, rolling my eyes as two of Vaughan's friends from a nearby table awarded me a couple of wolf whistles. I drank in the frothing winter flower arrangements on each table; the flowing, starched table cloths and the glint of cutlery. And then I began to speak, giving my gorgeous husband the occasional smile as he looked up at me and muttered his encouragement.

'When I was first thrust into the world of Glenlovatt, I was terrified. Hugo Carmichael had placed a huge amount of trust in me, which I didn't understand. The responsibility I felt to make this new tea room a success was immense, especially when it became obvious how much this beautiful place meant to Gordon and Vaughan.'

I took a steadying breath and continued. 'But what Hugo made me realise was that I could achieve more than I ever imagined if I just believed in myself and took a chance. I can't thank him enough for that.'

I looked down at Vaughan, who reached up to squeeze my hand and give me one of his incredibly sexy winks. 'And it's thanks to Hugo that I met a certain brooding sculptor,' I added, pausing briefly while my audience chuckled. 'I've had the chance to learn the strange and wonderful power of love, and I think we've both learned that love doesn't fade with the passing of time; it simply grows stronger.'

From down the wedding table, Gordon had a faraway look. No doubt he was thinking of his beloved Lydia.

I finished by saying, 'This very special house carries all the memories, hopes and dreams of those who have gone before. With Vaughan by my side, I feel honoured to be a part of her future.'

I sat down again, to be greeted by Vaughan's lips against mine and a thunderous round of applause.

And as my fingers searched for my silver bracelet, the four charms caressing my skin, I knew that Hugo, and Hettie too, would be making a toast to Vaughan and me.

Acknowledgements

Heartfelt thanks and gratitude to my phenomenal agent, and friend, Selwa Anthony. My thanks also go to Linda Anthony for her patience. I hope you both know how much I appreciate you.

A huge debt of gratitude to Allen & Unwin, especially my publisher, Annette Barlow; editor, Rebecca Allen; and copyeditor, Simone Ford. The whole A&U team are a very special and talented group of people.

Sincere thanks also to the Capaldi family and the lovely staff at the Honeybee Bakery, which was my inspiration for Thistles.

And, finally, to my much-missed mum, Helen, and mother-in-law, Anne, who are both loved forever.